Just/in Time

Just/in Time

BILLY DEE WILLIAMS
AND
ROB MACGREGOR

A TOM DOHERTY ASSOCIATES BOOK
NEW YORK

JUST/IN TIME

Copyright © 2000 by Billy Dee Williams and Rob MacGregor

A Forge Book
Published by Tom Doherty Associates, LLC
175 Fifth Avenue
New York, NY 10010

www.tor.com

Forge® is a registered trademark of Tom Doherty Associates, LLC.

Library of Congress Cataloging-in-Publication Data

Williams, Billy Dee.
    Just/ in Time / Billy Dee Williams & Rob MacGregor.—1st ed.
        p. cm.
    "A Tom Doherty Associates book."
    ISBN 0-312-87271-2 (alk. paper)
    1. Clairvoyants—Fiction.   2. Remote viewing (Parapsychology)—
Fiction.   3. New Age movement—Fiction.   4. Cults—Fiction.   I.
MacGregor, Rob.   II. Title.
PS3573.I4475 J87 2000
813'.54—dc21   00-039374

First Edition: August 2000

Printed in the United States of America

0 9 8 7 6 5 4 3 2 1

To my wife—Teruko
To Mom—Loretta Anne Williams
and my children—Corey, Dee, and Hanako Anne

To Trish and Megan

Just/in Time

Prologue

Camila Hidalgo riffled through the papers on the top of her desk, looking for the summary sheet with the president's itinerary for his upcoming eleven-day international tour. She'd made notes on the sheet and thought she'd left it right on her desk, but now she couldn't find it. She threw up her hands, feeling helpless. She snatched her briefcase off the floor and quickly explored every pocket. On any other day, she'd just ask Audrey, her secretary, or Watkins, her assistant, to get her a copy. But both had called in sick and she was left to fend for herself.

The hell with it.

She glanced at her watch, then opened her notebook computer. She went to the directory on press briefings, found the itinerary, and clicked print. While she was waiting, she noticed a new file from the chief of staff's office. Audrey or Watkins usually printed out any last-minute updates before she went to the pressroom. But not today.

She opened the file and read that Vice President Rollie Mitchell was hospitalized at 8:10 A.M. with a high fever and flu symptoms. The CDC would be issuing an advisory on the flu at 11 A.M. At the end of the bulletin, the national security advisor suggested that Camila in a note to downplay the flu, call it nothing out of the ordinary. She didn't like hearing that. If Harvey Howell wanted her to downplay it, that probably meant there was reason for concern.

She looked at her watch again and moved over to the full-length mirror. She ran her fingers through her shiny dark hair, adjusted her new suit. She'd picked this one out because she liked the way it accentuated her slender waist and the flare of her hips. At thirty-five, she still looked good, she told herself, and someday she'd have a life separate from her all-encompassing duties as the White House spokesperson. Meanwhile, she would continue stepping in front of the glaring lights and cameras day after day.

She was about to leave for the press conference when she remembered to check her voice mail. As usual, a string of calls awaited her attention. Most were from out-of-town reporters with questions that Audrey or Watkins could easily handle. The last call, however, was from Trent Calloway. When she heard his deep, resonant voice, she leaned forward and listened closely.

"Hey, I just want to tell you again how sorry I am about what happened yesterday. Jeez, if I would've had any idea that was going to happen . . . well, I didn't. I could kill that bastard. He's lucky he's behind bars and out of my reach. Well, enough said. I just hope everything's okay. Sorry again."

She hit the delete button as if it could erase her memory of what had happened yesterday afternoon. *Forget it,* she told herself. *Just forget it.* She loved Trent and would do anything for him, but working with him was risky business, best left to the professionals.

She should've known that getting involved with him again would inevitably lead to weirdness . . . serious weirdness. She used to be married to him after all. When it was over, she had tried to put the entire six-year experience behind her. Calloway had been a psychic spook, a military intelligence officer who used remote viewing or clairvoyance to spy. His work had dominated his life and ruined their marriage. Period. End of story.

But a year ago, he had sneaked back into her life when he'd desperately tried to convince her that a backpack nuclear bomb was heading for Washington. He was retired from the military and no longer involved with remote viewing, but the vision had nevertheless come to him. The ensuing events, which had proven him correct, had not only altered her perception of what was real and possible, but had also brought her back in contact with Calloway.

She leaned closer to the mirror and noticed the faint circles around her eyes. Not enough sleep. She straightened up and felt momentarily dizzy. She noticed a vague tickling in her throat. *No,* she commanded. *I am not getting sick.* Not now. Not when she was about to leave with the president for Europe.

She turned away from the mirror, arranged her notes. Among the several sheets of paper she discovered her original copy of the itinerary. She shook her head. She could've sworn it wasn't here. She shrugged, then abandoned her office and headed down the corridor. Of course, if she hadn't misplaced the itinerary, she wouldn't have picked up the news about the flu. Maybe that meant something, a warning that she should get away.

She shook her head and smiled to herself. David Dustin, with his quirky ideas, must be getting to her. The president was always telling her that answers to her concerns, large and small, could be found all around her. All she had to do was interpret the events and incidents in her life as if they were rich with hidden meaning. That was Dustin's Jungian side, as it was referred to in a recent article in the *Washingtonian*. It seemed Dustin could be as idiosyncratic as he wanted, because his standing in the polls remained strong. If all went well, he would be elected to a second term next year, and she would spend four more years in Washington, a fate that she could live with just fine, thank you.

The White House seemed eerily quiet, as if a hush had fallen over the building. Just her imagination, she told herself. She entered the conference room and approached the podium. She looked around as the camera crews turned on the lights and cameras. Reporters were still taking their seats, but she noticed several of the regular correspondents were missing. She decided to wait a couple of minutes.

She smiled and nodded to Tera Peters, a CNN reporter and a longtime friend, who sat in the second row. A high-spirited redhead with a warm smile, Peters was one of the cable network's rising stars. The two women had met when they were students at the University of Colorado. Later, Peters had worked as a reporter for a Denver television station, while Camila had served as an aide to then-Senator David Dustin. Even though they were sometimes at odds on stories, especially ones that didn't reflect well on Dustin, Camila trusted Peters and their friendship had never faltered over the years.

"Good job last night, in spite of everything. I know it must have been tough."

"Thanks," Tera responded. "I hope I never have anything like that happen again."

Tera had found herself in the center of a sensational story that had turned violent. Even though she had nearly been killed herself, she had taken considerable criticism from her colleagues even before the story aired. "I figured you would take some time off after that one."

"Maybe I should've stayed in Atlanta. I certainly don't want to catch this flu bug."

Camila frowned. "I'll second that. But there's probably nothing to worry about."

"I just heard there were three deaths this morning and hundreds of people in emergency rooms."

"Really." Wonderful. Camila had nothing prepared on the flu, no official response, except for Howell's request that she play it down.

"C'mon, Camila," a voice called out. "We're late. I've got a deadline, you know."

She smiled at Lenora Russell, the senior correspondent, who had reported on five presidents for Reuters. "I guess we can get started, Lenora. I don't want you missing your deadline and getting in trouble."

The crowd laughed. It was generally thought that Lenora would be here reporting on five more presidents before she retired. As Camila began her comments about the president's upcoming trip, she noticed a reporter in the back of the room stand up and move unsteadily toward the door. Someone else coughed.

She began by outlining the president's European agenda, frequently checking her notes. She moved on to some of the significant issues that would be raised during the trip. But just as she was about to take questions, she started to feel dizzy again.

One of the press aides suddenly appeared at her side. He slid a sheet of paper in front of her. She tried to focus on it. The words blurred, came into focus, blurred again. Finally, she found her bearings and quickly read the note written in large type and capital letters.

THE VICE PRESIDENT IS INFECTED WITH TULAREMIA, A DEADLY VIRUS. A BIOTERRORIST ATTACK IS SUSPECTED. QUARANTINE OF CITY IMMANENT. DD WILL MAKE STATEMENT AT NOON.

A wave of nausea washed over her. She tasted bile in her throat. Her head pounded, her knees felt weak. She leaned into the podium, steadied herself. Her face felt flushed; beads of perspiration formed on her brow. Her lungs felt as if they were filling with water.

She cleared her throat. "I have an important announcement to make. The president will be making . . ."

She heard more coughing. She looked up, trying to get her bearings. "I'm sorry, I'm . . ." The room spun. Her knees buckled. She stumbled, reached for the podium, but lost her balance. She dropped to one knee, then toppled over. Someone shouted that they needed a doctor.

Was it her imagination or were other people in the room also feeling ill? Chairs clattered. Someone hovered over her, a hand rested on her arm. She tried to stand up.

"Camila, it's me, Tera. Don't try to move. Just relax. We're getting a doctor for you."

With the bright lights illuminating Tera's red hair, Camila imagined she was talking to an angel, a lovely angel who was going to take her away. Another one of those symbols, she thought, a message that she wasn't going to make it. "No, I don't want to die," she whispered.

PART ONE

THE PRESENT

One

THREE WEEKS EARLIER

They finished lunch on a sandy beach in the warm sun and he started reloading the raft for the last leg of their two-day trip down the San Juan River. Trent Calloway had guided dozens of groups on this trip over the last couple of years, but he wished this one wouldn't end. He was going to miss his traveling companions, seven nurses from San Diego. He couldn't remember the last time he'd been surrounded by so many attractive women. Being the only man on the trip, and the main resource for information, definitely had its advantages.

Even his boss, Ed Miller, an old codger, had hung around Sand Island before they left, as if he'd wished he were guiding the trip. He'd elbowed Calloway before they'd left and jokingly warned him to make sure that he stopped at Mexican Hat. "Now I don't want you disappearing into the wilderness with these lovely ladies and never being seen again."

His reverie was broken as one of the women called out to him, "Trent, could you come over here for a moment?"

He ambled over to a tall, slender woman named Carol, who was standing over by a sheltered rock wall covered with petroglyphs. She wore her chestnut hair in a single, thick braid, with a turquoise necklace and silver hoop earrings. A persistent woman, she had asked the most questions and seemed more interested in his opinions on everything.

He reached into a waterproof pouch strapped to his belt and extracted several jelly beans. "What can I do for you?"

"You told us all about Kokopelli." She smiled and pointed to a carving of the mythical flute player with an enormous phallus. "It's easy to see that he's a fertility symbol, but I was wondering about these spirals I keep seeing every time we stop."

Calloway popped the jelly beans into his mouth as she talked. Here was his chance, he thought, to ask her if she was interested in going out to dinner with him this evening. He enjoyed her company and would like to get to know her better. She'd already suggested that he look her up the next time he passed through San Diego on his way to Baja, where he liked to spend his winters.

"Some of them are single spirals, like this one; others are two connected spirals. What are they about?"

He swallowed the jelly beans as he stared at the petroglyph. "Well, they've got a number of meanings, depending on who you talk to. Some say they represent the wind, others say water, still others say they are coiled snakes or snails. Those are sort of mundane explanations, though. I heard a Zuni Indian say that they stand for the journey to the center."

"The center of what?"

"The center is the home of the people. Remember the tribes migrated here and searched for their home, their center. But it could also be a search for the center of one's being, the journey inward."

Carol nodded thoughtfully. "I like that. Which explanation do you prefer?"

He shrugged. "None of them."

She looked at him curiously. "Why not?"

"I've used my intuition, you could say, in studying these petroglyphs and have come up with my own ideas. The spirals, I think, are related to the journey into eternity, the path the shaman takes. They carved these symbols for their people and their descendants so they could pass on the teachings. The message of the spiral is that there are always new realms to explore beyond the five senses."

She stared thoughtfully at him and nodded slowly. "I didn't know you were so deep, Trent. But is that their message, or is it yours?"

He smiled. "Maybe both."

She looked past him toward the raft. "Everyone's waiting. I guess we better get going."

"Yeah, say, Carol, would you be interested in going to dinner in town with me tonight?"

She smiled, touched his shoulder. "Gee, that's nice of you to ask, Trent. But I better not. I don't really think I should go off from the others. Rachel and Kate are going to put together a dinner tonight. You're certainly welcome to join us, though."

"Okay. But while they're making dinner, why don't you stop by the RV for a glass of wine?"

She frowned. "I'd like to Trent, but my boyfriend probably wouldn't care for it."

"Oh, you didn't mention a boyfriend. Yeah, he probably wouldn't like you messing around with some black cowboy in Utah."

"Hey, he's jealous about me spending time with any guy other than him. You know how it is."

"Yeah, I guess."

•   •   •

An hour later, they were nearing Mexican Hat, their final stop. Calloway still felt glum about getting rejected, but he should've figured that, with his luck, Carol would be unavailable. Living on the river guiding trips had brought him into contact with lots of people, but most of the women who interested him were already attached. For the most part, he was satisfied living on his own in his RV and having the freedom to do and go as he wanted, at least when he wasn't leading raft trips for Miller. But lately, he'd felt pangs of loneliness, and on more than one occasion, he'd wished that he had a woman around to share his life—at least part of the time.

"Okay, we're just about here," he called out from the back as he shifted the rudder and the raft drifted toward the shore on the right. The six women at the oars rowed hard.

"It was fun, but I won't miss the rowing," Kate responded.

"My shoulders couldn't take much more," Carol shouted.

They rounded a curve and Calloway glimpsed the flatbed truck waiting for them. Guy Shulpa, the teenager who helped him out from time to time, leaned against the truck. Calloway shaded his eyes and squinted against the bright afternoon light as he saw a woman in jeans with long, dark hair standing nearby. His heart leaped with joy as he recognized Camila Hidalgo.

Suddenly, he forgot about the nurses. He just wanted to get to shore.

Camila greeted him as he stepped out of the raft. He walked over and hugged her. "What a surprise."

"Yes, I see I've caught you with a raft full of young women. Sorry to spoil your fun."

He laughed. "Don't worry about it. The trip is over. So what brings you here?"

"Oh, I wanted to get away for a couple of days. I called Ed yesterday when I couldn't reach you. He told me you were out here, so I decided to fly out and meet you."

"I'm glad you did."

In the year since he'd renewed his relationship with Camila, they'd talked occasionally on the phone. But in spite of promises to the contrary, they'd only seen each other once, when she'd taken a raft trip with her boss, David Dustin, the president of the United States, and a throng of Secret Service agents.

"Besides, I figured if I was ever going to see you again, it was going to be up to me to come here."

He held up his hands. "Wait a minute. That's not true. I just didn't want to get in your way. You're very busy."

"Whatever. I'm here."

He smiled and saw that the others had gotten out of the raft and were looking over at him with obvious curiosity. "I want you to meet my fellow rafters."

Calloway introduced Camila as an old friend and left them to chat while he helped Guy carry the raft and gear to the truck. He told the nurses that he would see them in camp, and that Guy would take them back in the truck. Then, he left with Camila in her rented Grand Cherokee, leaving the Navajo boy to transport the nurses and gear back to Sand Island.

An hour later, in his RV, Calloway opened a bottle of wine and poured a glass for Camila and himself. They touched glasses. "To an enjoyable reunion," she said.

"Yeah, a reunion."

He liked the sound of that. He sipped his wine and watched her over the rim of his glass. She looked great, as always, with her mane of shiny black hair, high cheekbones, and generous mouth. Maybe there was a chance that things would warm up again. But he also sensed that Camila had some other motive for coming here, one that she hadn't shared with him yet.

"Would you like to go to town for dinner or do you want to raid my freezer for TV dinners?"

She cocked her head to the side. "Let's just stay here." She leaned forward and kissed him lightly on the lips.

Things were looking up, he thought. Memories of good times together surfaced from wherever they were stored. He wanted to repeat them and forget the gulf of years and distance and experience that separated them. He slipped his hands around her waist and kissed her, deeper this time.

She leaned back and tapped a finger against his chest. "You're not wasting any time, are you?"

"Should I be?"

"Well, just what are we talking about here, Mr. Calloway?"

"A reunion?"

"Oh, Trent. Our lives are so different now."

"Sure they are, for now. They might not always be, though."

"Let's not think about that now." She pulled him close and kissed him again. He tasted wine on her lips, felt her softness against him, and his desires rose. He walked her to the rear of the RV and into his bedroom. It all seemed so sudden, so unexpected.

They lay in the dark, satiated from their lovemaking. He felt a cool breeze from the open window caress his chest, and he heard the chirring of insects outside.

"I really wasn't expecting this to happen," Camila said from beside him. "I don't know what I was expecting, but I like what happened, and I don't know what it means."

"I like it, too, and I know what it means."

She raised up on her elbows. "Oh, what does it mean, Mr. Calloway?"

"That I want to see more of you. That I want things to work out again."

"Yes. But we can't rush it, Trent. Let's just see what happens."

"That's fine with me . . . as long as I don't have to wait another year to see you."

"Well, you may have to come and visit me, you know."

He leaned toward her and kissed her on the forehead. "I'll even put up with some city life again to be with you."

It didn't take long for Calloway to realize that life in the RV with Camila would shake up his world. She got up at six and started monitoring the news programs, flipping from one to the next. All the while, she made phone calls to her staff and to reporters, as if she were sitting in her office. After a report on the president's meeting with Mideast leaders in Washington, she called the reporter and chastised him for getting the president's position wrong and politely asked him to follow it up with a clarification.

"I'm really glad you've got that satellite dish. That's great," she said between calls.

He poured himself a cup of coffee. "It's a luxury, but I wanted it so I could see more of you."

She laid a hand over his and bussed him on the cheek. "You're sweet." She glanced at her watch. "Sorry, I've got another call to make."

"I guess this trip isn't really a vacation."

"A semivacation. Don't worry. I won't be doing this all day."

Calloway took his coffee and sat on a lawn chair outside the RV and enjoyed the quiet morning. Across the campground, the nurses were packing to leave, and he wandered over to say good-bye. When he hugged Carol, he wished her well. "You come back sometime and bring that boyfriend. I'll take you both on the river."

"I'll do that." In a conspiratorial tone, Carol added, "It's a good thing that I turned you down about dinner or you would've been in a big fix when Camila arrived."

He laughed. "That's true. It's odd how things work out sometimes."

Back in the RV, Calloway cooked cheese omelettes and pieces of thick fried bread. When he placed the meal on the table, Camila hit the mute on the television. "I'll go for the omelette, but that looks dangerous," she said, pointing to the fried bread.

"It's Navajo bread. It's good."

"I know it's good. Too good."

Camila's gaze strayed toward the television from time to time as they ate. She turned the sound on and focused on the screen as a news story began that showed a handsome man holding his hands above an elderly woman who was lying on a table. Then, as the camera panned a campground, a reporter said that as many as three thousand people were arriving each day at the New Mexico ranch.

"State of New Mexico Transportation Department officials are demanding that Melissa Dahl, who owns the ranch where Justin Logos is conducting his healing sessions, pay more than two million dollars for improvements on five miles of public roadway leading to the ranch. Lawyers for Dahl and Logos called the amounts 'extremely excessive' and plan to appeal the ruling.

They note that Logos works for modest fees and sometimes no fees at all."

Camila hit the mute again. "What do you think of him?"

Calloway shrugged. "I don't know much about him, but I think he's out of his mind saying that he's the Second Coming. That's just asking for trouble."

She nodded. "Especially if it isn't true. I don't know if you're aware of it, but he's been making some rather ominous remarks about the future of the so-called center of power, which probably means Washington."

Calloway shrugged. "Maybe he's getting it from Revelation."

Camila glanced at the television, where a reporter spoke from the floor of the New York Stock Exchange, then turned back to Calloway. "My concern is that it might be more than just loose talk or biblical commentary."

Suddenly, Calloway knew without a doubt that the primary purpose of Camila's trip related to Justin Logos, and he resented it. "What exactly do you have in mind, Camila?"

"What do you mean?"

"You're not telling me everything."

She smiled. "I think you already know. I'd like you to see what you can get on Justin Logos."

"Now?"

Camila measured her words. "Well, whenever you think you're ready."

He sat back in his chair. "So that's why you came here."

"That's not true. I could've just called you."

He didn't say anything.

"Listen, Trent, I didn't make love to you so that you would take this project, if that's what you're thinking. If you don't want to do it, say so."

"I promised Doc that I'd work with her on anything coming from you or from any branch of intelligence."

Camila nodded. "Of course. That's fine. This should be helpful for her when she takes her proposal to the committee. They'll have something recent to look at. I should add that Harvey Howell is very insistent on this one."

Howell, the president's national security advisor, was key to the success of Project Third Eye, a new remote-viewing program that would work with intelligence agencies on cases involving national security. It would replace the old remote-viewing projects from the eighties and nineties, which had ended in controversy. Doc, who would be the director, was particularly concerned with Howell's eagerness to use remote viewing for questionable purposes.

"I'll talk to Doc about it. I'll warn you, though, she may not go for it unless there's good reason to poke into this guy's life."

Camila met his gaze across the table. "I can't tell you everything, Trent, not right now, but believe me, it's important, very important, that you and Doc pursue this one."

Two

After a couple of days of damp weather in New Mexico's Sangre de Cristo Mountains, the low, rain-saturated clouds and cool temperatures had vanished as if someone had performed a rain dance in reverse. Calloway ambled across the makeshift campground, his boots sinking into the muddy earth. RVs, campers, and tents formed a circle around a large circus tent and a stage. A crowd had gathered near the stage, and the throng radiated a fervor that reminded him of an old-time revival.

A large man with a gray beard, shaved head, and suspenders holding up his jeans slapped him on the back like an old friend. "Hey, brother, it's really great to see you here today. Can I help you with anything?"

"Thanks. I'm fine. Just waiting for Justin."

"I know what you mean. I can't wait, either."

Suspenders, like so many here, figured Calloway was just like him, running on an inside track to a higher realm. They were seekers, believers, seemingly existing in a blissful state far from the concerns of everyday life. In Calloway's mind, they were well meaning, but vaguely obnoxious.

Calloway smiled back and wished him well.

"See you around."

In spite of all the fellowship, Calloway couldn't help feeling like the odd man out. It had nothing to do with race, even though there were few other Afro-Americans in the crowd. It was more about a state of mind. In other times and places, they might have been members of a UFO cult waiting for the prophesied fleet of ships to arrive and take them away to other worlds. Or they might have been followers of a charismatic Christian minister, who was leading them to the gateway of heaven. The atmosphere was so salted with giddy goodwill that if someone told him that laughing gas permeated the air, he would believe it.

Calloway scanned the crowd looking for Doc, who would probably be standing apart from everyone else to avoid the crush of bodies when Justin took the stage. He recognized a tall, attractive woman with dark hair, blue eyes, and a long, graceful neck moving his way. Accompanied by another woman, she eased through the crowd with the poise of a dancer and a sense of responsibility. At first glance, she looked thirty, but she was probably fifty or older.

Melissa, Justin's partner and manager, had welcomed Calloway and Doc when they'd arrived at the entrance and oriented them to the layout and the various activities. Although she'd been pleasant, something about her bothered him and he wanted to see if he sensed anything else.

Calloway stepped into her path. "Hello again, Melissa."

She paused and looked at Calloway, then responded in an officious manner. "Can I help you?"

"I was just wondering about something. I understand that some of these people have stayed on for months. What keeps them here after they've had a healing and heard Justin talk?"

She regarded him suspiciously. "That's an odd question. You've been here a couple of days. Don't you know?"

"No, I don't."

Distracted, she looked past him toward the stage. "What was your name again?"

He told her. He felt something deceptive about her, almost as if she were disguised.

"Yes, Trent. You'll have to excuse me." Her tone smacked of condescension. "Justin will be here at any moment and I've got to get to the stage." She turned to the other woman. "Claire, would you mind answering Trent's questions?"

"Not at all."

Calloway watched Melissa move away, then smiled at Claire, a petite blonde who bubbled with enthusiasm.

She introduced herself as Claire Bernard and said she was a nurse who had worked with Justin for the past eight months. "Some of us have dedicated ourselves to Justin Logos. We are here for the long run. We're not just curious tourists. We are committed. We would do anything for Justin. Anything. His time has come. He has returned." She smiled. "When you hear Justin talk, you'll understand better."

"Amen, sister," a tall, lanky man said as he shambled past.

Calloway nodded and thanked her. Odd, he thought. In spite of her ebullience, there was something hidden about Claire, too, as if she were playing a role. Just like him.

He decided to look for Doc in the huge circus tent that was erected near the stage. He wished Camila had joined him. He already missed her and wondered how she would react to Justin Logos. He stepped inside the enormous tent and was greeted by a large freestanding poster of Justin on the cover of *Time* magazine with the headline "The Revival of All Time."

He moved past it and reached into his pocket for a bag of jelly beans. He picked out several and popped one after another into his mouth. Camila had given him a bag of gourmet jelly beans last year, and ever since he'd been hooked on them. He figured the little colored beans curbed his desire for beer, which he used to drink in abundance. But lately he felt as if the jelly beans were a curse, and he'd been trying to limit himself to an eight-ounce bag a week.

He walked by the tables where new patients registered before a bus shuttled them to the clinic. He spotted Doc in the far corner, near the deserted information center where pamphlets about Justin and general information were handed out to new-comers. "Hey, Doc? What are you doing here? Justin's about to take the stage."

"What do you think I'm doing? I'm hiding out." She wore a loose cotton dress, covering her wide girth, and a big floppy hat. "This is interesting, though." She pointed at a video playing on a large screen.

Calloway looked up just in time to see the healer gouge out the eye of an elderly black man. Justin manipulated the eyeball with his fingers for several seconds, holding it just above the eye socket, then set it back in place. The video cut to an inter-view with the patient. A week had passed, and the seventy-two-year-old man could see clearly, his inoperable cataract gone. The man felt no pain and had felt none during the procedure, even though he received no anesthesia.

Next, the presentation cut to a well-known incident in which Justin told a group of followers standing on the opposite side of a stream that an "event" was about to happen. Within seconds, a 6.5 earthquake, centered 150 miles away, jolted the landscape. The waters briefly parted and Justin crossed the stream. The video cut to another well-publicized scene: Justin handing out more than three hundred sandwiches from a cooler that could not hold more than a couple of dozen.

A narrator, meanwhile, described Justin's life story. Aban-

doned shortly after birth, he was found in a Dumpster and raised
by an older couple in St. Paul, Minnesota. "Even as a child,
Justin emanated an unusual intensity. He knew things that had
not yet happened, things taking place elsewhere that he should
have had no knowledge of, and he had an uncanny knack for
healing injured animals.

"Justin left home at eighteen and traveled in Europe and Asia
for several years. No one he met in his travels ever forgot him. In
India, a guru proclaimed the young man to be the reincarnation of
Jesus of Nazareth. The news spread quickly, but soon the twenty-
three-year-old man disappeared. A year later, he reemerged in
New Mexico on a ranch owned by Melissa Dahl, a microbiologist
who retired from her profession to assist Justin in his healing sessions. By then, he had dropped his adopted last name and changed
it to Logos, which means 'the word of God' or 'the second person
of the Trinity,' incarnate in Jesus Christ. For the past six years,
Justin has worked ten hours a day, six days a week, in the ranch
clinic. Today, he turns down all requests for interviews and re-
fuses to comment on the speculation that he is the Son of God."

With that, the video ended. "I guess they didn't bother to
mention the television evangelist who called him the 'fornicating
Antichrist.' "

" 'The fornicating Antichrist who never quotes the Bible, and
who beds with the devils of the New Age,' " Doc said, reciting
the widely used quote.

Calloway held out the bag of jelly beans to Doc. "He's about
to take the stage. Let's go take a look."

Doc pushed the bag away. "I don't think I can handle it. I
was just trying to figure out how I could get back to the RV. I
wish I hadn't listened to you, Calloway."

Doc had a strong aversion to crowds, and she had spent most

of the time in the RV. He'd walked her over to the big tent forty-five minutes ago, hoping that she would gradually get used to the crowd. But it looked as if it wasn't working.

"C'mon, you've got to see him at least once while we're here. This is your chance."

"Oh, shit, Trent. Why did I ever agree to come here? This was a mistake."

"Well, we could've stayed at my place and remote viewed Justin, like Camila suggested in the first place," Calloway said.

"I'm sure she and Howell would've liked that, but I'm not playing Howell's game. If we remote viewed a healer just because he's getting lots of attention, it would be like telling Howell that we'll use the ability to spy on anyone for him."

"So, here we are. If we're going to evaluate Justin to see if he's a valid candidate, we should see what he has to say."

"Okay, okay. But let's stay by the outside edge, and if I start losing it, you've got to help me get back to the RV."

"That's a deal."

Applause and cheers rippled through the crowd as they stepped out of the tent. Justin had just approached the microphone. This would be the second talk Calloway had seen him give since arriving two days ago. Yesterday morning, he'd offered a parable about a man who walked out of the wilderness and was denied food and water because he looked and thought differently from the townspeople. He had an idea that could help the people overcome a drought, but they drove him away before he could help them. As a result, they perished in their ignorance.

Tall and slender, Justin wore jeans, cowboy boots, and a work shirt. He looked like a young Robert Redford and was every bit as charismatic as the actor. He warmed up the crowd with some friendly banter, saying that he was glad that the weather had finally turned pleasant, that the cold spell was over. If he hadn't been so busy with the healings, he would've tried to improve the weather earlier. But that wasn't his specialty, he added modestly. The crowd loved it.

"He can say anything he wants and get away with it," Doc muttered. "They just cheer and cheer."

Calloway saw that Doc was staring intently at her feet, which she was burrowing in the mud, doing her best to ignore the crowd.

"You know that I like to speak in metaphors," Justin continued. "But just because I use metaphors doesn't mean that what I am saying is not true. A metaphor just helps us understand the truth." He paused a few moments and everyone seemed to lean forward to hear what he would say next.

"I'm going to tell you about a great cosmic battle that is taking place right now that directly affects all of us. You see, the earth and all of its creatures, including man, were created by the Thunderbird, a great, majestic, awesome bird. The Thunderbird is the image that I see when I focus on this creative being. But I know that the Thunderbird is also a collection or group of wondrous beings of light who exist outside of time and space."

He held up his hands, patting the air. "Yes, I know. It's not the way you learned it in Sunday school. But don't worry about that. Am I speaking of God when I talk about the Thunderbird? No. Think of an architect who designs a building, an artist who paints a landscape, or a poet who writes a verse. You may recognize God's hand in their work. But we also know that the architect, the artist, and the poet are not God. So it is with the Thunderbird."

It sounded to Calloway as if Justin was drawing on a mix of Native American spiritualism and New Age philosophy. Was that how the reborn Jesus would express himself? He didn't know. But he recognized that Justin was a mesmerizing speaker, and it was easy to be swallowed up by his words and the luminous images within them.

"As I said, I was going to tell you about a great cosmic war, a conflict that exists beyond time and space. Just as individuals and nations face challenges and conflict from time to time, the same is true for the Thunderbird. The Thunderbird is engaged in a full-fledged battle with the Vulture."

Justin placed his hands on his hips, looked around, smiling. "So who is this other bird? The Vulture, my friends, does not mold new worlds. He is more concerned about control and domination. That's his thing. The Vulture is a warrior who long, long ago conquered this world and displaced the Thunderbird.

"The Vulture feeds on energy created by human emotions. The more emotional dramas and conflicts we create in our lives, the more the Vulture feeds. The Vulture actually helps create the circumstances leading to these dramas. It seems that we have free will, that we can make our own choices, and it's true to some extent. But you must realize that the Vulture keeps us penned like fat pigs. We've come to believe that the pen is a safe place, that to even think of venturing outside it would be foolhardy. That's the Vulture's influence, because he knows that if people ever get out of their pens, they become more alive and are not so easy to control and feed on."

Calloway looked around at the attentive faces. Everyone had grown still as Justin wove his tale. Even Doc seemed transfixed. She still stared downward, but he could tell that she was listening closely, and so far she showed no sign of the unbearable pressure she felt among crowds. Calloway, for his part, no longer felt like an outside observer. Like everyone else, he was interested in hearing the resolution to the story.

"I'm here to tell you that I have broken free of the pen and can fly between worlds and reach out to my many selves. You can do it, too. Don't revere me for who I am. Join me. Be like me. Now if you take up the challenge and try to escape from your pen, the Vulture will try to stop you. But remember the Thunderbird is within you, ready to awaken and guide you as you expand your awareness."

Justin grew excited and moved from side to side. "I want all of you to reach your hands up toward the heavens and pull in the power of the Thunderbird. Let the Thunderbird open your heart!"

Several thousand hands grasped at the air above their heads. A woman nearby started spinning in circles and shouting as she reached up. Then others around her followed her example, spinning, grasping, shouting.

"Yes, that's it!" Justin shouted. "Pull it it! Pull it in!"

Doc gripped Calloway's arm. "I've got to get out of here. I can't take it anymore."

Justin climbed down from the stage and moved among the crowd. Calloway started to lead Doc away as if she were a blind person, but he kept his gaze on Justin.

"What's he doing now?" Doc asked.

At that moment, Justin held a hand above a woman's neck, then he thumped his open palm hard against it. If she didn't have neck problems before, she did now, Calloway thought. Justin manipulated the woman's neck several times. When he let go, she turned it on her own, and Calloway could see her smiling broadly.

"It looks like he's healing people. I think he's just doing it at random."

"That's *so* kind of him."

"You don't sound very impressed."

"No, I am impressed. I'm also ready to wing my way out of here in the morning," Doc said. "But I'll tell you something, I'll never look at a vulture again without thinking about that story."

Calloway felt deeply unsettled by Justin's talk. He couldn't help thinking about the analogies to remote viewing. When he reached for a target, he left behind the boundaries of everyday life, the pen, so to speak, to explore the world beyond the five senses. He certainly knew there were dangers in his work, and the image of the Vulture definitely didn't make him feel any better about it.

Calloway suddenly stopped to avoid bumping into a woman. Doc looked up and her gaze took in the crowd for the first time. Panic spread across her features. "Oh, God. I had no idea there were this many people here. I'm losing it, Trent. Everything's pressing down. It's happening again. Get me out of here fast. Hurry!"

Her knees buckled and Calloway did his best to hold her up. He had no idea how he was going to get the big woman to the RV, which was parked nearly a quarter of a mile away. "C'mon, Doc, you can do it. Stay calm. Just focus on your breath."

"No, no," she whispered hoarsely. "It's horrible."

Calloway became aware of someone moving up next to him to give him a hand. He looked up in surprise as he saw it was Justin. "Let me help. Please allow me." Justin moved up behind Doc and clasped her upper arms. "Just let her go now. I've got her."

Calloway was certain that Doc would collapse to the ground

the moment he released his hands. But to his surprise, she stayed on her feet. Justin placed a hand on her side and it disappeared beneath a fleshy breast. He leaned close to her and whispered in her ear for nearly a minute. Although Calloway stood barely a yard away, he couldn't understand anything Justin said. It was as if the words went through a filter that made them incomprehensible.

Finally, Justin released her. He turned to Calloway and smiled broadly. "She'll be fine now. She can walk on her own back to your camp. She just needs a little rest."

Justin bent down and picked up the bag of jelly beans that Calloway had dropped and handed them to him. "You think they help you avoid something, like smokers who chew gum. But the truth is, you eat them to fill a void. The jelly beans are an attempt to make up for the lack of sweetness in your life." He patted Calloway on the shoulder. "Things are changing for the better, but you're resentful. So you still eat them."

Puzzled, Calloway jammed the bag of jelly beans into his pocket as Justin moved away.

"He's right," Doc said. "I'm feeling much better right now." She held out her arms, palms turned up, looked around, and nodded. "Damn good, in fact."

Calloway could hardly believe the change in Doc. "Are you kidding? You were on the verge of passing out a couple of minutes ago. What the hell did he do to you?"

Doc beamed. "I have no idea, Trent, but it feels like something has changed in me." She looked around and smiled. "I don't feel any particular concern about all the people."

"So he really can heal?"

"If I had any doubts before, I don't now."

Calloway nodded. He was impressed at the abrupt change in

Doc, but he wouldn't be convinced that she was truly healed until she faced another crowd at another time. "So what did he say to you?"

She frowned. "Didn't you hear him? First, he said the recurring pain I get in my side will go away in no time. Then he said not to worry about being afraid of crowds. They will never bother me again."

Calloway couldn't help feeling astonished by the turn of events. He was no longer aware of the crowd, of Justin, only of Doc and her miraculous recovery. "He not only healed you, Doc, but he did it without even being told what was wrong with you!"

"I know. He's incredible. He hit it on the nose about those jelly beans of yours, too. You know what else? I think we should go back to the RV right now and call Washington. I'll tell Harvey Howell that the government doesn't have any damn business spying on Justin Logos."

Calloway nodded. He had thought he would end up trying to convince Doc to target Logos, but now he didn't see any point to it. Still, he didn't want to offend Camila. "Why don't I call Camila first and explain how we feel. Maybe she can break it to Howell."

"No. Let me deal with Howell directly. I'm not going to tiptoe around him. Justin isn't a threat and I'm going to tell him as much."

"Okay. I'll talk to Camila tomorrow."

For chrissake, Calloway. What a wimp. You're afraid to target Jesus. Now that's really pathetic.

Calloway looked over at Doc, a startled expression on his face. He started to say something, but stopped.

"What is it?"

He shook his head. "Nothing."

The voice had been inside his head, a brief, fleeting impression, like a part of himself that disagreed with their decision. But that didn't feel right. It felt foreign, a thought implanted from outside of him. *No, not that.* He tried again to convince himself it was just a stray thought. But he had a nagging sense that someone had just looked in on him, someone he didn't want to think about.

Go away, he ordered silently. *Just go away and stay away.*

Three

*R*itter *here. Yeah, me again. Coming back at ya. Full power. Directly into your cerebral cortex. We're linked up and it feels good. So good. God, it's been nearly a year, gang.*

Oh, surprised, are we? No one speaking up. I know you're tuned in. This is no Steve Ritter fantasy. No way. I'm beyond that. I can sense you, almost as if we were all in the same room together, holding one of our meetings, just like the old days at Eagle's Nest. Yes, sir, Captain Maxwell. Yeah, too bad about Max. He created us and his creations destroyed him. But that's ancient history. Let's stay with now.

What's that? Henderson, is that you? A little peep out of ol' Hendy, the animal man. Nine dogs and seventeen cats at last count. And only one horse. Cutting back, I see. So you want to know why you're hearing from me now after nearly a year in solitary confinement. You probably don't even know it, but the bastards beamed an electromagnetic field into my cell day and night. It stopped me cold. I couldn't get out.

But that's over. Funny thing. Ha ha ha! I can't help laughing about it. My lazy-ass lawyer finally got them to turn it off. He showed the judge some studies on the dangers of EMF, but the clincher came when the judge realized that the entire prison pop-

ulation was being exposed. That's when he ordered it shut off. He said that if they want to blast an electromagnetic field at me, they've got to set up a separate facility just for me. No way they're going to do that, just too costly for little ol' Steve Ritter.

So now I'm ready to flex our psychic muscles, and, boys, I can tell already that we've gotten stronger. I sit here day after day staring at the wall in my locked room, and all I want to do is fry Calloway's brain. That's what I live for now. I want you three working with me, and I've got a hot idea that I think we should all pursue.

Okay, Johnstone, I hear ya. You're worried that Calloway and Doc might be listening in, and you don't want the FBI hassling you again. Hey, I know they gave you guys a hard time after General Wiley and I went down. You bet I know that. But they couldn't do anything to you guys. It was all too unbelievable for a court of law. My case was different, of course. I was in the plane over Washington with Wiley and the goddamn bomb, after all.

But not to worry, Johnstone. You're right in thinking that our two former colleagues are still wired in, connected to us at the psychic hip, thanks to Maxwell and his drugs. But we've got a secure line. Clear and secure. I figured out a way of cutting them off when I need to talk to you. It's easy. Real easy.

I target Calloway and as soon as he starts to pick me up, I put an imaginary EMF around him. Only thing is, it's not so imaginary. As long as it's in place, he can't reach us and we can't get him. The same goes for Doc. I did her, too.

Yeah, that's right, Johnstone. It's like magic, and that it is. Yeah, that it is.

Now you guys got me sidetracked. Where was I? Oh, yes. My bright idea. Do we all know who Justin Logos is? Yeah, the guy some people are saying is Jesus. Oh, I see I've struck a nerve. We don't like him. Now Timmons, don't be so quick to judge. Let's not scoff until we know more about him.

Why bother, Hendy? Is that what you want to know? Here's why. The White House is worried about Logos. They wanted Calloway and Doc to target him, but our old buddies won't touch Mr. Son of God, which makes me laugh. So Calloway has a weakness.

Let's play on it. If he won't do it, then it's up to us, boys, to do our patriotic duty. So let's flex our muscles and play the field for a while. Let's go to work.

No, Timmons. We're not working for General Wiley any longer. He's not in this game. Pay attention now. We're targeting Justin Logos.

Okay. I'm getting a building, like a warehouse, but different. It's a huge open hall with rows of folding chairs. The place must seat more than a thousand people. But all the seats are empty now. I see a long counter by the door. At the other end of the hall I see cubicles, a half dozen or so, with tables behind them. This is where Logos works; it must be his clinic. Big place.

Nobody's here, but I'm drawn toward the back wall. I see a couple of doors. One goes into a room with boxes, a supply room. Okay, let's focus on the other door. Stay with me now. I already know he's behind it. Let's go take a peek. Yeah, it's his private room and there he is sitting on the floor on a cushion like some kind of guru. He's burning incense and a candle on a low table in front of him. What an asshole.

Moving closer now. Let's go inside and see what makes this guy tick. Stay with me.

He stared straight ahead into the cobalt darkness. He awaited the word, the message. His Father always brought a message, direction, guidance, but today, in the aftermath of his talk, he heard nothing. Only silence.

In the center of the table, a hundred-year-old, cobalt-blue

bottle rested on a blue velvet cloth. He always stared at the old perfume bottle when he called on his Father, whom he likened to a powerful genie. Something about that deep blue color entranced him. He'd first seen this bottle in his mother's room when he was five years old. He'd stared in fascination at it, and that was when his Father had appeared to him. He'd materialized as an old man with a white beard, the very image of God that his mother had instilled in him.

By the time he was a teenager, Justin had begun to doubt that the bearded one, whom he still called Father, was actually God. He wanted proof, and once he demanded it, his Father no longer appeared to him. He became a voice, who continued to guide him when he asked for help, and eventually he began to understand that his Father was not the one and only God, but a master creator who lived outside time and space and who created worlds. He now preferred to think of his Father as the Thunderbird, the defier of the Vulture, because the image was more meaningful than that of an old, bearded man.

He called out again to his Father, and again he was answered by silence. "Why, Father, have you abandoned me? I've done everything you've asked. I warned them about the Vulture. I did as you said."

He knew that something was blocking him from moving ahead. Sometimes, he felt that he was a fraud, not because he didn't actually heal people, but because the power so obviously came from elsewhere. He was a mere conduit, and still people followed him and even pledged their lives to him.

Know thyself. That was one of the key messages he offered in his talk. Yet, ironically, he didn't really believe that he knew himself. He was aware of something in him that confused and frightened him, a hidden part of himself that he didn't understand—the part of him that manifested when he didn't take his medication. He had lost contact with that part of himself, or maybe he had never made contact. That, too, made him feel like a fraud. At some point, he needed to explore that side of himself. Soon.

He released the thought and focused on the bottle, but within seconds a disturbing thought insinuated its way into his mind. A betrayer had infiltrated his inner circle. He knew then, without a doubt, that to move ahead the betrayer had to be exposed. An image suddenly appeared in the bottle, the face of a woman. He closed his eyes, blocking it out. Within the hour, he was expected to attend a dinner with the apostles, and the woman, the betrayer, would be among them.

Now this is interesting. It sounds to me like the Son of God is heading for the Last Supper. I can't wait. I wonder what's on the menu. Ah, Johnstone thinks he's a vegetarian.

What's that, Hendy, you don't want me calling him the Son of God? Sorry, but that's his handle.

Timmons, speak up. What's on your mind? You think that if he were really the Son of God, then he would've known we were in his head. Maybe he did know. Maybe he just doesn't care. What interests me is that in his mind, he's not the Son of God at all. He's more like the son of god with a small g, a lesser god.

That's a good point, Johnstone. His god might not be the God, but he's big enough to create worlds, including our own. That impresses the hell out of me.

Timmons, the skeptic, would like to wash his hands of this whole thing. But he wonders what medication the Son of God is on. I don't know the answer to that yet, but I think it's the key that opens doors. Now I need to rest a few minutes before the big dinner.

Four

Melissa Dahl picked at her dessert, feeling anxious. Justin, who sat at the head of the long table, had seemed particularly introspective this evening, barely looking at his apostles. Everyone seemed vaguely uneasy, probably because Justin's speech earlier today had caught everyone by surprise. Out of nowhere, it seemed, he had started talking about big cosmic birds, something he'd never before mentioned.

They'd eaten a sumptuous meal made by an East Indian chef Melissa had hired. The food, with its ginger and curry seasoning, reminded her of her time in India, where she had discovered Justin. He encouraged her to arrange the dinners at the ranch house to honor his apostles, some of whom had volunteered their services for several years. But now she wondered if she should end this monthly tradition. The apostles were useful, but she'd always felt vaguely threatened by them, as if their helpful deeds weakened her power.

Suddenly, Justin began speaking in a low voice as if he were talking to himself. Everyone leaned forward to hear his words. "One of you will leave the ranch very soon. But this one will return wearing the robes of an inquisitor."

A hush fell over the table. "Justin, what did you say?" Melissa asked, frowning.

"This one has been sent by the government to orchestrate my downfall."

She watched his eyes to see if he would reveal the betrayer, but he stared down at his plate. Then he sampled his green-tea ice cream as if he'd said nothing unusual.

Justin's comments left Melissa stunned, but she managed to smoothly shift the subject before the matter got out of hand. She would wait until everyone had left before she talked to him about the supposed betrayer. "Justin, I think everyone would like to hear more about the Thunderbird and the Vulture. I, for one, am curious about why you have never used those terms until now."

He stared at his dessert a moment, swirling it with his spoon. Then he stood up. "I don't know why I do what I do sometimes. Most of what I say is directed to me from the Father, yes, the Thunderbird. I speak for him. He said it was time to move people away from the images of the past and tell everyone about how I see him. That provided me with a way of explaining the Vulture.

"For the past two thousand years, we have talked about the Vulture in terms of a horned creature from a place called hell. But that analogy is no longer relevant. The planet is moving into a higher vibrational level that will allow us to expand our awareness of the nature of nonphysical reality and its relationship with the physical world.

"Long before the birth of Christ, spiritual leaders in the Mideast attempted to end the divisiveness among peoples by moving past the concept of the many competing gods to the one God. It was a worthy effort. But in truth, both explanations are true. There is the one God and there are also many higher beings who are godlike in their existence. The Thunderbird is a collection of these beings who are aligned with the master creator, God, the Father. Other beings, who in the past might have been known as fallen angels, follow another path, one that denies the existence of the master God.

"This group of beings is known as the Vulture. It is strong, so strong that the Vulture will kill me. That time is very near. So this may be our last gathering here at this table."

Several seconds of silence passed. Then someone shouted, "No!" A second, then a third person erupted, then all the apostles responded nearly in unison. "No . . . no . . . no!"

A spontaneous outpouring of emotion rippled around the table. Some grew agitated; others began to weep. One woman, Claire Bernard, looked away. Melissa, caught off guard again, remained dumbfounded.

Justin raised his hands. "No, please, don't mourn me. I know that the Thunderbird will prevail, I will rise from the ashes to be with you again. In a sense, I will never leave."

"But will we recognize you? Will we see you as you look now?" one of the disciples asked.

"I will be as I am now," he said in a resonant voice.

Melissa saw the glazed look in Justin's eyes and she knew that his proclamations were coming from outside of him. In fact, his comments about resurrection clearly contradicted his own beliefs. He'd said many times that he didn't believe that Jesus had been physically resurrected from the dead. Yet, now he had told everyone that he would be back.

He held out his arms as if to embrace everyone. "Remember, I love you and I will always be with you."

Melissa closed the door as the last of the apostles left. Finally, she could talk to Justin alone. Although everyone had been upset about his comments on his own death and the existence of a betrayer among them, Justin had refused to answer any questions. He only reaffirmed what he'd said, that there was nothing to worry about, that he would return from the dead. But he'd damned well better give her a more detailed explanation.

"Justin, we need to talk," she said, catching up to him as he climbed the stairs.

"I'm tired, Melissa. I need rest."

"So do I, but you've got to tell me why you said those things. Did you take your medication this morning?"

He stopped halfway up the stairs. "Melissa, you don't have to treat me like your child."

Oh, yes, I do, she thought. He was so caught up in his work that if she didn't keep close tabs on him, he wouldn't eat, he wouldn't sleep. He would work until he collapsed. He definitely wouldn't remember his medication, and when he forgot, all sorts of strange things happened. It was as if he became another person.

"Justin, if you think your life is in danger, please tell me. We'll beef up the security. J.D. can hire extra help or we can cancel the clinic for a week. Whatever it takes."

He continued up the stairs. "You're overreacting, Melissa."

She hurried after him as he reached the top of the stairs and headed down the hall toward his room. "No, I'm not. I'm just trying to understand what you meant."

He stopped and took her hand. They walked down the hall past her room. They'd kept separate bedrooms for three years now, because Justin preferred sleeping alone. He said he required little sleep and didn't want to bother her. She didn't like it, but she went along with it. They stepped into his bedroom and she marveled at the difference between their rooms. Hers was cluttered with furniture, framed photos, mementos, stacks of books, and usually a basket of clothes. His room always looked spotless, as if he had just checked into a hotel room and hadn't unpacked his bag.

He sat on the edge of the bed and patted the spot next to him. She sat down and immediately felt uncomfortable. It had been months since they'd had sex together, and she often wondered if he suspected that her needs were being satisfied by someone else.

"So what do you want to know?"

"Everything. Why did you say that you're going to die? What about all of our plans?"

"We all die, Melissa, in our time. It's nothing to worry about." He frowned, looking puzzled about something. "But in my case I will return from the dead."

"How will you do that? If you can't make someone's lost arm or leg come back, how can you come back from death?"

He lay back on the bed and clasped his hands behind his head. "It's a totally different matter. It will simply seem as if I never died. Don't ask me how I know that, because I don't know the answer. Not yet. I just know that it's true."

She turned to him, mystified and unsettled by his calm acceptance of his impending death and the contradictions it created with his vision of their glorious future. But his last comment left her with a glimmer of hope. If it seemed as if he never died, then maybe everything was okay. He reached up to her. She leaned over him and folded into his arms. She held him, more for security and comfort than a desire for sex. She no longer even thought of him as a sexual partner.

He ran his hands down over her hips, and she felt his growing interest in her. He kissed her; their tongues dueled for a few moments, then he nuzzled her neck and nibbled on her ear. He slid his hands along the inside of her thigh and between her legs.

He rubbed her gently, circling his fingers through the fabric of her slacks.

She slid her hands along his chest, down over his flat belly, and then felt his erection threaten to burst through his khakis. Maybe if she made love as in the old days, he would stop talking about death. Maybe it was all a subconscious ploy to get her attention, to win back her affections.

She dug deep for the old feelings that always used to excite her. Who else made love to the reborn Savior? No one. She was his only lover and she knew that other women were endlessly curious about what that experience was like. She didn't want to encourage or disappoint them, so she never gave even the slightest intimation about his prowess as a lover.

She was about to climb on top of him when he whispered in her ear, "This may be our last time, you know."

She rolled away. "Why did you say that? I don't want you to die. Besides, you just said you were coming back, that we wouldn't even know you died."

"I know what I said. I *will* be back. But I also know that our life as sexual partners is about to end."

"Damn you, Justin. Why are you doing this to me?" Did he know about her secret liaisons, that she had taken a lover? Maybe that was why he was antagonizing her with his threats.

She lay back down, intent on following through with what they had started as if she could erase everything that had happened this evening. She kissed him again, but this time there was no passion.

She rested her head on his chest. Then she recalled something else he'd said at dinner. "Justin?"

"Hm?"

"The betrayer. You said that one of the apostles would betray you."

"That's right." He sounded cautious now.

She thought about each of the apostles. They all seemed so dedicated and loyal. "Which one? Who is it?"

"It will become apparent."

"Just tell me. I want to know."

Justin closed his eyes and she didn't think he was going to answer. Then, in a quiet voice, he said, "She who lacks faults is too good to be true. Enthusiasm and energy abound and so does ability."

Riddles. He was giving her riddles, making her guess. "Who is it—a woman?"

Eight of the twelve were women, and that had been a source of numerous jokes since the apostles from the time of Jesus had been men. As she thought over the possibilities, she eliminated each of them until one remained, one who was talented, abundantly energetic, and resourceful. *Too good to be true.*

"Damn. It's Claire. It's got to be Claire Bernard. She's your most dedicated nurse, and she's only been here seven or eight months. She wants to do everything. We're always joking that she should run this place."

"I don't have to look far to find betrayal," he muttered, almost to himself.

"What was that, Justin?"

This time he didn't respond. His breath was deep and slow. He'd fallen asleep. It didn't matter. She was confident she'd pinpointed the one.

Melissa moved through the night toward the guesthouses, simple one-room cabins. She assigned them to special guests or to volunteers who didn't have RVs or trailers. She headed directly to number three, the cabin where Claire had been staying.

She rapped her knuckles against the door.

The compact blonde peered through the doorway. "Melissa! What's going on?"

"Can I come in?"

Claire hesitated. "It's kind of a mess right now. I was just getting ready for bed."

"I insist. Please let me in."

Claire stepped aside and Melissa moved into the cabin. The nurse had changed into jeans and a sweatshirt, and Melissa caught her breath as she saw that Claire wore a handgun on a strap under her arm. Suddenly, Melissa realized that she didn't know who or what she was up against.

She looked around and saw that she'd interrupted Claire in the midst of packing her luggage. "Where are you going?"

"I decided it's time I leave."

Melissa looked at the gun again. "Without telling us?"

"I was planning to say good-bye in the morning."

"I don't think you were going to tell us anything. I think you were leaving tonight. You're the betrayer."

Claire took a step closer to her. Her blue eyes bore into Melissa as if she were excavating her innermost thoughts. "Is it me, or could it be you, Melissa? Is there something you are hiding that could bring down Justin and everything he stands for?"

"What are you talking about?"

"I think you know."

"Who are you, anyhow? What's the gun about?"

Even though she was short, Claire looked tough now, a distinct shift from the gentle, enthusiastic nurse that Melissa knew. "I'm a federal agent. But I'm also a registered nurse who provided free care and assistance for eight months. You got a good deal."

Melissa backed toward the door. "I want you out of here. I'll give you fifteen minutes. If you're not gone by then, I'm sending J.D. down here to escort you off the ranch."

Melissa turned and left. She struggled to keep herself from shaking with anger and confusion as she walked back to the house. What did the bitch know? How much did she know? She realized that Claire had spent considerable time with her as well as with Justin. She couldn't help wondering if she was the target and Claire intended to destroy Justin by undermining her.

Five

For the last hour, the landscape had been monotonously similar, flat and dry and empty. A sparse forest of oil rigs offered the only relief. But Calloway knew that within minutes, the scenery would abruptly shift as Mother Earth opened her lips and the road curved downward into a fertile valley on the banks of the San Juan River.

"I hope we made the right decision," Calloway said as they neared Bluff, Utah, after a comfortable four-hour drive in his RV. They'd left the ranch right after breakfast and taken their time by stopping at a couple of small towns en route.

"What do you mean?" Doc asked.

"I hope what we did doesn't damage your plans." After returning to the RV, Doc had left a terse message for Harvey Howell. She explained that after three days at Justin's ranch, she and Calloway still felt Justin Logos was not a valid target for remote viewing. Furthermore, they respectfully declined the request to pursue the project any further.

"My plans? You mean *our* plans. I need your help, Trent. The new guys aren't going to be ready for a while."

"Like I told you, I'll help if I can. But you've got to understand, I've got other commitments now with Ed Miller and the river-rafting business." Calloway had ended his remote-viewing career several years ago when he retired from the air force, and he wasn't about to go back to it, at least not full-time.

"Take it easy, Trent. I know your agenda. As far as Howell goes, I'm not going to worry about it. I've said all along that if I'm running a remote-viewing program, I'm not going to be manipulated by politicians or bureaucrats. If Howell doesn't like it, tough."

Doc's position seemed fixed. He knew her as stubborn and overbearing at times, but she usually allowed some flexibility in her positions. He was surprised that she would be willing to give up everything she'd been working for in recent months. Maybe her close call with death a year ago, when a bullet had missed her heart by an eighth of an inch, had changed her attitude. Or maybe her encounter with Justin Logos had altered something in her.

Calloway was not so worried about Doc's project as he was about the future of his tentative new relationship with Camila. Their rejection of her efforts could put a damper on it. "Doc, there's something I've been meaning to tell you."

"Oh, you're finally going to say something about you and Camila. You didn't think I picked that up?"

"You know?"

"Are you forgetting that I've got some talent myself, Trent? I feel it every time you mention her name. You two have reconciled."

"That's right. Well, sort of. It's not written in stone or anything."

"Is it ever?"

"Camila and I are not exactly living similar lives right now. I'm just concerned that she might take it the wrong way when she finds out we turned down the project."

"Hey, when you mix work and pleasure, it can get sticky."

"Yeah."

He pushed aside his concerns and focused on the road as they descended toward the river and the town of Bluff. Built by Mormons in the late nineteenth century, the tiny town's red sandstone exteriors matched the bluffs rising on either side of the river. As they entered the town, Calloway looked up at the Twin Navajos, two spires of red rock that towered above the town's trading post and were backed against rugged sandstone cliffs. They drove along one of the town's narrow streets and passed a couple of tacky trailers that had taken up residence alongside the sandstone houses. Calloway pulled up to Miller's two-story house and eased the RV off the road.

Located on a large corner lot, the house looked out onto a dilapidated ball field where grass refused to grow. Behind the field, the landscape rose abruptly to a flat-topped hill where an Anasazi Indian village had once been located. Broken bits of pottery could still be found without much trouble, and Miller kept an old washtub on his porch half-filled with shards of pottery and arrowheads that he'd picked up. In the distance, the majestic reddish brown bluffs could be seen high above the river in the afternoon sun.

As he climbed out of the RV, Calloway stretched his legs. They walked around Calloway's Jeep Wrangler and Doc's Explorer, both parked in the gravel driveway near a massive cottonwood tree. Then he noticed a familiar old, rusted pickup belonging to Guy Shulpa and a new Dodge Durango with a coat of dust on its shiny white surface. He wondered who was visiting Miller.

"Hi, Trent. How are you?"

Calloway glanced toward the shed near the back of the property where the Navajo boy was unloading a truck piled with rafting gear. "Hi, Guy! I'm fine."

"Who's that?" Doc asked.

"He's a local kid who's been helping out. His uncle is another river guide, but he's got a problem with the bottle."

"Ah, so you've got an assistant," Doc said with a laugh.

"Right. I guess I'm moving up in the world." Calloway knocked on the porch door, then opened it.

"Hey, Ed. You here?"

"C'mon in."

Miller stood in the doorway to the kitchen. His watery blue eyes gazed out at Calloway from his leathery face. He was a tall, large-boned man with thick white hair, which fell over his collar. He often complained about his bad knees, but was remarkably fit for his age.

A retired silver miner from Aspen, he had moved here thirty years ago, started a river-rafting business, and now he was grooming Calloway to take it over. He'd even talked about selling his business and his house, probably the best kept of the old Mormon sandstone houses, to Calloway and moving to Florida. But Calloway figured that Miller was too much of a desert rat to ever abandon Bluff. Besides, Calloway wasn't sure that he wanted to stay here. Some days, he felt dedicated to his work on the river and was satisfied with his life. On other days, he felt the urge to roam as he'd done ever since leaving Project Eagle's Nest and the air force. Now there was also Camila to consider.

Miller smiled as if withholding a secret. "Got someone waitin' for ya."

They stepped inside and Calloway saw a dark-haired woman sitting at the kitchen table. "Camila!"

Surprised and somewhat baffled, he walked over and hugged her as she stood up. Seeing her again, especially without any warning, sent him into emotional turmoil. "Good to see you again so soon."

"Yeah, I'm back."

He heard a note of reserve in her voice and sensed stiffness in her movements. He knew her arrival related directly to Doc's call to Howell.

"I'm here to see you . . . both of you." She hugged Doc and exchanged greetings with her.

She looked slender in her tight black jeans, especially standing next to Doc. Her dark, curly hair was tied back, accenting her striking facial features, the high cheekbones, aquiline nose, and warm brown eyes.

"When did you get here?" Calloway asked.

"Within the hour."

"But I bet it's not a pleasure trip," Doc put in as they all sat down.

"Good guess. We do need to talk. I finally got you scheduled for a very important meeting next week in Washington. It's going to determine how much support you're going to get for Third Eye."

"Great. I want Trent there, too."

"Of course." Camila smiled. "That's important."

It annoyed him that Doc just took for granted that he would drop everything and fly to Washington, that she assumed he would be ready to work for her new project. He had never wanted psychic abilities, nor was he born with the talent. A lightning strike had rewired his brain, and his life had never returned to normal. Long ago, he had resigned himself to his visions and the voices that whispered in his ears. But that didn't mean he was always available, always waiting for the next opportunity to show what he could do. In spite of his reservations, he conceded he would help Doc, especially since it would give him a chance to spend more time with Camila.

Calloway turned to Miller and patted him on the shoulder. "I hope everything went okay."

"No problem. I took a group out this morning."

"I thought Charlie was going to handle that one."

Miller rolled his eyes. "Charlie was unavailable, if you know what I mean. So I'm glad you're back. We've got two more going out in the morning."

"I'm afraid I've been keeping Ed from his work," Camila said.

"Oh, no. I've enjoyed every minute of it. Damn, it's not every day that someone steps right out of the television and into my kitchen. I see you all the time on the tube speaking up for the president."

"Yeah, Ed watches CNN all day," Calloway said with a laugh.

"Ed says he doesn't mind if you take another couple of days off next week," Camila added.

"Hell, Trent worked every day for nearly two months until he took off to New Mexico. I don't mind if he takes another couple of days as long as he can help out tomorrow. I can't handle two trips by myself."

"I'll be there." Calloway was actually more interested in getting back on the river than he was in going to Washington. But, in deference to Doc, he kept his thoughts to himself.

Miller laid a hand on his shoulder. "Well, I'll let you guys talk. I've got some equipment to put away."

"You want me to help?" Calloway asked, starting to stand up.

"Naw. I've got Guy back there doing the heavy stuff. He's

working out well. Camila, Doc, you're both welcome to stay.
I've got plenty of room here." Miller started to leave, but stopped
at the door. "By the way, this Jesus fellow in New Mexico. Is
he for real?"

"Justin Logos is a real, bona fide healer," Doc said force-
fully, looking from Miller to Camila. "That much I can vouch
for. If he wants to say he's the reincarnation of Jesus, well, so
what."

Miller shrugged, surprised by Doc's emotional response.
"Well, I just asked."

After he left, Doc turned to Camila. "Okay, let me guess.
You heard about our report to Harvey Howell."

"Exactly, and I'm disappointed. I'm sorry to barge in like
this, but we need to straighten this out right away."

Calloway didn't mind her barging in at all. He hoped that
she'd also made the trip so she could spend some time with him.
They needed time together to work things out or their tentative
reconciliation would fall away as if it had never happened.

Doc crossed her arms. "I think you're wasting your time
coming here, Camila. We've made up our minds."

Before Doc could say anything more, Calloway interrupted,
"Camila, I know that Harvey Howell is pressuring you, but we
just don't feel that Justin Logos is a viable target. Sure, he's
weird. He claims he's the Messiah, the Son of God. He's attracting a lot of attention, and he's even made predictions of a disaster. But a lot of people make predictions like that. It doesn't
mean we should invade his privacy."

Doc nodded. "That's right. We've got to draw the line somewhere, and I think this is a good starting point. I personally do
not want to go into Third Eye with a precedent like that hanging
over my head."

Camila listened closely, but Calloway could tell she wasn't convinced. "I understand your concerns, Doc. But you don't have the full picture. There's more to this than you realize."

"If you know something we don't, maybe you should tell us," Calloway said.

Camila shook her head. "It's privileged information, and besides, I'd like to see if you can verify it psychically."

Calloway recalled something that had occurred to him while he'd been listening to Justin yesterday afternoon. "I think I already know what you're getting at. Logos sees himself becoming some sort of world leader, very influential."

"Maybe so. But how does he expect to achieve that goal?" Camila asked.

Calloway thought a moment. "I don't think he knows how it's going to happen. He's leaving it to divine intervention."

Camila didn't like the answer. "If you looked a little deeper, you might find out more pertinent information that doesn't have anything to do with divine intervention."

Calloway could tell that Doc was about to explode. Her body tensed, her massive bosom swelled with indignation. "I can't believe I'm hearing this from you, Camila. So what if the guy wants power? So do a lot of people. Today, it's Justin Logos. Next week we'll be asked to remote view presidential candidates who want to knock David Dustin out of office. I'm sorry. This is totally unacceptable."

Calloway wished that Doc would control herself. Even though he and Camila had been apart seven years, he knew that she didn't respond well to intimidation. Doc, on the other hand, had always been quick to speak her mind, regardless of the consequences. She also had endearing qualities, a sense of compassion and caring that had made her one of the most well liked and respected members of Eagle's Nest, the old remote-viewing program. But those aspects of her personality weren't visible at the moment.

Camila, to her credit, seemed unperturbed by Doc's outburst. "Listen to me closely. What I'm saying is that remote viewing would be a noninvasive way to make certain that Justin Logos and his partner, Melissa Dahl, aren't planning any acts of violence of a similar nature to what happened last year with George Wiley and Freedom Nation. We don't want to spy on their private lives or go on a fishing expedition for dirt. We just want to protect the country, particularly the capital, which might be a target again."

Ironic, Calloway thought. A year ago, he had pleaded with Camila, trying to get her to believe that a backpack nuke was en route to Washington. At first Camila didn't want to believe him. But with the help of Doc and their former colleague Eduardo Perez, Calloway had not only managed to find the bomb and stop it from reaching its destination, but Wiley, the Freedom Nation leader, was captured and his plans to create a new country in the American West were left in disarray.

Their success, though, had not been without its costs. Perez had died in an attack by the Freedom Nation militia, and Doc had been wounded. When Doc had recovered from her wound, she was encouraged to start a new government-sponsored remote-viewing program. Calloway, whose Airstream trailer had been destroyed by Wiley's thugs, had bought a new RV and a Jeep Wrangler with the generous payment that he'd been awarded.

Now Calloway felt torn between Doc's insistence that they not allow Harvey Howell to misuse remote viewing and Camila's concerns about national security. He also couldn't help wondering if his tentative new relationship with Camila was at stake.

"I have one question. Has Howell told you exactly what he knows or suspects about Justin Logos?"

Camila hesitated. "Not in detail, no. He thought it best that I didn't know. He wants to see what you come up with on your own."

Calloway nodded. "I'm sorry, Camila, but it just doesn't seem like the right thing to do. I have to go along with Doc on this one."

Camila abruptly stood up. "Well, it's obvious to me that you two have fallen under Justin's spell. I don't think either of you are seeing very clearly right now."

Belatedly, Calloway realized that, in spite of her self-control, Camila had been deeply offended by Doc's remarks and the way he had seconded them. He quickly tried to repair the damage. "Why don't we all rest awhile, then talk some more over dinner down at the café. They've got great Navajo pizza. We can all get a new perspective on things."

Camila glanced at her watch. "No thanks. I think I've heard enough already. I've got a plane to catch." She headed toward the door. "I'll talk to you later."

So much for asking her to join him on the raft trip tomorrow, he thought.

Calloway started after her, but Doc grabbed his arm. "Let her be, Trent. She'll get over it."

He started to pull away from Doc, but then he saw Miller walk up to Camila as she reached her rented Durango. He stared morosely out the open door. "Well, we really impressed her."

"If she's so offended that she gets the program canceled, then that's their loss," Doc said. "Something else will work out for us, if it's meant to."

Calloway was thinking more about how things would work out between him and Camila than any future remote-viewing program. On the one hand, he was disturbed that she seemed to link his take on Logos with their relationship. But he also understood her anger. From her perspective they were acting overly stubborn. Somehow, he would make it up to her.

"Don't look so glum. It ain't the end of the world, Trent, ol' buddy, no matter what she says. She'll come around."

But it felt like the end of the world, of his world. "I hope you're right."

Six

era Peters wandered through the Native American market in downtown Santa Fe. She enjoyed the town's ambience with its adobe buildings, Southwest decor, and the Native American influence. The relaxed atmosphere was a nice change from the high energy/high stress of Washington, D.C. Earlier, she'd spent an hour working on her notes. She would interview Justin Logos later this afternoon for the third and final time, but first she needed to make a stop, an important one.

She stepped outside from the maze of indoor booths and shops and found her rented 4Runner parked a block away. She put on the turquoise earrings she'd bought from an old Apache woman, brushed her auburn hair, then drove toward the bus station. She prided herself on getting people to open up and expose their weaknesses, their human foibles. Justin Logos, however, had been a tough subject, and his sidekick, Melissa Dahl, hadn't helped.

As she waited at a red light in downtown traffic, she called her friend Camila Hidalgo, on her cell phone. She knew Camila was also in the Four Corners area, and they'd talked about getting together this evening in some little town in Utah. But maybe it was too far for Tera to drive. She always forgot how big the

Southwest was and how much time it took to drive from place to place.

"What's wrong, Camila? You sound upset. Aren't you with Trent?"

"I left in disgust."

"Oh, no. You mean it's not working out?" Camila had told Tera that she and Trent had reconciled after seven years apart. Tera was happy for Camila, but it had seemed like a difficult situation, considering the distance and differences in lifestyles.

"It's complicated, Tera. I can't talk about it now."

She knew that Calloway had been one of the CIA's psychic spies when they were married, and she wanted to ask if his talents were being used again. But she respected Camila's privacy. If she wanted to talk, she would do it in her own time.

"So where are you now?"

"I'm en route to Albuquerque to catch a plane back this evening," Camila replied. "How about you? What are you doing?"

"I'm just heading out of Santa Fe to see the so-called Messiah again.

The third time in six weeks. Just wrapping it up."

"I think you just like staying in Santa Fe."

Tera laughed. "I do, but this is a good story, a very good story. Do you want a quick preview? I think you'll be surprised."

"As a matter of fact, I would like to hear it. You sound a little more suspicious of him now."

"You bet I do. He and Dahl haven't revealed their entire story." Tera then related what she knew.

The combination of research and luck had paid off. She had documented Justin's true heritage, and she was literally ready to tell the world. In her interactions with Dahl, she had sensed that the woman had been abused as a child, and that, too, had turned out to be true in a way that Tera could never have guessed.

"Are you kidding?" Camila said when Tera finished. "Does she know? She must know."

"It's possible that she doesn't, but not likely. That's what I want to find out."

"I'm stunned, Tera. I'm really stunned. That is an incredible story. Are you sure that you've got it down?"

"Definitely."

"When will we see it?"

"It's coming right up. Next week. We've got a two-hour slot for it. We're calling it *The Man Who Would Be Jesus*. It's the most in-depth story that's been done on him."

"It sounds like the story of your career. But what do you think is going to happen to them?"

"I've thought a lot about it. Justin might survive as a healer, but the story will probably end his Messiah claim. As for Melissa Dahl, I don't know. It worries me. But I think it's time for the truth."

"Hey, anyone who claims to be the embodiment of the Second Coming is definitely open to scrutiny," Camila said. "Don't lose any sleep over it."

Tera spotted the bus station and turned into the parking lot. "Thanks, Camila. I appreciate that. It's just a matter of confronting them with their accuser, along with the evidence, and getting their reaction, his and Dahl's. I wouldn't do it this way except that it's so damned hard getting any kind of emotional reaction out of him, and it's been tough getting Dahl on camera at all."

"Good luck. I'll be watching, and I won't say anything to anyone, of course."

"I'll talk to you in a couple of days." Tera knew that Camila appreciated the advance notice, and she also knew that her friend would tip her off on a story sooner or later, giving her a jump on the competition. But Tera had never exploited her friendship and considered Camila a friend first and a news source second.

Tera eased the 4Runner in front of the building and stopped by a sign that said No Parking or Standing. A woman leaned against the wall smoking a cigarette. Tera recognized Betsy Lambert and rolled down the passenger window. She leaned over the seat.

"Betsy! Over here."

The woman peered at her, then hesitantly stepped toward the vehicle. She exhaled a cloud of smoke, dropped her cigarette on the sidewalk, and rubbed it out with her heel. She climbed into the vehicle. "Well, I'm here. Just like I said I would be."

"Have you been waiting long?" Tera pulled away from the curb.

"About ten, fifteen minutes by the door. The bus got here at ten-thirty this morning. I tried to sleep in a chair, but you know how that goes."

"Oh, I'm sorry. If I'd known that, I would've picked you up sooner. You should've gotten a room."

Betsy gave her a surprised look. "A room for three hours during the day? They'd think I was a hooker. Besides, that's a waste of money."

At forty-five, Betsy Lambert appeared a decade older. Her short, dirty-blond hair looked dry and coarse and was made worse by a choppy homemade cut. Wrinkles spread out from the corners of her wounded blue eyes. No makeup covered her weathered face. Tera tried to imagine what she had looked like at fourteen, but could find no telltale signs of the girl Betsy had once been. It was as if that part of her life had been wiped away. *Destroyed* was a more realistic description, Tera thought. Betsy had had a rough life, and she would soon revisit a terrible part of her past.

"How was the bus ride?"

"I don't like sleeping in buses much. So I'm kind of tired. Real tired. I'm not really looking forward to this, either."

"Don't worry, Betsy. I'll be right there with you." Tera drove away from the bus station and headed out of town. She tried to make small talk with the woman, but Betsy seemed guarded. Something was on her mind, something she wasn't revealing. Then Tera realized it must be the money. She'd sent Betsy $200 to cover her expenses and had told her there would be another $500 for her time and effort.

Tera reached over into her purse and felt for her wallet. She worked it open with one hand and found the check. "By the way, here's your payment. I really appreciate your help."

Betsy took the check and stared at it for a long time. "I used to always go to the check-cashing store, you know. But they keep too much of your money just to cash the check for you."

Tera nodded, tried to think of something positive to say. She'd already visited Betsy's dreary two-room apartment in Denver and knew her lifestyle. "But you've got a checking account now, right?"

"Naw. The bank wouldn't give me one. I hate bank people, the way they look at you. They knew damned well I didn't have much money, and I'm sure they thought that I'd bounce their checks. At least they let me have a savings account."

"That's good. So you've got some savings now."

"No, I just use it to put the checks in, then I take the money right out as soon as the check clears. But, like I said, it's better than the check-cashing store."

Tera was learning from Betsy that banks and telephone companies treated poor people differently from other people, and she wondered if there might be a story there. Betsy had called her last week to ask for an advance on the travel-expense money so she could buy her bus ticket. Even though she had a phone in her apartment, she'd used a pay phone outside a convenience store and had to keep feeding it coins. She'd explained that the phone company didn't allow her to make any long-distance calls. Betsy put the check into her purse, then took out a pack of Eves and started to knock one out.

"Ah, Betsy, I'd prefer if you didn't smoke in the car. It's part of the rental agreement." Besides which, she couldn't stand smoky cars.

Betsy shrugged and put the cigarettes away. "I guess I can do without. The pack will last longer, too."

"We can stop if you want to smoke. Just let me know." Betsy nodded and turned quiet, but Tera could tell she was mulling over something. "What are you thinking about?"

"Me? I was just thinking, you know, that you're a nice lady, coming to my crummy apartment the way you did, and sittin' there listening to me talk about my life. You believed me, too. That's the incredible thing. I knew that writing that letter to CNN would be a good idea."

"Thank you, Betsy. I'm glad you wrote that letter, and I'm glad that you've trusted me, too."

Actually, her story had been so outrageous that Tera had initially refused to believe it. But Tera, who had worked several years for the leading television station in Denver, had called upon her contacts in state and county government. She'd dug into the records, and to her amazement, Betsy's story had checked out.

"Trust? Yeah, I guess I trust you," Betsy said. "You are going to tell the truth, aren't you?"

"Of course I am."

Tera noticed Betsy studying her as if she were a sculpture in a museum. "I bet a lot of men come onto you, don't they?"

Betsy asked in her low, husky smoker's voice. "That pretty red hair, those good looks, that smile. Nice body, too."

Tera tensed. She resented the personal commentary, but quickly covered her anger. "Not really that much. I guess I'm too busy."

"No boyfriend?"

"There's a guy I see from time to time. But we're both reporters and usually running off in different directions. I was married for a couple of years out of college. It didn't work out, though. He was a producer and quite a bit older than me."

"A movie producer?"

Tera shook her head, smiled. "No, just a TV news producer."

Betsy considered what she'd heard. "Well, I think that fellow you're seeing ought to keep an eye on you. You are a real looker and someone's going to fall all over you one of these days."

Tera laughed. "I'll tell him."

"You know, I've worked in restaurants all my life, mostly truck stops actually. When I was younger, these guys used to hit on me all the time. The truckers always wanted to take me out to their cabs, you know, after I got off, or even on breaks."

"Really?" Tera tried not to sound judgmental.

"I was never that much into sex, though. Especially not with fat, married truckers." Betsy's husky voice turned into a growl. "But the ones that had drugs, you can bet that I went out there with them."

"Didn't the drugs make it hard for you to keep your job?"

"I didn't say I did 'em while I was workin', for chrissake. Except for the black dex. Speed, you know. Mostly, I liked the cocaine. I'd get high after work with the other girls." Betsy grinned. "We had some good times." Her smile faded. "But it got old . . . and so did I."

Tera stole a glance at her watch. Another forty minutes. It was going to be a long ride.

"Are you sure they're going to let us in?" Betsy asked. "I hear you've got to have a ticket to get in there and it takes weeks, even months now."

"Don't worry. They're expecting me."

"Yeah, but I got the feeling they're not expecting to see me."

Betsy was right about that. Tera wanted to surprise Justin, and she knew that if she introduced Betsy in advance, there would be no interview. Justin's controller, as she thought of Melissa Dahl, wouldn't allow it.

"That's what I want to talk to you about. We'll be meeting Louie, my cameraman. We're getting you inside as part of the crew. You're going to be working with him, helping him with the sound and lighting. You'll like him. He's nice."

"I don't know nothing about any of that."

Tera patted Betsy on the arm. "Don't worry. Louis will show you everything. You'll do fine."

"What I'm worried about is him. I've heard some real bad things about him."

"Justin? What have you heard?"

Betsy explained that she'd been going to a church that met in an elementary school on Sunday mornings, and the preacher regularly attacked Justin as the Antichrist. "He said Justin Logos was the heart of all evil in the world, and that he fools everyone because he can heal."

"But if he's healing people, he can't be all bad, can he?"

"That's just the way the devil works. He tricks us," Betsy said confidentially.

She was probably repeating her minister's words. Tera had interviewed a couple of ministers with similar opinions. The gist of their argument seemed to be that Justin was too non-Christian to be the returned Jesus. He dismissed the Bible as mostly rubbish. He believed in reincarnation, like the Hindus. He was too unorthodox, too New Age. They considered his beliefs to be contrary to virtually everything they stood for. He was making a mockery of their teachings and their churches, and they felt threatened.

Tera knew that her portrait of Justin would fuel their beliefs about him, and she felt bad about that. Her own opinion, the one she felt was shared by most intelligent people, designated Justin as neither Jesus nor the Antichrist, but as a talented healer who was being misguided by Melissa Dahl. Her story would definitely reveal his incredible abilities.

While Justin appeared vaguely detached from his surroundings, Dahl portrayed herself as a behind-the-scenes visionary. Even though Tera found Dahl's know-it-all attitude annoying, Peters had played to her ego and convinced her to go on camera along with Justin. Now, her own strange story would be revealed, and neither Melissa nor Justin would come out of it unscathed.

Tera glanced over at Betsy and picked up the thread of the conversation. "Did you tell the minister what you know?"

She hesitated. "At first I was afraid to say anything. I thought he would kick me out of the church. But finally one day after church, I let it all out."

"What did he say?"

"He said he would help me."

"Did he?"

Betsy nodded. "You bet he did. He helped me write that letter to you. In fact, he wrote most of it. I just told him sort of what I wanted to say."

Neither one spoke for a few minutes until Betsy broke the silence. "Yeah, I'm really glad we're doing this."

"Why?"

"Because we're going to show the world who that bastard really is." Betsy's voice faded to a whisper. "Everyone will know and that will be the end of him. I'm going to make sure of that." Tera frowned. "What do you mean?"

Betsy stared ahead, a sullen look on her face, as if she hadn't heard the question.

"Okay, that should do it," Calloway said as he and Guy finished loading the supplies in the kid's old pickup. "I'll see you then at seven sharp."

"I'll be there." Guy climbed into the pickup and drove off.

Calloway walked back to Miller's house. Now he was anxious to get back to Sand Island and spend a peaceful evening alone in his RV. He would've preferred spending it with Camila and taking her on the trip tomorrow, but thanks to Doc and her belligerence, there was no point in even thinking about that. Before he left, he needed to wake Doc up and send her on her way.

He found her sleeping on the couch in Miller's family room where he'd left her an hour ago. He was about to shake her shoulder, but he hesitated. He watched her sleep, listening to her slow, shallow breathing, and suddenly felt sorry for her. He recalled that shortly before he'd met her, Doc's husband of twelve years and her ten-year-old son had died in a traffic accident. As far as he knew, she'd never been involved with anyone in the intervening years.

"Hey, Doc. Time to wake up," he said, touching her shoulder.

She awakened with a start and looked around, a surprised expression on her face. She focused on him. "Trent! Why did you wake me up?"

"Because you wanted me to wake you up at four. It's five after."

She sat up. "I was having this incredible dream."

"Oh, a sex dream?"

"No, a remote-viewing dream."

"What's that called, a busman's nightmare?"

"Very funny. No, this was interesting. I dreamed about a group of remote viewers who were living sometime in the future. They were trying to tell me something. It was important, a message of some sort. But now I can't remember it."

"Too bad."

"Wait a minute." She buried her face in her hands. Then she looked up at him. "Something happened in the future that changes everything."

He stared at her. "That's it?"

She made a face. "Yeah. It seemed so important, but it doesn't make much sense now, does it?"

"Dreams are like that."

She looked up. "Now I remember something else. I think they want to talk to you."

Calloway laughed. "Then I'll see them in my dreams."

Seven

From the second-story bedroom window, the crowd at the center of the camp-ground looked like a blob of multicolored ants—lots of blues, yellows, and reds. If she put her eye to the telescope, Melissa Dahl knew that the tiny creatures would magically transform to men and women dressed in jackets, sweaters, and T-shirts. But right now she didn't want to look any closer. Her focus, after all, needed to be right here in the ranch house where she and Justin would be interviewed in a few minutes.

Her stomach ached and she felt like telling Tera Peters that she'd changed her mind, that she didn't want to go on camera. She preferred staying out of sight, at least for now. But then again she wanted Peters to see her as cooperative. The special on Justin, after all, could be the turning point. It would be the most thorough examination yet of his work and his life, and if Justin was right, dramatic changes would result from it. But now when she thought of the future, she couldn't get by the nagging thought that Justin had also predicted his own death.

"What do you see out there?"

She turned and looked across the room at J.D. Kirby, her security chief. His broad shoulders and massive chest filled the doorway of her bedroom. "I see the end."

"What do you mean?" The husky, handsome bodybuilder took a couple of steps closer.

"Whenever I look out this window, I can't help thinking back to the days when there were only a couple of hundred people in the campground and we didn't take reservations or charge anything. Now it's a big, chaotic mess, a full-time job. But that's going to end. I'm not going to be a campground director much longer, J.D. That is definitely not my role in life."

"You could hire someone. I'm sure one of the apostles would be happy to run the camp."

"You mean someone like Claire?" she said after a pause.

Kirby frowned. "Claire's gone. She left last night without a word to anyone. There's talk that she was going to betray Justin. I think we've seen the last of her."

"I think the talk is right. She was an undercover agent, a fed spying on us." Melissa shook her head. "There are going to be a lot of changes. Justin says that we've got to buckle our seat belts, because it could be a rocky road for a while."

Kirby was about to say something when a beep from his two-way radio interrupted him. He excused himself and quickly moved into the hallway.

She caught a glimpse of herself in the full-length mirror. With her long, slender frame and narrow hips, she might be mistaken for a teenager. But anyone who took a close look would quickly see the lines around her lips and eyes. She would probably look like an old lady on television. Much too old for Justin. In spite of the separate rooms and the fact that she was his manager, not his wife, she had freely admitted to interviewers that they were lovers, that Justin functioned as a normal man. But their relationship had been controversial, especially after she had proclaimed Justin's true identity. Some people didn't want the Messiah to have a sex life.

"Tera Peters and her crew are here," Kirby said. "They're setting up in the media room."

"Where's Justin?"

"On his way from the clinic."

"I'll be glad when this one is over."

Kirby walked over to her. From the front, his brown hair looked short and neatly trimmed, no sign of the ponytail that fell over his collar. He met her gaze, held it. His brown, puppy-dog eyes watched her. So different from Justin. Naive, but kind. Primitive, but well mannered. Poorly educated, but thoughtful. Ultimately, she liked him because he was uncomplicated, understandable. She needed that. She knew she would never fully understand Justin, no matter how hard she tried.

Kirby reached out and touched her hand. "Don't worry about it. You'll do fine, just fine."

She smiled and clasped his hand. "I hope so. If everything goes well, we're going to be free of this ranch, this campground, and these endless healings."

"Gee, I don't know if I like the sound of that. I'll miss my job and I'll miss you, too."

She smiled up at him. "Don't worry about that. I'm not giving you up. I'm going to need you more than ever."

She heard a noise down the hall. She straightened and dropped Kirby's hand. Without another word, Kirby exited through a doorway that led into Melissa's study. "Justin, is that you?"

She walked out to the hallway. His shoulders drooped, he looked tired. "Oh, look at those circles around your eyes." She touched his face. "I thought you were going to quit early today. It's almost time for the interview, you know."

He shrugged as if it didn't matter. "There were a lot of people who needed help."

"You work too hard. You've got to rest more."

"Not much longer."

"I know. Pretty soon we'll be flying from country to country, meeting ambassadors, presidents, and premiers. Right?"

He swept a hand through his blond hair and studied her for a moment, a faint smile on his lips. "How glamorous you make it sound. Is that the lifestyle you're striving for?"

"Justin, you know me better than that. We're moving into a much wider scope. Pretty soon you'll be healing nations and the planet, rather than individuals."

"It still comes down to individuals."

"I know. But you can affect masses. You can reach millions. You can change their lives. You can change the world."

He gave her an odd look, one she couldn't decipher. "It won't happen until after my resurrection. I don't know why that's true, but I sense that it is." He turned and walked down the hall to his room.

Every time Justin made reference to his death or his resurrection, Melissa felt herself spinning out of control into depression. She struggled to push it away again, but it was getting more and more difficult.

In spite of being closer to him than to anyone else, Melissa conceded that a substantial part of Justin would always be out of her reach. That part of him meditated each morning before sunrise and another hour at noon. Justin often spent his evenings in his room alone, and sometimes, while in a deep meditative state, he spoke in an archaic language. When she'd asked him about it, he'd said he was unaware of it and asked for proof.

With his cooperation, she'd managed to record a couple of minutes of his babbling. She'd taken the tape to a linguist in Los Angeles, who had identified it as Aramaic, an archaic language that was spoken at the time of Jesus Christ. The scholar had recognized several words, including the word for time, which had been repeated over and over, but he couldn't make much sense of the monologue. Justin shrugged off the incident. He said he didn't know the language and had no idea what he was saying.

Melissa glanced at her watch, then looked in on Justin. He had taken off his shoes and was lying on his bed staring upward, his eyes open. She knew it was no use prodding him.

"You don't want to go through with this interview, do you?" he said.

"I think we should, but I'm concerned that Peters is going to get tough this time."

He stared blankly toward the ceiling. "Whatever happens was meant to happen."

"She's probably going to ask about our relationship, which we can handle. It's better to be open than to appear to be hiding something."

"That's what you've always said," Justin responded.

"If Claire, or whatever her real name is, talked to Tera today, then she might know what you said about dying."

"I don't think she was undercover for CNN."

"I know, but she still might have talked to her. After all, she knew that Tera was coming back today."

He gazed off a moment. "I don't think they've been in contact. But I wouldn't put it past Tera to use whatever means she can to get her story."

"Well, just in case, we should talk about that. How would you respond if she asked about rumors that you've predicted your death?"

He looked at her as if she were a curious object. "I would say that we can all predict our deaths and eventually we would all be correct."

"Except you said that you were going to die very soon."

"It's a rumor, my rumor, until it happens. Then it's fact."

"Stop it, Justin." Melissa's voice rose an octave. "You're frightening me again."

His eyes slowly closed. "No need for it. There's nothing you can do about it."

She sank into a chair and watched him as he closed his eyes and drifted off. She knew that it was no use questioning Justin any further.

A few minutes later, Justin began to stir. He sat up and smiled. He looked as if he'd lost ten years in ten minutes. He stretched his arms.

"Are you ready, my love?" she asked.

"Of course."

If Justin was aware of any change in Tera Peters, he didn't show it. He greeted her warmly and the interview started off smoothly with Justin answering a few questions about his healing prowess. But Peters wanted to get Melissa involved in the interview, so she turned to her, smiling.

"Melissa, this ranch is a wonderful place for Justin to do his work. I understand that you grew up here and inherited the ranch from your parents. I was wondering if, while you were growing up, the name of the mountains here—Sangre de Cristo—the Blood of Christ—had any special meaning to you?"

"That's an interesting question. I always thought of the land as part American, part Native American, and part Spanish, and it was the Spanish monks, in particular, who brought the Christian flavor to the area, for better or worse."

"For better or worse." Peters nodded thoughtfully. "Could you explain what you mean?"

"Of course, if you ask the traditional Native Americans, the ones interested in maintaining their heritage, about the legacy of Christianity, you'll hear about torture and slavery and forced schooling, bans on speaking the native tongue, and even mandatory haircuts to help destroy their cultures. The lessons of Christianity were often not very Christian in nature."

Peters turned to Justin. "Do you agree?"

"As I've said before, Christianity today has little to do with the teachings of Jesus Christ. They've been greatly altered. All references to reincarnation were removed from the Bible at the Council of Constantinople in the sixth century."

"Why would they do that?"

"It's about controlling the flock. If people think there's only one life, then heaven or hell, it was easier for the priests to keep them in line."

"So you're saying that's not the way Jesus originally conceived Christianity."

He laughed. "Jesus didn't conceive Christianity at all. He didn't want his followers to worship him or build a religion around him. He was an advanced soul who simply wanted people to emulate him, to realize that we are all the sons and daughters of God. But that message was misconstrued and reshaped into Christianity, for better or worse. If you look at the life of the Cappadocian mystic named Balinas, a near contemporary of Jesus, you'll get a much better understanding of Jesus."

"Tell us about Balinas."

"He was a holy man who was interested in all religious teachings, but he didn't embrace any particular one. He traveled the world from Greece and Rome to India and back. He was so advanced in his meditative skills that he had the ability to appear in two places at once."

"He sounds a little bit like you. I've heard stories of you

appearing at a patient's bedside to check on them. But at the same time you were known to be working at the clinic."

He smiled. "Yes, there are those stories, but as the skeptics say, they are hard to prove, especially since I will not perform any such tricks on demand. I'm neither an entertainer nor a guinea pig. Actually, what I admire most about Balinas is that he spoke out against the decadent rulers of the time, like Nero, and he stood virtually alone in condemning the popular Roman games where thousands of humans and animals were killed."

"You also have challenged the leadership of your own country to abandon petty politics and to lead the country into an era of personal transformation. Could you explain what you mean by that?"

"I am simply challenging our leaders to wake up. Most of them are working for the one I call the Vulture, but they don't know it because they're still asleep." Justin took a minute to explain the nature of the Vulture, and its counterpart, the Thunderbird.

"What about David Dustin? Is he working for the Vulture?"

"He has moments of wakefulness. But then his trusted advisors, who are counseled by the Vulture, tell him to go back to sleep."

"You have predicted that the center of power, which I assume is Washington, D.C., is going to be struck by some disaster. Is that because Washington is corrupt, like Rome during the time of Balinas?"

"I don't make such predictions lightly, Tera, and I don't do it as some sort of condemnation of our leaders. Their own actions speak for themselves. What I'm doing is warning people of what is to come."

"But do you definitely see this disaster happening?"

"I would call it a probable event. I don't know when it will happen or what form it will take, but I think it will be fairly soon."

"Can you stop it?"

"I'm a healer. That's my talent. I've also seen my own death. I won't attempt to stop it. If I die, it was meant to happen. If the center of power collapses, that, too, was destined."

"So, you are predicting your own death. When will it happen?"

"Shortly. I'm not only saying that I will die, but I will rise from the ashes."

Tera seemed caught off guard. But she didn't let the revelation pass. "Are you saying that you will be resurrected?"

Justin gathered his thoughts. "We think of time as linear, one event following another. Yet, there is a larger reality where time is much more fluid and where future events can actually alter the past. In this context, I will die and rise again."

"I'm not sure I understand. Are you saying that your death will be the result of something that happens in the future *after* your death?"

"That's right. I know that sounds odd and confusing, but that's all that can be said about it."

"How do you know these things?"

"That's a good question. All I know is that something in me is pushing this information to the surface."

Tera turned to Melissa. "How do you feel about this prediction by Justin?"

"I don't want to see Justin die. I hope he is wrong. If I could prevent his death, I would do it. But he tells me that I can't."

Tera nodded sympathetically. "Melissa, could you tell us, in your own words, how you first met Justin?"

"I'd be happy to."

Omar, Melissa's calico cat, wandered into the room and jumped into her lap. She smiled and stroked its silky fur and gathered her thoughts. "At the time, I was dedicated to my profession as a microbiologist. I was conducting experiments in India on advanced yoga practitioners who were exposed to a flu virus."

"Did they get sick?" Tera asked.

"Actually, most of the yogis were able to either thwart the virus completely or minimize its effects in comparison with a control group exposed to the same virus."

"So where did Justin fit in?"

"He had been traveling throughout Asia and was staying in an ashram not far from where I was working. One of the yogis pointed him out to me as an advanced soul on the level of a young Buddha or Jesus Christ."

Tera nodded encouragingly. "What did you think?"

Melissa laughed. "At first, I thought it was preposterous. He was an American guy with boyish good looks, but then I saw the long line of people waiting to see him. I spent three weeks watching him heal and talking with him between his meditations and healing sessions."

"What was your conclusion?"

"I didn't want to believe that he was the reincarnated Jesus, the essence of the Second Coming. It was just too outrageous. But then he gave me a sign that I couldn't overlook."

Tera leaned forward. "A sign. What kind?"

"One day we were sitting by a small lake where he liked to meditate and I asked him if he believed that he was the returned Savior. He turned to me and opened his hands, and I was shocked to see that his palms were bleeding. Then he raised his shirt and there was a hole in his side. I couldn't believe it. I looked away, and when I looked back, his palms and his side were fine. The blood and injuries had vanished."

Tera glanced between Justin and Melissa. "What did he say to you?"

"Just one thing: 'Sangre de Cristo.' That was when I knew I had to take him home with me."

"Justin, what was that like? Has that happened often?"

"To this day, I have no recollection of the incident. I just remember how upset she was when she described what she saw. To my knowledge, it has never reoccurred."

"So, did Justin readily agree to come here to the ranch with you to set up a healing practice?" Tera asked.

Omar jumped down from Melissa's lap and sauntered away. "No, he didn't. We talked about it, but he didn't want to be the reborn Messiah. He fled to Nepal and I didn't see him for months."

"Is that right?"

Melissa had never told a reporter this part of the story. There was more to it, but she wasn't about to tell Tera Peters how she had found Justin begging on the street and cursing people. That was when she learned about his bipolar syndrome and realized that he needed protection and guidance.

"Yes, I ran off," Justin said, "because I wasn't ready. It was too much to comprehend. But, by the time she found me, which was months later, I was ready to move on. I've been here ever since."

"Interesting." Tera looked thoughtfully at Justin. "Now you readily claim to be the essence of the Second Coming, the returned Messiah, and many people are taking you seriously. A recent CNN poll shows that nearly one in five people believe you are the Messiah, and forty-one percent say that they are open to that possibility. So what can you tell us about your Father, God?"

Justin smiled. "Thanks for asking. First of all, I am the re-incarnation of Jesus the man, not the mythical religious figure we all know about who is so often seen as one and the same as God. God is my father and he is your father, too. I assure you that all of us, whether we recognize it or not, have bottomless holes in our hearts that need to be constantly filled with the knowledge of God."

Tera turned to Melissa again, and something changed in Tera's expression. "Do you see yourself as closer to Mary, the mother of Jesus, or to Mary Magdalene, the devoted follower of Jesus, who Luke, I believe, called the sinner?"

"Well, I'm not his mother, and neither Justin nor I go around calling people sinners," Melissa responded firmly. "That's the verbiage of the past that was related to controlling and deni-grating people. I'm human, and like everyone else, I have my faults. But I suppose, symbolically, I'm a little of both Marys."

"You are aware, of course, that you have offended some Christians because you call Justin the reincarnation of Jesus Christ and yet you live with him as husband and wife, even though you are not married."

"Justin was not meant to take a wife. He is married to hu-manity and its future. I consider myself his first follower, and, yes, I won't deny it, his lover. He needs love like anyone else."

Peters nodded, seemingly agreeing with her. But Melissa could already tell that she was being set up for a follow-up ques-tion. "Now this leads to the matter of Justin's birth. He was found within hours of his birth in a Dumpster behind a restaurant in Chicago."

"That's been documented," Melissa said.

"Do you know anything about his mother?"

"Nothing. No one has come forward, and we suspect she may be dead. It's really a moot issue. As you know, Justin has never claimed that his mother was a virgin, or anything like that."

"That's right," Justin put in. "The concept of virgin births goes against nature and we are all a part of nature, just as we are all linked to God. I respect other people's beliefs, but Jesus Christ was a man of nature, just like me."

Peters turned up her hands. "So you are really just like the rest of us? Is that what you're saying?"

"I'll answer that," Melissa said. "Justin's life is divinely inspired. He is human, but he is far from an ordinary man. The same could be said of Jesus Christ."

"And what about you, Melissa? Are you an ordinary woman?"

Melissa noticed a sudden sharpness in Peters's tone. "As ordinary as they come."

"I have evidence to the contrary."

Melissa looked confused. She noticed one of the crew members moving forward. The woman lowered the microphone that was attached to a long boom as if it were a weapon. Something about the woman bothered her. In the other interviews, she remembered, they had worn miniature microphones on their clothes.

"What are you talking about?" Melissa asked defensively, looking from the woman to Tera.

"Do you remember Betsy Lambert, your old friend from Chicago, back when you were a teenager?"

The name triggered a vague memory. "No, I can't say I do."

"You should remember me, Melissa. We were best friends."

Melissa peered toward the soundwoman, who handed the microphone to the cameraman. She took off her headphones and walked up to Melissa.

"It's me, Betsy. Don't you remember what happened to us

that terrible night? You couldn't have forgotten. We met the guy at a bowling alley, and when it was time to leave, he offered to drive us home. I didn't want to go with him, but you thought he was okay."

Melissa looked at Peters, exasperated. "What exactly is this about? Am I supposed to know what she's talking about?"

"I think you know. I've seen the evidence. Hard evidence."

Tera glanced at Justin, then turned back to Melissa.

"Please explain to us what you're talking about," Justin said patiently.

Peters turned to him. "Melissa and Betsy were both raped by a man they met at the bowling alley when they were fourteen. They were lucky to get away with their lives. He was an escaped convict. He went on a killing spree after the rape and murdered four people before he was shot by the police."

Melissa felt baffled and angry and wanted nothing more than to throttle Peters. "I don't remember. If it did happen, as you say, I blocked it out of my mind." Melissa turned to Peters. "So what's the point of dredging into my past? These are astonishingly inappropriate questions, and bringing this woman here in the guise of one of your crew members . . . I don't understand."

"Melissa, your blood sample is in the county records and so is Justin's. I've had the DNA from both samples analyzed. There's a ninety-nine percent chance that you are Justin's mother."

Melissa bolted to her feet. "That's crazy. This is ridiculous. This interview is over."

"Did you go looking for your lost son, Melissa? Is that why you found Justin?"

"Of course not."

Suddenly, the memories flooded over Melissa. The overwhelming fear as the man strangled and raped her. Hiding her pregnancy from her parents. The birth in a bathroom of a restaurant. And finally, disposing of the newborn.

"That's difficult to fathom, Melissa. But if that's true, you're meeting Justin is a very bizarre coincidence. Don't you agree?" Melissa struggled to stay poised. She felt light-headed. She started to shake, her throat tightened. Perspiration beaded on her brow. She couldn't respond. She looked at Justin. To her amazement, he remained calm.

"Justin, what do you think about what I just said?" Peters asked.

"I think that God acts in strange ways, beyond the understanding of man."

"Beyond yours, too?"

"Like I said, I am a man." He smiled. "And you've just proved it."

Eight

Calloway tried his best to be friendly· and upbeat with the group of Scouts that he took rafting the next day. But he felt miserable from the moment they pushed off from shore until the trip ended late in the afternoon. He felt caught in a bind between his love for Camila and the concern that he shared with Doc regarding the dark side of remote viewing. Calloway, after all, treasured his privacy, and he didn't want to serve as a vehicle for depriving others of theirs. That was the gist of it.

It was after six when he finally finished helping Miller with some mundane scheduling activities and restocking supplies. Calloway looked over the schedule and realized only one trip was planned over the next eight days. He decided to ask Miller for a week off.

"A week, for chrissake, Trent!" Miller scratched the back of his brown neck as they stood outside on his porch. The sun hovered above the distant ridge of bluffs on the far side of the river, and the slanting rays highlighted the patterns of wrinkles on Miller's face.

"Hell, you just took three days off. Then you're going to Washington next week. I don't know."

"I want to go to Washington tomorrow. I have to patch things up with Camila."

"Again?"

"Yeah, again," Calloway said sullenly.

"Oh, I guess I can get Guy to help me out, and maybe Charlie will sober up. But I hate to depend on him."

"There's only one trip coming up."

"That we know of right now. Who knows what's coming up tomorrow."

Calloway started to get annoyed with Miller. "Look, if you don't want me to go, just say so." Now he was ready to quit and drive his RV to Washington, if that's what it took.

But Miller backed off. "Go ahead. Take a week off, damn it. But after this, I expect you to be here the rest of the season with no running around the country. I can't rely on Charlie, and now I'm starting to wonder about you."

Calloway drove his Wrangler back to Sand Island and called Camila. When he heard the recording on her cell phone, he started to hang up. Then he changed his mind. "Camila, it's me. I've got a week off. I'm coming to see you. I'll call your office when I get into town sometime tomorrow. We need to talk." He cleared his throat. "Listen, I love you. I don't want to lose you again. I want to make up for everything that happened, not only yesterday, but all the way back. Well, I'll see you."

"Christ," he muttered after jabbing his thumb against the power button. He sounded like a lovesick idiot.

He pulled into the campground and headed for the RV. He needed to call a couple of airlines for prices and make a reservation right away. He would eat a quick meal, then drive to Albuquerque and take the first flight out in the morning. With so little advance notice, he would pay the full price, probably close to $1,500. But he didn't care. He just wanted to get there and see Camila as soon as he could.

He put on water for pasta and called Doc to tell her what he was doing. "I can't let the Justin matter mess up things between Camila and me, Doc. She made two trips out here this month. I need to reciprocate and spend some time with her."

"I understand. It's important. But don't drive to Albuquerque. Fly out of Durango. That way we can come back together like we were planning. Besides, I already ordered our tickets. You can just change the departure date."

"That's great."

"In fact, let me take care of it through my travel agent. You just get into your Jeep and drive. Stay here tonight."

He shrugged. "Okay, Doc. I'll see you in a couple of hours or so."

She heard the pounding at her bedroom door and her name called, but she ignored it. When it continued, Melissa clasped her hands over her ears and turned her back to the door. She didn't want to see Justin and didn't want his sympathy. She just wanted to die. There was no reason to go on. She had the means to end her life, and the only thing holding her back was her own weakness. If she had any guts at all, she would've pulled the trigger by now.

"Melissa, you're going to starve yourself," Justin pleaded. "You can't stay in your room forever. It's going to be all right. Please, let me in. I can help you."

In spite of her effort to block out the sound of his voice, she could still hear him as if he had invaded her head. "Bullshit! Go away! I told you before to just leave me alone."

Shortly after the interview, Melissa had retreated to her

room, shut the windows, and closed the blinds, cutting off the sight and sounds from the campground. She'd gone to bed and buried herself in deep despair and despondency. Justin had come by twice, but she'd told him to go away.

Meanwhile, Kirby had left dinner outside her room, but she hadn't touched it.

Now, the day after was no better than those first dreadful hours that had followed her encounter with Betsy Lambert. Maybe it was even worse. She sank further and further into her gloom. There was nothing left for her, nothing at all. Her life was over. No one could help her. She had lost everything—her future, her dignity, her sense of well-being, her will to live. It was just a matter of time before she found the nerve to end her life.

Meanwhile, Tera Peters was back in Washington, no doubt laughing and bragging about her exclusive. She would win her awards while shredding Melissa to bits. There would be nothing left of her when it was over.

She could just imagine how the CNN special would show a close-up of her as she admitted she and Justin were lovers. That would be followed by her horrified reaction when she was told he was her son. She and Justin would be ridiculed. She would always be seen as the mother-lover of the so-called Son of God. Her life would be one of infamy, her name synonymous with any horrid or dreadful surprise. They would say that she had risen rapidly, bringing Justin Logos to the world's attention, and then nose-dived into her personal hell. The whole thing had been a huge cosmic kick in the ass, a bad joke, and she was the butt of it.

She heard Justin talking to someone else, then recognized Kirby's voice. The bastards were planning to break down the door.

"J.D., don't you dare!" she shouted. "Don't even try it. I've got a gun and I'll use it, damn it."

"Melissa, listen to me. Don't do it," Kirby pleaded. "I won't break open the door. I promise."

"Okay, just leave me alone."

She walked to the far side of the room, the little pearl-handled .38 bouncing against her thigh through the pocket of her robe. She stood by the window, closed her eyes, and covered her ears again. She didn't relax until she was sure that they were gone.

How had she allowed this to happen to her? Maybe Betsy Lambert was right. Maybe some part of her knew who Justin was. He was the child whom she had lost and wiped from her mind. But that was a lie. She could never erase the memory of that child. It lived deeply buried within her. She must've known and somehow found her child through means beyond the five senses.

But how could she have mistaken her own child for . . . for what? A lover, the Savior? What madness.

She took out the gun and held it to her head. She wondered if her life would flash before her when she pulled the trigger. Maybe she would see herself as a child growing up in Chicago. Would she relive the rape and the birth of her child? She hoped not, but she would like to see herself meeting Justin and to reexperience her early magical days with him. Maybe she would also see herself as a college student and in the lab during her years as a microbiologist.

She lowered the weapon as a thought occurred to her. If she killed herself now, she would leave behind her secret lab. When Justin or someone else discovered it, that person might inadvertently expose himself to a deadly virus. She had left her career behind several years ago, and the stolen viruses were nearly forgotten leftovers of another time. She should get rid of her supply of viruses. Or maybe not. Maybe it was time to consider the unthinkable. It would be a just revenge.

Camila wasn't looking forward to her meeting with Harvey Howell, but the quicker she told him the bad news, the better. She stepped into his office, and Darren, his secretary, greeted her, then picked up the phone and announced her arrival.

"He'd like you to go right in."

She entered Howell's office. The national security advisor waved, pointed to a chair, then continued a telephone conversation. Howell, an average-sized man, was in his midfifties. He had short hair, a receding hairline, and wore round, wire-frame glasses. He was leaning back in his chair, his feet up on his desk. He listened intently to his caller, but said little.

Her thoughts drifted to Calloway. She'd gotten his message and wasn't happy about it. The timing couldn't be worse. She didn't know when she was going to see him. She should've never allowed herself to fall for him again. She thought she loved him, but she conceded it was probably a lost cause.

Finally, Howell told the caller to update him again next week, then rang off. He looked up at her. "Sorry. So, what do we know?"

"Nothing."

He folded his hands on his desk and made an annoying twiddling motion with his thumbs, something he did when he was nervous. "Oh. Tell me about nothing."

"They wouldn't do it. Doc, in particular, is concerned about controls and limitations on remote viewing to protect individual rights. As you know, they can pry pretty deep into their targets."

Howell twiddled again. "For chrissake, Camila. Didn't you tell them the man is a terrorist, or potentially one?"

"I told them as much as you told me. They spent three days on the ranch. They didn't pick up anything."

"They didn't try." Howell glared at Camila. "This annoys the hell out of me. Does Doc really expect to come here next week and ask for money when they won't work for us?"

"I think she does."

"Well, she's going to find out that she can't pick and choose her assignments willy-nilly without knowing anything about them."

He looked at Camila waiting for a reaction. She almost told him that no one said *willy-nilly* anymore, but she held off. That was the sort of thing she told the president, because he had asked her to monitor his speech and watch for words or phrases that were grammatically incorrect or out-of-date. She nodded, encouraging Howell to continue.

"Cancel the meeting. I don't see any point in going any further. As far as I'm concerned, this proposed project is dead."

"Harvey, first of all, I'm not your secretary. I went out there to follow up on Doc's report to you as a favor. I'm not even part of that committee."

"Sorry, I got carried away," he said curtly.

She held up her hands. "It's okay. But I'd like you to do me a favor now. Give them one more day. Let me talk to Trent."

Howell twiddled his thumbs again. "What good will that do?"

"Maybe nothing. But I want Trent to understand the consequences. He can reason with Doc. They may come around yet." Even though Howell had been tight-lipped regarding the reasons for his concern about Justin, she knew that he was onto something. It wasn't just curiosity about the Logos phenomenon.

"I want results, Camila. Not promises."

If not for her interest in Calloway, she doubted that she would make another effort. But she wasn't going to tell that to Howell. She hadn't mentioned their attempt to reconcile to him and didn't plan to, either. "I'll see what I can do. Don't forget that David is behind this project. He wants to see it fly."

"I'm well aware of that, Camila, and I plan to keep him fully informed."

Five minutes after Camila returned to her office, her secretary buzzed her. "Trent Calloway's on line one. Do you want me to take a message?"

"I'll take it, Audrey." Camila glanced at her watch. "Hi, Trent."

"Listen, I just checked into a Holiday Inn near the beltway. I don't want to impose myself on you, but I do want to see you."

"Trent, I wish you could have given me a little more notice. I'm really tied up. Tonight I've got a dinner engagement."

"You mean a date?"

"No. Well, sort of. A couple of weeks ago, before I went out to see you the first time, Hal Russell, Tera Peters's producer at CNN, invited me to a dinner party at the home of the secretary of state. I don't feel like I can cancel it now."

"Okay. Have you been going out with him for long?"

"No, I haven't. I barely know him."

"So, can we get together tomorrow?"

Camila sighed. "My schedule is a nightmare, and my sister, Rita, is arriving from Oregon tomorrow evening. She's staying with me for three days."

"I never got along with her."

"I know."

"Bad timing."

"Yeah."

"I'll wait. I've got an idea how I can accommodate you and Howell on the Justin Logos matter without causing any problems with Doc."

"You do? How?"

"I'll explain it when I see you. I think it'll work."

"Good. Can you do it on your own and call me tomorrow with the results?"

Camila listened to the silence and regretted her remark. "That's not exactly what I had in mind, Camila. I was hoping you'd monitor me. I work best that way."

"Okay. Let me see what I can work out. But it's going to be a couple of days, at least."

"I'll visit some museums."

Nine

Waiting. It reminded him of his former military life where counting the days to go on leave or to get his discharge papers was a tradition as common as rising at reveille. He should be enjoying himself, Calloway thought as he wandered the halls of the National Gallery of Art on his second morning in Washington. But his eyes glazed over as he stared at the paintings. He was preoccupied with the nagging thought that Camila didn't really want to see him, that she was putting off their meeting because she didn't know how to say that she had made a mistake thinking that they could get back together. That it was over, before it started.

He left the museum and took out his cell phone as he descended the steps. He punched her number, but got the recording. He stabbed the power button. He could try her office number, but the chances of reaching her were slim. He walked purposefully along The Mall, even though he had no direction in mind. When he reached the Capitol Reflecting Pool, he stopped. He called her cell phone again. This time he waited until the message ended.

"Camila, when can I see you? I mean, if you think this matter with Justin Logos is so damned important, then let's get together and do something about it."

He reached into his pocket and hurled jelly beans, one after another, into the pool. "Stop littering!" ordered an old woman in a baggy sweater and sneakers.

He was about to tell her to mind her own business when his phone rang. He turned away from the woman and answered it.

"Trent, it's me. I'm sorry. I know you think I've been ignoring you, but I've been busy every minute. What have you been doing?"

He heard the blare of a horn behind her voice and knew she was in a vehicle. "Trying to act like a tourist. Yesterday, I did the National Air and Space Museum and the National Museum of African Art."

"Very good. And today?"

Today I want to see you. "You know how it goes, another day, another museum." He looked around and saw the old woman watching him from a bench a few yards away.

"Rita and I are on our way to lunch at Gadsby's Tavern in Old Alexandria. But I've got the afternoon free."

"That sounds good. In fact, I moved to a bed-and-breakfast in Old Alexandria on Prince Street three or four blocks from Gadsby's."

"Hey, synchronicity. We're on track, right?"

He laughed. "I certainly hope so. Camila, I really want things to work out between us. That's why I'm here."

"I know."

He wanted to say more, to tell her again that he didn't want to lose her a second time, that he wanted to make up for everything that had gone wrong, but he knew it wasn't the right time. "Call me when you're ready."

She stepped into her walk-in closet and shooed away Omar, who had been her only companion during her self-imposed confinement. The cat wound between her legs and disappeared into her room. Two days had passed since her interview with Tera Peters, and now she was emerging from her depression.

But the path to a renewed sense of direction had come after a descent into a gloom from which she thought she might never emerge. After all, everything she had worked for during the past six years had been lost. Her entire life had collapsed around her. But last night, she had eaten the meal that Kirby had left for her and contemplated a new path. This morning, she had awakened with a clear mission in mind. She wanted revenge. She would fight back. Maybe her life was over and her dreams destroyed, but she wasn't leaving without making one more explosive impact.

She carefully pushed aside the clothing at the rear of the closet, exposing a paneled wall. She reached up, found the latch, and pushed it to one side. A slight opening appeared in the center of the wall. She reached her fingernails into the crack. The two panels slid apart like accordions, revealing a second, smaller closet in which a white outfit resembling a space suit hung from a hook. A thirty-minute oxygen tank connected to the suit. She wore it whenever she was working in her lab with viruses.

She started to reach for the protective suit, then changed her mind. She'd take her chances in the lab, something she'd never done before. She pushed past the suit and moved directly to a four-foot-tall, curved steel door with a combination lock. She quickly worked the combination and opened the door. She moved into a plastic hatch and closed the door behind her. She spent a couple of minutes sealing the outside of the hatch and unsealing the inside. Then she stepped into her five-by-ten-foot lab. A single empty counter grew out of the far wall.

Shortly after she had met Justin, Melissa had joined a tight-knit network of viral researchers who had created clandestine supplies of deadly viruses. Initially, their reasons were professional. They felt that political pressure would be brought on them to destroy stocks of all the viruses, especially variola, the smallpox virus. When that happened, all research would end.

Variola, in particular, had fascinated her. It possessed one of the largest genetic blueprints of any virus and was highly stable outside its host. It could retain its powers of infection over long periods, aiding its spread among victims. She believed that variola and other viruses might actually be human genetic material that had escaped the confines of the human body and had evolved on its own.

She leaned down and opened one of the cabinets below the counter where she kept a compact refrigerator. She took out a sealed, insulated container from inside the refrigerator and set it on the counter. She unlatched it and carefully lifted the top. The lined interior was segmented into six compartments, each containing a dozen plastic mist dispensers that looked identical to either cheap cigarette lighters or expensive fountain pens. Coded labels were attached to each dispenser.

She noticed that a couple of the labels on the fountain-pen dispensers in the section containing variola virus were peeling off. Melissa prided herself on being orderly and precise, and of course, she didn't want any confusion about which dispensers carried which viruses. She bent down and opened the supply cabinet below the counter to get new labels. She immediately noticed something was wrong. One of her packets of pen-shaped mist dispensers was gone. She clearly remembered that she had had two packets left. She tried to think what could have happened to them. It didn't make any sense.

Just as she picked up one of the dispensers containing the variola, she heard a faint knock from the hallway. Probably Kirby with her breakfast, she thought. Good timing. He was just the person she needed to talk to. She put the dispenser back in place and closed the top on the container. She unsealed the hatch and left the steel door open, but closed the closet door as she stepped back into her room. It was clearly sloppy procedure, but she didn't really give a damn. If a virus leaked out and infected her, so be it.

"Hang on. I'm coming," she called out as the pounding continued. She would surprise Kirby today with a smile.

She turned the lock and started to open the door. Suddenly, a naked Justin Logos burst into the room. He brushed past her and spun in a circle. Omar hissed and ran under the bed for cover. Justin spun around, peering in every direction. He ran a hand through his mussed hair.

"Okay. Where is he? Where's your macho man now? I've had it with him. He's out of here."

"What are you talking about? Where are your clothes? Have you been walking around like that?"

"You know, your big hunk, Mr. Galaxy. Speak up, where is he? Did you think I was totally blind? You amaze me, Melissa. I am the Son of God, the greatest human being on earth, who is not really human at all, but a superbeing, and what do you do? You fall all over some dumb, pea-brained bodybuilder. Is that any way for the mother of God to behave?"

His eyes seemed to bug out of his head. He looked crazed, out of control; *manic* was the word, and she guessed that he hadn't taken his lithium tablets since she'd locked herself away in the room.

"Stop it, Justin! Stop it right now!"

When she'd found Justin in Kathmandu, Nepal, he was begging on the streets and cursing people who ignored him. He wasn't performing any miracles or healing anyone. At first, he resisted her offers of help, but after a couple of days, he meekly returned to the States with her, where they took up residence at her ranch. By that time, she had discovered the secret to Justin's uneven behavior and promised him that she would guide him through his rough points, but he had to do exactly what she said, and that included changing his surname from Davis to Logos. Ever since, she had managed his healing work and nurtured him for the greater role that he saw himself playing, and she made sure that he took his lithium every day to counteract his bipolar syndrome.

Now Justin walked over to the window and pulled aside the heavy curtains. Bright sunlight momentarily blinded her. She closed her eyes and felt pressure on the sides of her head that had nothing to do with the light. The air in the room turned cold and she gasped for breath as if there were no longer enough oxygen available. She knew something was about to happen.

She'd almost forgotten how frightening he could become when he was off his medication. The most bizarre incident had involved a man who had come to Justin complaining that he was impotent. A week after the healing, Justin had infused a part of himself into the man's body while he was making love to his wife. In his manic enthusiasm, Justin had lifted both of them off the bed and spun them around. The man died of a heart attack and the woman ended up in a mental institution. Melissa knew about it because during the incident Justin had seized her head in his hands and projected the incredible scene onto her mind, like a movie playing in her head. She'd recognized the man and found out about his death a couple of days later.

She opened her eyes. Justin stood facing her in front of the window, his arms outstretched to the sides. He had raised up high on his toes and she couldn't understand how the tips of his toes could possibly hold his weight. Then she noticed his feet were bleeding. She looked up and saw a hole in his side and a trail of blood. Then she saw the blood dripping from his palms. She backed away, shaking her head. "Stop it, Justin. Stop it." She turned to the door to get Kirby, but before she could open it, Justin called out, "Where are you going?"

She looked back and he stood calmly by her closet door with no trace of blood on his body. The room seemed normal again. "Are you okay?"

"I feel wonderful. I suppose I should get dressed."

He peered into the closet and she remembered she'd left the lab open. If he got his hands on those mist dispensers, he would probably start spraying.

"Those are my clothes. Here, put this on."

She took off her robe and handed it to him. For an instant, they stood together, like old times. But now there was nothing sexual in their mutual nudity. She felt naked, exposed, and quickly reached into the closet. She grabbed an oversize sweatshirt and pulled it over her head and down over her thighs. She shut the closet door, then moved over to her dresser where she kept a supply of lithium. She shook out two tablets and handed them to him.

"Take this. You need it." She took a closer look at his palms and saw no sign of the stigmata.

He frowned. "You know, I feel so much more creative when I'm not taking this stuff. I have a much better understanding of myself. It's the real me that comes out."

"Take it," she ordered, walking into the bathroom for water. "You were just bleeding like that time by the lake in India."

"Things happen to me."

"I know. It's over now. But you can't run around naked like a madman. Think about who you are."

"Naked is natural and I don't give a damn who I'm supposed to be," he said defiantly. "That's just ego, anyhow."

She handed him a cup of water. He looked at it, then popped

the two pills into his mouth. He swallowed them obediently, like an old pro, without water, then tilted the cup, pouring the water on the carpeting.

She snagged the cup from his hand before he threw it. "Why don't we go down to the kitchen and talk. I could use a cup of coffee."

"A little chat over coffee." Justin grinned. "That sounds just wonderful, my little Melissa."

The robe clung to his armpits and the sleeves only reached the middle of his forearms. She tried to think of him as her son. But she couldn't see any similarities between them. His straight blond hair contrasted with her curly, dark brown hair. His face was fuller than hers. His nostrils flared slightly, while her nose was long and thin. But she remembered someone mentioning once that their blue eyes mirrored each other.

"Sure, we could even invite your buddy, J.D., to join us and see what he has to say about your perverted sex life."

She slapped his face. "Damn you, Justin. How dare you talk to me like that. I should walk out on you and let you figure it all out on your own. Your Jesus career would be over in a week. I guarantee it."

"Sorry, Ma," he said contritely. Then a grin crept over his face. "I kind of like calling you that."

"You knew, didn't you? You bastard. You knew." She shoved him with such force that he stumbled back. His head cracked against the wall.

She rushed up to him and took his hand. "I'm sorry, Justin. Are you okay? Did I hurt you?"

He looked stunned, but straightened up. "Melissa, I felt a strong love for you from the moment we met, but believe me when I say that I had no reason to think you might be anyone other than a beautiful researcher who was interested in my work."

He seemed perfectly calm, normal. A tidal wave of confusion and frustration washed over her as she realized her love toward him hadn't changed in spite of her knowledge of their relationship and his outrageous behavior.

"I just don't understand how this could have happened. Why, Justin? Why? We were about to move on to something much bigger."

"I told you that there were changes coming."

She nodded. "You said there would be rough times ahead, but I hardly expected anything like this. I feel like I'm not even the same person anymore. How can we do anything together in public without being ridiculed?"

Justin considered the question. The wild look on his face had faded. "People ridicule me every day."

"But the ones around you are constantly praising you. What's going to happen now? Tell me that."

"Sometimes I feel like I know too much. It's a burden that's getting harder to bear. But I won't be here much longer. So you're going to have to go on with your life without me."

"I don't want to hear that, Justin," she snapped. "I don't believe it. In fact, I refuse to believe it." Just minutes ago, she'd threatened to leave him. Now she felt panicked that his predictions of his own death might actually be true.

"Excuse me. Would you like me to come back later?"

They both turned toward the door to see Kirby holding a platter with Melissa's breakfast.

"Ah, J.D., come in." Justin smiled and didn't seem the least bit concerned about Kirby. "I was just about to tell Melissa that I've got to get dressed and get to the clinic. I have patients waiting, hundreds of them."

With that, Justin nodded and walked out of the room, still wearing Melissa's pink robe.

Ten

C alloway turned the corner onto Cameron Street and saw Camila standing outside Gadsby's. In front of her, a taxi pulled away and she waved. "I guess I just missed Rita," he said, walking up to Camila.

She turned, smiled, and gave him a hug. "You don't sound too disappointed."

"Can't say I am."

Camila's sister, Rita, had never given him a chance. She'd actually told him, in a moment of anger, that he should never have married Camila, that he'd torn their family apart. It was all about race, of course, and there was nothing he could do about that.

"Well, Rita was shocked when I told her who I was calling. She can't believe that I would see you again."

"Can you believe it?"

Camila met his gaze. "I believe in you and I'm glad you had faith in me. If it were me and you said we couldn't get together for a couple of days, I might have turned around and gone home."

They walked away from the restaurant, heading toward his place. "Truthfully, the thought did enter my mind. But I'm supposed to meet Doc here in a few days, anyhow. So I waited."

"That meeting is in jeopardy, Trent. Howell wants to cancel it and kill the project. He's prepared to take the heat from the president."

Calloway frowned. "I was afraid of that. Can we still change his mind?"

"I got him to hold off awhile. He wants to see what you get, then he'll decide whether or not there will be a meeting."

They turned the corner and headed down Prince Street past a row of majestic old houses. "Then let me tell you what I've got in mind. First of all, I'm not going to remote view Justin Logos. Not yet at least."

She looked sharply at him. "Then what are you going to do?"

"I want to target Washington in the future to see if I pick up on any sort of disaster. I mean, that's what we're concerned about, aren't we?"

"Yes, but . . ."

"That's how it started last year. I had a vision of a disaster coming to Washington and I worked backwards to the source."

She nodded. "Okay, let's try it. But I don't know if I'm supposed to be pleased or disappointed if you don't see anything."

He pointed to a three-story, wood-frame house behind an iron gate. "Here we are. It's an old sea captain's house. I'm got a room up in the tower on the third floor."

"Is it haunted?"

"I don't know. We're not doing ghosts."

She laughed. "That's right. We're doing the future."

They entered the house, and as they climbed a creaky, winding staircase, he took her hand. He stopped in front of his door and turned to her. "So before we get started, I need to know how you feel about us."

She placed her hands on his shoulders. "I feel good right now. But I want to tell you something. No matter what it looks like, I'm not tying *our* future with your willingness to remote view for me. Is that understood?"

He made a face as if he'd just bit into a lemon. "Well, you did walk off rather abruptly back in Bluff."

"It wasn't personal. It was a professional matter. You and Doc left me in a precarious position."

"Okay, I accept that." He unlocked the door and they moved into the room.

"You don't sound like you accept it."

He smiled. "I'm trying." He bent over and kissed her. She pulled back after a couple of seconds. "We need to work."

Boys, I've been touring the capital with Calloway. The guy has really lost it. He's a lovesick pup and a tourist on top of it. He's just hanging out in D.C. waiting for his honey. He'll do anything for her. In fact, I think he's going to go for Justin Logos, even though he told Doc he wouldn't do it.

I tried Justin myself earlier today, but couldn't get through. He's a mystery man. I felt a totally different energy. Nearly knocked me on my ass. Couldn't get near him. So I backed off and checked on Calloway.

If our boy goes for Justin, I hope the Son of God blows his brains out. Yeah, blow them right out his ears. Whatever he's about to do, I want to watch and I want you guys with me.

Hello, wake up. I know you're listening. Hello, Johnstone. No, Calloway won't know we're looking. Neither will Doc. I've

*blocked them out. Blocked 'em good. So no one's going to find
out that you're working again and beam poison rays at you.
Why bother, Henderson? Why not? Besides, if there's a
chance to mess him up, let's do it.*

Calloway sat up on his bed, resting his back against the headboard. The afternoon sun filtered through the blinds, forming a
striped pattern on the bed. Camila sat in a chair next to the
bed.

Calloway slowly inhaled several long breaths. He cleared his
mind, and every time a new thought crept into his awareness he
released it, sending it on its way. After several minutes, he
reached a deeply relaxed state. His mind remained alert yet free
of distractions. He lifted a finger indicating that he was ready
for Camila to direct him to his target.

"Okay, I've selected three targets, like you suggested," Camila said. "I've written each one down on separate sheets of paper
and folded them into quarters. One of them is the target we are
interested in."

"After I find Washington, then I want you to direct me to
an important incident in the future of the city, one that might
adversely affect large numbers of people."

He hoped that was specific enough. He watched her as she
held her hand over the three pieces of folded paper. Even though
she hadn't chosen one yet, he glimpsed an image of the Golden
Gate Bridge. "That's San Francisco," he said as soon as she
picked up one of the pieces of paper.

She smiled, unfolded the paper. "That it is."

She picked up another one. This time everything went blank.
He pushed hard. Nothing happened. No images appeared, no
impressions whatsoever. He felt as if a thick, impenetrable wall

had been erected around him. He shook his head. "I'm not getting anything now. I don't know why."

"Just let the images come to you. Don't try to force it."

He tried again, but he felt something dark and oppressive, probably his own concern about failure.

"Let's do the other one," Camila said calmly after a couple of minutes. She picked up the third piece of paper.

This time he closed his eyes and tried to image a screen in front of him. He had used this technique in his early practice of remote viewing, a simple tool to help stimulate the images. He could imagine the screen, but nothing appeared on it. Then he sensed a barrier around him, shutting him off. He felt trapped, psychically paralyzed. He opened his eyes, shook his head.

"I don't know which one of them was Washington, but it doesn't matter. I'm not getting anything and I don't think I'm going to, either. Not today."

"What's wrong, Trent?"

He shrugged, confused. "I don't know."

"I should've never told you what Howell said. It put too much pressure on you."

He shook his head. "I don't think it's that."

Can't see the future now, Calloway?

"Get out of my head," he whispered.

That voice again. It sounded, or rather felt, like Steve Ritter. But how was he getting past the electromagnetic field, and if he was really working again, why hadn't Calloway sensed more activity?

"What did you say?" Camila frowned, leaning forward.

He covered his face with his hands. "Nothing." His fingers slid down his face. "I'm sorry, Camila. I can't do this now."

Camila didn't respond. She stood up, and for a moment he thought she would leave. Then she climbed onto the bed and wrapped an arm around him. "We'll figure something out. I'm going to talk to Howell again. If I have to, I'll go to the president. I want you and Doc to talk to the committee."

Eleven

He seems better now," Kirby said in a concerned tone as he set her breakfast on the table.

Melissa sat down on the edge of the bed, exhausted from her encounter with Justin and concerned about what he would do next. "Why, what was he doing before?"

"He wanted to go to the clinic without getting dressed. I stopped him and he got upset. He called me names and said he knew about us. I told him that he was wrong and that he should talk to you after he got dressed. I hoped that was the right thing to do."

Melissa tried to keep from panicking. She had to stay in control or everything would fall apart. "You did fine, J.D."

"What's wrong with him, anyhow? I've never seen him act like that."

"Never mind. He's okay now."

"Yeah, as long as he doesn't go to the clinic in that robe. It's a size or two small on him."

Melissa stared coldly at Kirby, then a smile spread across her face and she starting laughing and couldn't stop. "That's good, J.D. Very good. Let's hope he finds something that fits better."

Kirby looked relieved. "Boy, am I ever glad to see that you're feeling better. I was getting worried for a while that you weren't going to make it."

"I'm bouncing back, in spite of it all. But I want to talk to you."

He turned up his palms. "Okay. I'm listening."

She poured herself a cup of coffee. "Do you know why I've been staying in my room?"

"It's about you and Justin."

"Did he tell you?"

He shook his head. "I heard it in the campground. The word has gotten out. People don't believe it, don't want to believe. They think it must be a mistake. You don't seem old enough to be . . . to be his mother." Kirby stumbled over the words and looked away, embarrassed or confused or both.

"Well, apparently I am that. Tera Peters said she has proof."

"But you didn't know?" The words spilled out of him.

"Of course not," she said in an admonishing tone. "What kind of person do you think I am?"

"Sorry."

Kirby shook his head, then let go of the reserved manner in which he'd been treating her. "I don't get it, Melissa. If he's so great and wonderful, why didn't *he* know? I thought he was supposed to know stuff like that, and why the hell is he running around naked now?"

The way he said it reminded her that Kirby was jealous of Justin's abilities, that he hated the way Justin's life was always center stage. When they made love and she was ecstatically at his mercy, he would whisper, "Can the Jesus boy-wonder do this to you, Melissa? Can he make you feel like this? Tell me, can the pretty boy make you come over and over?" And of course she would say, "No, no, no. You're the best."

"J.D., he doesn't know everything. He's not God."

"Just the *Son* of God," Kirby said with a snicker. "I'm sorry, Melissa, but I don't think Jesus would fuck his mother. No offense."

She stared at him a moment, stunned by his bluntness. Then the tension in her face faded and she laughed. "You wouldn't think so, would you. Especially not with *her* reputation."

Now Kirby seemed surprised. "What are you saying, it's all a lie, that you've been fooling everyone?"

"No, not at all. You're like so many people, J.D. You want to believe that the reincarnated Jesus is just like the Bible stories. Justin is not like that, and you know what, neither was Jesus."

Kirby seemed disturbed. He had told her that he wasn't religious when he took the job and that was fine with her. But now his religious background had surfaced. "Sometimes I wonder what I've gotten involved in here. I've seen Justin do things I can't explain. Like that day he handed out all those sandwiches. I was standing right there next to him, and every time he opened that cooler, there were more sandwiches in there. That was no trick."

"That was a manifestation." Melissa knew that she needed to keep Kirby thinking about the miracles and healings that he had witnessed. "He has incredible abilities. It's a shame that it will all be lost."

"What do you mean?"

"Once that interview goes on the air, everyone will think that Justin is a fraud. A man who sleeps with his mother, after all, is nothing but an outcast. No one will trust him or believe in him, and when people lose their faith in Justin, he won't be able to heal anymore."

Kirby stared at Melissa's untouched plate of scrambled eggs. "Maybe Justin could make it all disappear. If he can heal people and do all these incredible things, maybe he could stop CNN from broadcasting the program. Make it like it never happened." "You mean like a fairy tale?" She shook her head. "Even if Justin could do that, he wouldn't. He believes in fate or destiny. He's going to just let everything collapse around him." "That's too bad," Kirby said in a low voice.

"But there is something you and I could do together that might change everything around yet."

He let out a nervous laugh. "What's that?"

"First of all, we'll let it out that you are my lover, and that I never actually had sex with Justin. You see, I've tried to make it seem like he was a normal man, but it didn't work. Now I understand the reason. He needed a mother more than a wife."

Kirby nodded. "You think Justin will go for that?"

"Look at the alternative. I think he will accept it. Hell, I bet he gladly endorses it. He'll be relieved, because it gives us a way out of this mess." As an afterthought, she added, "Besides, he already knows, so I don't think that's going to be a problem."

Kirby nodded warily. "What else do you have in mind?"

"Yes, there is something else. I see it as part of the master plan, a necessary road we must traverse."

"What road is that?"

"Remember how Justin has said that there will be a time of chaos, that the seat of power will collapse? Well, it's time for the chaos to begin, the chaos that will lead to a thousand years of peace that will be set off by Justin Logos. You and I will pull the trigger, so to speak. I've had the means all along, but I never realized that I would be the one."

Kirby frowned and looked around as if searching for a way out. "What are you talking about, Melissa? I don't follow you. What would I do?"

She smiled. "You, along with some of the apostles—the

most loyal and faithful ones—will be the vehicle. You'll make it happen."

She let Kirby process that bit of information before she continued. Several of the apostles had let it be known that they would be willing to do anything for Justin, and the implication had been that the offer included breaking laws. Claire Bernard, the betrayer, had been among them, and now Melissa wondered how much Claire had instigated such sentiments. Melissa, for her part, fostered a healthy suspicion of this inner circle of followers and had ordered Kirby to keep an eye on them. But gradually, she'd come to accept them as necessary, though she'd remained watchful and wary of anyone who attempted to usurp her powers. But now with Claire flushed out, with her own life in total disarray, she knew it was time to act, and the apostles were the appropriate vehicle.

"I still don't know what you're talking about."

"Come here. I want to show you something."

She led him through the closet and into the lab. Kirby's bulk filled the space, making it seem smaller than it was.

"Wow, I never knew you had a lab here."

"Now you do." Melissa opened the case on the counter and took out one of the dispensers containing the variola virus. "Do you know what this is?"

He shook his head. "A fountain pen?"

"It looks like one. It's a dispenser containing one of the last supplies of the smallpox virus left in the world."

"What's it doing here?"

"Never mind."

She held the dispenser up to Kirby's face. "There's nothing to it. You and the apostles will take tours of the halls of power—the White House and Congress, the Justice Department and the

Supreme Court, and of course the Pentagon. You'll discreetly spray the assortment of viruses as you go."

"It sounds like a suicide mission to me."

"It's not. Each of you will be vaccinated against all the viruses."

"It's still dangerous, if you ask me. Besides, others in the campground will know that we all left for Washington. It'll look suspicious."

Good. He seemed to accept the idea. Just the details needed to be clarified. "That's easy. We'll create a cover story for anyone who gets snoopy. As a bonus for their work, we will send the apostles to a retreat in North Carolina. But first they will tour Washington, D.C. You spray as you tour, and the airborne viruses will do the rest. It's easy. So what do you think?"

Kirby frowned and rubbed his fist into his palm, something he did whenever he was confused or nervous. "What do I think? I think you're insane, Melissa. You know me better than that. I would never do anything of the sort. Besides, I thought you were on a spiritual mission. What are you, some kind of born-again killer?"

"That's clever, J.D. Clever for you." She took off the cap and aimed the fountain pen at Kirby. "Squirt. That's all it would take, you see, and you would be infected."

He gave her a hurt look. "You wouldn't do anything like that to me, would you?"

"Wouldn't I?"

He reached out and grabbed her hand. He tried to push her finger off the top of the fountain pen, but instead forced it down. To her surprise, nothing happened.

"What are you doing?" she shouted. "You could've infected both of us."

He smiled sheepishly. "Sorry. For a moment there, I thought you were really going to do it."

She was more concerned now with the fountain-pen dispenser itself. Now she could tell by its weight that it was empty. She picked up another and another. They were all empty. The variola was gone, her dispensers replaced by empty ones using her original labels. Now she knew why some of the labels had been peeling off and why a package of dispensers was missing.

She tried to think what could have happened. She immediately suspected that one of the other researchers had somehow managed to break into her lab. Melissa had cut off relations with the others after two of her colleagues destroyed their stocks of viruses, including variola, and had threatened to expose the network if the others didn't follow suit. Their action had followed rumors that one member of the network had secretly sold parts of his stock to foreign agents. Both researchers died a short time later under mysterious circumstances.

With their deaths, Melissa became the only member of the network who maintained a stock of variola, which was why she suspected her former colleagues were behind the theft. But how could they have gotten through her security system?

She put the dispensers back into the case. She had a dreadful feeling that all the viruses were gone. Frantic now, she picked up a dispenser shaped like diposable lighter and recklessly sprayed it at Kirby. He sputtered and wiped his face with his shirtsleeve as a fine mist struck him.

"What is that?"

"Anthrax"

"Jesus Christ. It's a joke, right? It's got to be a joke." He laughed nervously as he continued wiping his face.

"It is not."

"Wait a minute. If that was really anthrax, you would be infected, too."

She put the cap back on the dispenser and put it away. "No, I've been immunized."

He grabbed her by the shoulder and roughly jerked her out of the closet. Her sweatshirt hitched up over her hips. "What are you telling me? Stop playing games. I don't like it." He slid his hand to her throat. "I could snap your neck like a twig. You know I could."

She gasped for breath. "Sure, and then we would both die." He loosened his grip. "Face it, you're infected, J.D., and you are going to die unless you get the vaccine immediately."

He let go of her neck. "Then that's what I'll do and I'll expose your little lab, too."

She pulled her sweatshirt down tightly over her thighs, then rubbed her throat. "It's not that easy, my big rough-and-tumble friend. No one will believe you until you come down with the symptoms. Then it might be too late. But I can save you right now. I've got the vaccine."

"Then do it."

"Only if you agree to carry out my plan. If you don't do it, I'll work with the apostles myself. It's going to happen one way or another."

She watched him closely. She was counting on him not to think it through. She knew she was vulnerable, that Kirby could put her behind bars and destroy the entire plan and might still save himself.

"Okay, I'll do it, but give me that vaccine. I want it now, not later."

"Of course."

She moved closer to him and ran a hand over the swell of his chest, down over his ribs, and along his muscular thigh. "I want you to live. I want you as part of my future. Do you understand that?"

"Yeah. I guess so."

She looked up into his eyes. "I'm sorry I had to do it this way."

"Me, too."

She took him into her study where she kept a small refrigerator beneath her desk. At the rear of it on the lower shelf were the vaccines, coded and disguised as bottles of liquid herbal remedies—cat's claw, ginkgo, and goldenseal.

She took out the vaccine for anthrax and filled a syringe. As she prepped his arm, she could feel him shaking. She expertly injected the vaccine. "Okay. That should do it."

"Are you sure? How do I know it's going to work? How do I know you're not tricking me?"

"I wish you would have a little more trust in me, J.D. Just remember, we're working together. If I didn't give you the vaccine, then you are going to be getting very sick by the time you reach Washington. In that case, you don't follow through with your side of the agreement."

He considered what she said. "Okay. So when do you want me to leave?"

"Today. No sense waiting. Pick out just three of the apostles, one man, two women, the most loyal and fanatical of the bunch. You know the ones. You will work in couples."

"What do I tell them?" he said helplessly.

"Leave that to me."

"So, will Justin talk to them, too?"

"No need for it. He's working."

Kirby twitched uneasily. "Does he even know what you're doing?"

Now she had to lie to him. "Of course he does. He's well

aware of the plan. In fact, he will use his powers to watch you. He can do that, you know. He has the same abilities as those psychics who used to work for the CIA, those remote viewers. He can find you and see what you're doing. He can even be in two places at once."

Kirby's gaze narrowed. "And what if we don't do it?"

She considered his question. "You've already seen a little bit of Justin's dark side this morning. You know that it's not very nice." She smiled. "It's like the Jesus freaks like to say: "You're either with Jesus or you're with the devil. You're either with Justin or you're in a very bad place."

Kirby frowned. "That kind of talk doesn't make him sound much like Jesus."

"I'm sure even Jesus of Nazareth had his bad days."

Twelve

I'm free as a bird in my isolation cell in this hellhole prison. Free as a bird. Speaking of birds, what do you make of God-son Justin and his bird talk? He's an odd duck, that one, with his Thunderbird god and his nasty Vulture.

Hello, boys, come in. I know you're there. Don't start crapping out on me already. I know you can hear me. Okay, that's better.

Timmons thinks it's a sacrilege turning God into an animal. What do you think about that, Hendy, our animal man?

Ah, no comment. He doesn't want to offend his menagerie. Let's move on. We've got business to attend to.

So, after we messed up Calloway the other day, I took a peek at Melissa Dahl. A real schemer, that one. I picked up on her plans, and now I want to see how they are being carried out.

Focus, boys. What do you see? Where are we?

Ah, Timmons sees roses. That's good. Roses have bugs, bugs carry germs. Don't worry about it, Timmons. You can wash your hands later.

Johnstone says it's a rose garden. Interesting connection, but not quite right. It's the White House Visitors Center. There's probably a vase of roses on a counter or table. But maybe we'll see the Rose Garden.

We're going on a tour of the White House courtesy of the somewhat weak mind of J. D. Kirby, special assistant to Melissa Dahl. A very special assistant.

No, Johnstone. I've got Calloway and Doc covered. They won't know you're working, and we do need to work. Kirby needs help. He's acting too nervous. Same with the woman he's with, a real nutcase, totally brainwashed by Logos. But they've got a job to do and I want to see them succeed.

Why? Well, Timmons, let's say it's in my blood.

Okay, they've got their free tickets for the tour and they're walking up to the East Gate. I'm with Kirby. He's shaking, worried about getting caught with the goods. He has to empty his pockets just like everyone else.

Getting close now. I don't like this gatekeeper. Secret Service. He's already eyeing our guy. Okay, he's emptying his pockets. Let's push on the agent. Tell him that the big guy's okay. No problem. It's just a cigarette lighter. Push ... push ... push. Let him go.

Whew! That wasn't so easy. But now they're in and ready to spray. Gee, maybe we'll see the Lincoln Bedroom. Let's go live into Kirby's head. I'm pushing my way inside.

Lots of guards. Too much waiting. Boring introduction by smiling blond babe. Wonder how she got her job. A Secret Service tour officer in every room. Wonderful.

Suzie, stop looking around. Act normal. What a bitch I've got for a so-called wife. The others all said Suzie Carlson looked good with me. A robust blonde with muscular shoulders, works out every day. Looks don't go far, though. She acts like I don't even exist and warned me to keep my hands off her. She's a fanatic. She never even questioned whether this was right or not. All she does is talk about Justin, her God-man, and how this is all for him. Tired of hearing it.

Moving now. Down a ground-floor corridor. Okay, into the Vermeil Room. Don't know about this. Suzie looks scared. Two Secret Service officers here. Oh, now she takes my hand. Isn't that sweet. Act like a couple, she whispers.

Jesus. She's got the dispenser in her hand. I can feel it. Hm, maybe this will work. A little squeeze against her fingers. That did it. Point her hand up more. Watch where the spray goes. Move it around. Good. This works. Melissa said the virus would spread on its own. No need for direct hits. Now upstairs to the State Floor and on to more rooms—the East, Green, Blue, Red, and State Dining Rooms, where a big dinner is planned tonight. I'll definitely save some for that last one.

Wake up, boys. This guy is doing what we couldn't do. Give him some credit. He's a big, dumb guy, but he's got balls. He and the others are spraying the town. Watch what happens in a week or so when the virus gets a foothold on Washington.

Okay, we'll stop here. Timmons is getting sick. He's afraid his mind is touching the virus. Right. Go take a shower. Clean your body. Then meditate and purify your mind. I promise none of us will catch anything. What a guy.

Thirteen

It was the last place he wanted to hang out, Calloway thought as he and Doc were guided down a long wide hallway by a young second lieutenant. Electric golf carts whizzed past, occasionally beeping to warn of their approach from behind. After walking for five minutes and turning down a third or fourth hallway in the Pentagon maze, Doc asked their guide why they didn't take a golf cart.

"We're almost there," he answered brusquely. "Maybe we can get you a cart for the return trip."

"I'd appreciate it," Doc said.

"I remember the first time I came here," Calloway recalled. "I'd just finished my training for Eagle's Nest, but I was still doing practice targets. Maxwell brought me and Ritter here to show off our stuff. I was pretty damned nervous I remember."

"I bet Max knew you were the best even then." Doc watched another cart go by. "Did you get to ride in a golf cart?"

"No, actually they didn't have these carts back then. They had big tricycles with baskets. It was pretty weird seeing all these uniforms tooling down the hallways on trikes."

"I can imagine."

"Here we are," the officer said, turning into an alcove. He opened a door that led down a short hallway to a large, impressive steel door with a combination lock and handle instead of a doorknob. Another second lieutenant saluted, then worked the combination.

"It looks like we're going into a vault," Doc said.

The officer pulled open the heavy door. "It is a vault, ma'am. Step inside, please."

The room was surprisingly large with a long table encircled by red leather armchairs. The steel walls were covered with heavy, dark curtains that looked as if they belonged in a theater. About a dozen of the chairs were occupied by uniforms, decorated with bars and medals, and several gray suits. In addition, several staff members, both military and civilian, sat on metal chairs that bordered the curtains. Legal pads or notebook computers rested on their laps.

Even though Calloway had abandoned the world of military intelligence, specifically psychic duty for the CIA and NSA, it hadn't done much good. It seemed that no matter how many times he dropped out of the elite corps of psychic spies, his membership kept getting renewed. So here he was deep in the Pentagon, surrounded by serious men and women, and none of them looked too happy.

One of the gray suits stood up and extended a hand. Calloway recognized Harvey Howell, the president's national security advisor. "Good to see you again, Trent. Hello, Doc. Please sit down. Let me introduce you to everyone."

Calloway wanted to ask him about Camila, but held off. He'd assumed she would be here, but he hadn't talked to her since Doc had arrived yesterday afternoon. He'd called her last night, but she hadn't returned the call. Maybe she was too busy to attend or considered the meeting outside of her realm. At least, she'd managed to keep the meeting scheduled. They'd also spent two nights together, one at his place, the other at hers, and Calloway felt much better about their relationship. Doc, for her part, seemed more annoyed that he'd attempted to work with Camila than the fact that Howell had nearly scuttled the project.

After introductions, they sat down and Calloway dug his hand into his pocket and quickly popped a couple of jelly beans into his mouth. He'd promised Doc that he wouldn't eat them at the meeting, but at the last minute he'd slipped a small bag into his pocket. Maybe Justin Logos was right about the jelly beans and lack of sweetness in his life. He stopped eating them after he'd seen Camila, but when he didn't hear from her last night, he went out and bought a bag.

He leaned toward Doc. "Are you okay?"

She beamed at him. "Just fine."

Amazing, he thought. Justin was an extraordinary healer. Until Doc's encounter with Justin, she had worried that she might not be able to remain in the meeting for more than a few minutes and that her absence would ruin her chances of getting a government contract to set up the new project.

"Doc, go ahead with your presentation," Howell said after conferring with a general next to him. "We're ready."

She spoke for about twenty minutes on the background of remote viewing and her proposal for the new project. She ended with a dramatic explanation of how she and Calloway had used remote viewing to stop an attempt to set off a nuclear bomb in Washington. Everyone in the room knew about the bomb, but Calloway figured that most of them had never heard the details, and definitely not from the ones involved. While they were digesting the story, Doc added that one of the most important roles of the project director would be to make sure that remote viewing was not misused for political or unethical purposes.

No one responded immediately when she sat down. Then the general seated next to Howell stood up. Light glinted off his chestful of medals. "I realize, of course, that we have to balance ethical matters with those of national security, but frankly, Dr. Boyle, I'm concerned about your willingness to carry out our requests."

Calloway stared ahead and played with his necktie, a jelly bean trapped in his sweating palm. He coughed into his hand and the jelly bean slid into his mouth. As he listened to the general, he stared at the smear of red on of his palm. More than once he'd suggested to Doc that creating a new remote-viewing program might be a mistake, that those with access to the tool might misuse the abilities and cut off funds if their requests were turned down. If it were up to him, he'd be tempted to tell the general that his concern was well taken, because they weren't about to play along with these games. But he reminded himself that he was here to support Doc, and he would do his best to help her get the new program off the ground.

As Doc responded to the general, Calloway occupied himself by transforming the table into a raft. He imagined they were all bounding over rapids as sunshine gleamed off the racing water and a cold spray bathed their faces. Instead of sitting silently, they were all whooping it up, shouting joyfully. But the image faded as Harvey Howell voiced his own concerns.

"On this same topic, I'm also uncomfortable with the director of the remote-viewing program deciding what is and what is not in the interest of national security. There will be instances where we will not be able to reveal the full ramifications of the situation." Howell took off his round, wire-frame glasses and inspected them in the overhead light as if they held some answers to his concerns. He wore his hair so short that it was difficult to tell exactly where his receding hairline ended.

"Of course we would establish an agreed-upon set of parameters," Doc explained. "We can start with the ones used in Eagle's Nest and revise them. I have some ideas I'd like to present on the matter."

But before she could continue, Howell interrupted, "I think we're jumping too far ahead here, Doc. I want to hear from some of the others at the table."

For the next several minutes, Doc fielded a variety of questions and complaints. To Calloway, it seemed that the bastards were tearing apart every detail of the plans Doc had prepared. They didn't like the name, Third Eye, because it didn't provide enough cover, even in a black-bag budget. Neither did they care for Doc's plans to move the operation from Maryland to Colorado within a year, nor did they want to spend the money to renovate the underground mansion that the government had purchased from Eduardo Perez's estate. The deceased remote viewer's abode would make a perfect headquarters, but now it seemed that anything Doc wanted would be rejected, all because Calloway and Doc had refused to remote view Justin Logos and Melissa Dahl.

Calloway could see that Howell, in particular, with his petulant questioning, annoyed Doc, and she was about to counterattack. "I have a question," she said in a voice that sounded too tense, too shrill. "Can someone tell us what you folks are so damned concerned about regarding Justin Logos? Do you think he's really a threat to the U.S. government, to democracy, to the American way? What exactly is it?"

Several heads turned toward a two-star general with short salt-and-pepper hair. "Ms. Boyle, I can assure you that what we know about Logos and his partner, Melissa Dahl, clearly fits the profile of potential terrorists."

"We still feel he is a threat," Howell added, "even though this CNN special tomorrow night is supposed to unveil him as some sort mother-frigging pervert." He glanced at Doc. "No offense."

"If you mean to say *motherfucker,* just say it," Doc snapped. "I don't know anything about his relationships, but from what I saw of him, he doesn't have time to be a terrorist. He's too busy healing people and performing some damned sensational miracles."

"We have other information," Two Star reiterated.

"What information?" Doc persisted.

"That's classified." Howell folded his hands and discreetly twiddled his thumbs. "Besides, if you had done what we had asked, you probably would've been able to figure it out by now."

"Damn it, Howell!" Calloway erupted. He'd heard enough.

Everyone shifted their attention toward him. The room turned silent, except for someone who coughed several times.

"If you want blind obedience, then I think you've got the wrong people. I know Doc very well and I know that she is accepting this position as administrator of Third Eye—or whatever you want to call it—to use remote viewing to protect this nation. Remote viewing is a unique weapon, but we've got to avoid shooting ourselves in the feet with it. If we enter people's minds and manipulate their thoughts and actions, there better be a damned good reason for doing so. We don't want to know your secrets about Justin Logos. But we do want clear guidelines established that will prevent abuse. That's all I have to say."

"Okay, Trent, I think we understand your point," Howell said tersely. "But I think we're jumping ahead too quickly. Not everyone in this room is convinced this tool is even viable. I've seen you work so I know you have abilities. But I think that a demonstration would be in order before we go any further."

Christ. Calloway should've figured as much. Howell wanted to entertain his buddies. Calloway felt like walking out. These people all knew his track record. They knew that remote viewing worked or they wouldn't be here discussing the strategy for a secret multimillion-dollar project. But again he deferred to Doc and her interests in working with the intelligence community. He sat back and crossed his arms. "So what do you have in mind?"

Howell smiled and twiddled again. "I want you to find Camila Hidalgo and describe her surroundings."

No wonder she wasn't here. They'd planned this exhibition. Maybe Howell didn't trust him anymore after Camila had reported his failure to see anything when he tried to remote view Washington in the future. So now they would perform some basic remote viewing, as they'd done years ago. He'd performed similar experiments for observers on dozens of occasions. He looked over at Doc, who shrugged.

"Now let me ask you, Trent," Howell said, "have you talked to Ms. Hidalgo in the last twenty-four hours?"

"No, and I have no idea where she is now, if she's not in her office."

Howell looked over at the others at the table, a faint smile curled on his lips. "I don't know where Ms. Hidalgo is heading, either. That was intentional, because remote viewing is not about telepathy. Trent will not be able to read my mind. He must send an invisible, nonphysical part of himself out to find her."

"Okay, let's get on with it," Doc said impatiently. She handed Calloway a notepad and a pen so he could sketch what he saw. "If we can have silence now, I'm going to take Trent down into his zone, the relaxed state from which he will remote view."

Usually, Calloway favored his Native American flute music in the background, but they would have to do without it. They hadn't come prepared. Neither of them had even considered the possibility of being asked to prove themselves, not after all they'd been through. Calloway looked around at everyone watching him, and that was when he started worrying. If he was blocked again and unable to pick up anything, the meeting would turn into a disaster.

He closed his eyes and began taking long, slow, deep breaths as Doc led him into a relaxed state. She started with the bottom of his feet and his toes and slowly worked upward. He cleared his head of any thoughts and just followed the tone of Doc's voice. By the time she was telling him to relax the crown of his head, he was ready to look for his target.

But someone coughed, an annoying hack over and over again, and he abruptly came fully back into the room. Again, the thought of failure crept into his mind. Maybe with all these guys staring at him he wouldn't be able to go as deep as he needed. Maybe he wouldn't get anything worthwhile. Stop worrying, he told himself. Use what you already know. Turn adversity to advantage.

He focused on his breath, and when he heard the cough again, he immediately incorporated it into his relaxation. He told himself that every cough he heard would take him deeper and deeper. Finally, he released all his concerns about proving himself. Within seconds, the room and everyone in it faded from his awareness. He heard a distant sound, a cough, and he heard Doc's soothing voice. He slipped deeper into his zone. After a minute of silence, he raised a finger indicating he was ready to proceed to his target.

"Okay, Trent," Doc said in a soft voice. "I want you to go to Camila Hidalgo. See where she is and what she's doing."

Calloway drifted for a couple of minutes before he sensed

her. He couldn't see Camila or her surroundings, but he was aware of one word or one thought that emanated from her. Crepes . . . crepes.

At first, his analytical mind intruded. It was close to noon. Camila must have gone to lunch and was going to order crepes. It made sense, a logical deduction, but it didn't feel right. He gently told himself to stop analyzing and go deeper. He didn't sense Camila being in a restaurant, and he didn't get any impression of food being prepared.

Crepes . . . creeps . . . they're all creeps! Don't want to be here. Creepy guys. They're crazy.

Odd, he thought. Usually, he picked up images, and only after going deeper would he pick up thoughts. But then he was targeting his former wife, who had been closer to him in his adult years than any other person. But her thoughts baffled him. He reached out for her surroundings. Walls. Sterile walls. Institutional. A hospital?

He wrote *Creeps* on the notepad and circled it. Then he drew a building, surrounded by a fence. He jotted down two words that came to him: *Hospital-Prison*. No, not quite right. Mentally ill people. Criminally ill. A state hospital.

"I'm going east, about forty minutes from here to a mental ward, a lockup. Dangerous people. Camila thinks they're creeps or creepy. She's interested in one particular person here. I see her now watching him through a window."

His lips moved, but none of the words were spoken aloud. It was as if he'd lost his voice. He was picking up all the surrounding circumstances, but he was still having a hard time focusing on the target. Then to his surprise, the target appeared to him. At the same moment, he heard a voice in his head.

Bravo, Calloway. Bravo. You found me. Long time no see,

pal. Well, maybe not so long. We'll have to get together more often. Love your ex, by the way.

Calloway tensed and nearly came out of his zone. How could Camila have done this? She'd taken him to Steve Ritter, a psychotic remote viewer and his onetime colleague. Ritter had been convicted of conspiracy and attempted murder after he was captured with George Wiley when their attempt to nuke Washington was thwarted. He'd heard that Ritter had entered a near catatonic state, rarely spoke or did anything but stare at the walls. As far as Calloway knew, an electromagnetic field surrounded his cell, blocking him from remote viewing. Calloway hadn't felt him around at all, at least not until he and Doc had gone to the ranch to visit Justin Logos. Even then, he'd thought it might be his imagination.

All of his thoughts about Ritter flashed through his mind in an instant. Then he heard a familiar grating cackle.

Look, Ma, no EMF! Yeah, I'm free, so to speak, and we're all still connected in our sticky little psychic web, like a multiple psychic entity. Far out! Way far out!

Ritter's jabber reached Calloway like a whisper in his ear and was immediately identifiable as an outside impression. As long as he was able to sense Ritter and the others, he had a chance to defend himself. But if Ritter's thoughts ever merged with his so that he couldn't tell which was which, he would be heading toward the same insanity that had engulfed the former air force major.

At that moment, he felt Doc's hand clamp onto his wrist. *Pull back, Trent. Get out now. Get away from him. I'm right here with you.*

She jerked his arm and he opened his eyes. It took him a moment to orient himself in the meeting room again. A dozen pairs of eyes stared at him.

"What happened?" Howell said, disappointment souring his tone. "You didn't say anything."

"Quiet!" Doc snapped. She leaned toward Calloway, patting his arm. "Are you all right, Trent?"

He rubbed his face. "Yeah, I think so."

"Sorry I pulled you back that way, but I saw him, too. I didn't want you there a second longer."

"What are you talking about?" Howell asked. "Saw who? What the hell's going on?"

Calloway found his bearings, looked around, focused on Howell. "Camila is at a state hospital in Maryland, the one where Steve Ritter is being held."

"What? She went there?" Howell sounded doubtful. "That's a very odd choice."

"That's for sure, especially since Ritter's not getting the EMF anymore. What the hell happened to it?"

"Oh, that," Howell said uneasily. "Last week a judge ordered it turned off. It violated the other prisoners' rights." He turned up his hands. "We haven't had a chance to look at any alternatives."

"Oh, great," Doc moaned.

Calloway slammed his fist on the table. "Hey! Hello! Listen to me, God damn it. He's got to her. He pulled Camila there. It wasn't where she was going at all. Get her out, get her out of there now!"

Howell looked stunned, but only for a moment. Then he turned to one of his aides, a young woman sitting in a chair near the wall. "You heard him. Call the hospital. Find out if she's there and get her on the phone."

Fourteen

teve Ritter, my name is Harvey Howell.
I work for the president of the United
States and I'd like to talk to you about your unique abilities."

Howell hesitated, then extended his hand across the table.
Ritter stared at the hand, then reached out, clasped it, and held
it too long. When he let go, he knew the man was telling the
truth about his identity.

"I'm all ears." Ritter laughed.

"What's so funny?"

"What I said. Just imagine if it were true. You'd be sitting
across the table from a pair of big ears. So what do you want?"

*Can you believe this, boys? Now we're cooking. I'm sitting
in a private visitor's room with yet another visitor from the White
House. Yesterday, it was Ms. Hidalgo, the president's own
spokesperson, and today let's welcome a voluntary visitor, none
other than the president's own national security advisor.*

*Let's show him how cooperative we can be. If Calloway
won't work for him, we will.*

*Johnstone. Cool it! When I said "we," I meant me. He
doesn't know you guys are active again. Oh, he might guess.
But I'll be happy to take all the credit. So don't worry. Besides,
we're on their side this time. Sort of.*

Focus directly on me now. Pay attention. See what you can pick up.

"Mr. Ritter? Do you hear me?"

"Sorry, sorry. I drift off sometimes. What were you saying?" Howell smiled and peered at Ritter through wire-framed glasses. His short hair and receding hairline accented the roundness of his head. "I asked you how you tricked Ms. Hidalgo into coming to this prison yesterday."

"Oh, that. Calloway led me to her. I peeked in on her and found out what she was planning. Then I nudged her in a new direction, right here, of course."

"That's quite extraordinary."

"That's me—extra ordinary." Ritter smiled, leaned forward. "I liked looking at her, and into her, too. I don't see many women, not even on television. They give me one hour a day to watch the tube, if I want it. But I never go to that little room. I don't like it."

"You make it sound so easy."

Timmons wants to know how Calloway and Doc found her since we put a block on them. Good question. But here's how it seems to work. The block stopped them from seeing what we were doing. They were completely surprised. But, you see, after we focused on Hidalgo, the two of them were free to do their own work.

We could've stopped them, of course. Blocked them right out when we first felt Calloway coming our way. But once I detected our boy, I wanted him to find Camila. He succeeded for the generals, but now they know who rules. That's why Howell is here today.

"Excuse me, Mr. Ritter? Did you hear me?"

Ritter blinked and saw Howell waving a hand in front of his

face. "You don't need to do that. Just repeat your question. I drifted off again."

"Yes, I can see that. I was just pondering your abilities. Is it really that easy for you? Can you just peek into someone's life and adjust his or her thinking? If that's so, you are an incredible resource."

"Yeah, I'm a natural resource and one of the ten wonders of the world, too. But the shrinks also say that I'm out of my mind." Ritter grinned and stared at Howell's folded hands, watching him twiddle his thumbs. "I like that, 'out of my mind.' I like it a lot."

Howell nervously cleared his throat. "Well, I'd like to see if you could try something for me. A little experiment."

"What's in it for me?" Ritter folded his hands and aggressively twiddled his thumbs.

"I can't get you out of here, but I can keep the EMF turned off."

"It's already off. That's like telling me I can have a piece of pie that I ate yesterday."

"Listen to me closely. There are plans in the works to move you to a military facility where you will be in isolation and the EMF will be turned back on. If you cooperate, I can forgo that plan."

"Good. So let me guess. Calloway and his sidekick won't play ball with you, and you see me as a solid relief pitcher who can go an inning or two. Is that what you had in mind, sport?"

"Something like that. Would you go after Justin Logos for me? I need to know what he's planning."

"Harvey, Harvey, Harvey. You want to know what Justin is planning." Ritter bent down and looked under the table.

"What are you doing? You know I have a buzzer in my hand and I can get a guard in here in seconds."

"I'm sure you can. I was just wondering if you're wearing those slinky nylons you like so much. You're a real doll when you're made up, you know."

"Stop it, Steve. I want you to focus on Justin Logos. This is about him, not me."

"Oh, I know. It's just that you're too late. The damage is already done."

Howell rapped his fingers nervously on the table. "What are you talking about?"

"Have you heard about any of your friends getting sick yet, coming down with a virus? No? You will. Very soon. Like I said, the damage is done. Justin's people did their duty."

"You're just making that up. You're lazy, Ritter, and you're wasting my time. I can see that now."

"I'm just telling you the truth, which is more than I can say for you. As soon as I prove myself to you and make a few hits, you're going to send me to that military prison. You'll say that I'm too dangerous. I might go after the prez again."

"That's not it at all," Howell protested. "I want you to help us."

"You want to suck me dry, then turn the EMF back on."

"That's not true."

"Lie all you want, Harvey. You're going to come down with a very deadly virus tomorrow. You'll be dead within forty-eight hours."

Ritter stood up, walked over to the door, and tapped on it. "Guard, take me back to my cell."

"You'll pay for this, Ritter." Howell stood up. "I'll see that the EMF gets back on. You won't be able to remote view the end of your nose."

"Like I said, that was your plan all along."

Fifteen

As soon as she stepped into the crowded clinic, Melissa wondered if she and Justin had made a mistake when they'd decided to hold a public healing session. The seats were all filled and bright light flooded the entire examination area, illuminating every corner as television camera crews scurried about with their last-minute preparations. The privacy partitions had been removed to make more room and better visibility. Everything looked exposed and chaotic, and Melissa wondered how Justin would work under these conditions.

She headed down the central aisle and felt more and more wary with every step. Three nurses moved among the patients, who were already assembled, taking down pertinent information about their conditions. In spite of all the activity, someone quickly identified her as she moved into the lights.

"That's her, the tall one over there."

Suddenly, reporters and cameras descended on her. "Melissa, hello. Art Drysdale from KRML-TV. Why are you holding this public session at the same time that the CNN special on Justin is being broadcast? Are you trying to direct attention away from the program?"

A microphone, held on a long boom, suddenly hovered

above her head and reminded her of Betsy Lambert. Caught off guard, Melissa faltered and stepped back. She looked around for a way out, but knew there was no place to hide. She hadn't planned to make any statement, but now she had to say something. She cleared her throat, steadied herself, and looked directly at the reporter.

"CNN, as I'm sure you know, has been showing clips from the interview for the past two days and the major revelations are already known. So, no, we're not trying to hide anything. All we're doing here tonight is showing something positive and helping people heal. As you'll see, in spite of the controversy, Justin is continuing his work, his good deeds, for all to see."

Before anyone could ask another question, she added, "One of the reasons Justin wanted a public appearance relates to recent questions that have been raised about his ability to heal. Some people have suggested that it's all tricks, sleight of hand, that Justin is really a magician, not a healer. So tonight he's putting his abilities on the line."

"You now say that you were never sexually involved with Justin," another reporter called out. "If that's the case, why did you say before that you were?"

She held up her hands. "I'm sorry. I can't answer any more questions right now. We have to get ready. We'll be starting in a few minutes. Justin plans to answer questions after the session is over."

She quickly turned away and looked around for Kirby. When she spotted him standing off to the side, she hurried over to him. "Are they here yet? Did you find them?"

He nodded calmly. "They're sitting right over there." He pointed toward a set of folding chairs near the front. "They're ready to go anytime you are."

"Great. Where's Justin?"

"He's on his way. He should be here in a few minutes."

She glanced around, noticing the row of beds near the back wall where some of the patients waited. Others were gathered in two clusters, those sitting on folding chairs on one side, others in wheelchairs on the opposite side. Melissa's gaze narrowed to one of the woman sitting on a chair.

She moved several steps closer and recognized Betsy Lambert. The woman stared back at her from across the stage. She wanted to grab Lambert by the arm and drag her away. But that wouldn't work, not with the television crews ready to film anything out of the ordinary, whether it was an extraordinary healing or two women pulling out each other's hair.

Melissa made up her mind and walked over to Betsy. "I see you're back again. I hope they're paying you a lot of money."

The woman, who was a vague and distorted reminder of Melissa's teenage companion, looked frightened and defensive. She held up the badge that she wore around her neck. "You can't kick me out. I came to be healed. I'm with KRML. I'm one of their patients."

To avoid suspicions of fraud and to counteract the new charges, each of the three television crews were asked to bring three volunteers who wanted to be healed. Another couple of hundred people waited for an opportunity to see Justin when he'd finished with the select patients. One of the stations was broadcasting the entire event live, and it was being shown on large-screen televisions in the big tent, where several hundred people had gathered.

"Who said I want to kick you out?" Melissa said in the calmest voice she could muster. "But I'm curious. What's wrong with you?"

"None of your business. I already talked to the nurse." Betsy literally spat the words at her.

Melissa shook her head. "I hope whatever's wrong with you gets healed."

"You knew, didn't you?" Betsy called out as Melissa started away. "You knew he was your son and the son of that demon killer. You left your baby in that Dumpster and that's exactly where they say they found him. Same city. Same part of town. Same year. Of course you knew."

Melissa's hands curled into fists. She hunched over in front of the woman. "I did not know. I'd forgotten all about that. I was young. It was like it had never happened."

Betsy looked at her incredulously. "I don't believe you."

"Believe whatever you want."

Melissa turned away and walked over to where Kirby was talking to two men. In the past few days, she'd concluded that all the events that were taking place were part of a larger plan to get Justin to the place where he belonged. Without her traumatic encounter with Betsy, she wouldn't have sent Kirby to Washington with the viruses. He'd returned four days later and assured her that he and the apostles had done their job. She hoped he was telling the truth. She hadn't told Justin about it, not a word. She wanted him to be completely detached from the event. But that meant Justin hadn't monitored Kirby's activities either, and anything could have happened in Washington.

So far, she had heard nothing about a viral outbreak, and she knew a thousand things could've gone wrong. A part of her recognized the pain and suffering she would cause and hoped that there would be no deadly epidemic. But another part of her, the part that dominated most of the time, still wanted revenge and wanted to set in motion the chaos that Justin had predicted.

Melissa smiled at the two guest speakers who would begin the session and shook their hands. "Sorry about all the confusion, gentlemen. I know we're running late, so why don't we begin. Reverend, would you like to go first?"

The tall, white-haired, mustachioed man smiled. "Of course. Anytime."

Melissa moved to the podium that had been set up in front of the area where Justin would work. The cameras all turned toward her. The chatter from the patients and the television crews ceased. "Okay, we're about to start this extraordinary session tonight. But before Justin Logos begins healing the patients who are waiting here, I want to introduce to you the Reverend James Everett of Carbondale, Illinois."

Everett, who carried a Bible, took the microphone and began his smooth, practiced banter. He explained how he had been observing Justin for several weeks and had become one of his most ardent supporters. "But it wasn't just observation of strangers that made me a believer in Justin Logos. I first came here with my seven-year-old grandson, Kevin. I pushed him in a wheelchair up to Justin and told him that a bullet was lodged next to Kevin's spine and that doctors couldn't remove it because they feared he would be permanently paralyzed.

"Justin spent no more than sixty seconds with Kevin. Then he told me to take him home and get another X ray. The boy seemed unchanged and I thought Justin Logos was a fraud. But he began improving by the hour. By the time the X ray was taken, he could walk again. When that X ray came back, the doctors were astonished. The bullet had somehow dislodged from the spine and was just below the skin. It was removed in a five-minute office procedure."

Everett went on to tell how he had returned in his RV and made daily visits to the clinic, speaking with patients before and after they saw Justin. He added that thirty-seven members of his own congregation had come to Justin, and thirty-three of them had had positive results.

"Now Justin does not preach from the Bible because he is a modest man. That would be like a boastful author reading from his own biography to everyone he met just to show how wonderful he was. Justin is not like that, not at all. He's deeply sincere, honest, and above all, a high spiritual being who is not only of Jesus, but he *is* Jesus."

Not a bad endorsement, Melissa thought. Just as she was wondering what the minister thought of the CNN revelations, he answered her question.

"Now, you may have been hearing some bad things about Justin, both from other men of the cloth and from the media. The strongest of those accusations are being made this very evening. Good Friday of all days. Think about that. They are attempting to kill the bearer of the Almighty's word on the day Jesus died on the cross.

"Don't be misled by their message. The devil is out there, on the loose, trying to turn everyone away from the word of God. Don't pay any attention to the nonsense. Don't allow yourself to get caught up in the negativity and callous words coming from the loose tongues of those who want to create drama so the ratings of their networks will go up. I say nonsense to all of it."

Thunderous applause and cheers erupted from the onlookers in the clinic. The reaction reminded Melissa that what was taking place was being seen not only by those here and the hundreds in the large tent, but by millions of others. She looked over at Betsy. Her head was bowed, her hands clasped together in prayer.

"Now let us pray." The minister started with the Lord's Prayer and continued on for several minutes. Shouts of "Amen!"

and "Hallelujah!" resounded each time the litany reached a crescendo. Betsy now stared straight ahead, her hands at her sides as everyone else prayed. She had clearly sided against Justin and would probably later proclaim to the cameras that he hadn't healed her.

Everett cleared his throat. "Now I want to finish with a verse of my own that I call 'Holy Vibrations.' "

> *"Hail to Justin Logos,*
> *Spirit of the Second Coming,*
> *Reborn Messiah,*
> *Author of Divine Light.*

> *"Holy vibrations!*
> *He comes in the name of the Lord.*
> *Hail to Justin Logos!*
> *He heals us all at the end of the world."*

Amid more shouts and applause, Everett stepped away and Melissa returned to the podium. If Betsy Lambert didn't like the good minister, wait until she saw who was next, Melissa thought. "Now I want to introduce you to another healer. His name is Enrique, and he comes to us from the Peruvian Andes. He is a shaman in the Inca tradition, and he will invoke the spirits of the four winds to give us guidance this evening."

A man with dark, elongated features, wearing a colorful poncho and a pointed stocking cap, stepped to the center of the stage. Enrique had shown up at the camp two days ago with a group of Americans who had taken a shamanism workshop with him and toured Canyon de Chelly and Chaco Canyon. Justin had not only embraced Enrique, but insisted he be allowed to speak.

He began in Quechua, the Incan language, as he held his

palms together above his head and turned to face each direction. Then he nodded to Melissa and switched to Spanish. She moved next to him and translated as he spoke.

"Enrique says that we are entering a period of tumultuous changes. The world, as we know it, will no longer greet us each morning. You must listen to this man, Justin Logos, and decide for yourself who he is. He is related to these changes.

"There is more than one future. Some of you will be able to move into a future that is free of many of the horrors that will be taking place. But the window to that future is through the place of no time, the place that contains both the past and future. Those of you who find this place may be able to help others through the window to that future."

He finished by giving thanks to Pachamama, the Mother Earth; Inti Taita, the sun; and again, the spirits of the four winds. He walked offstage under a veil of awkward silence. Betsy prayed again, her hands to her forehead. The shaman was a mistake, Melissa thought. Even though she had translated his words, she didn't understand them and she knew she wasn't alone. He hadn't even endorsed Justin, but then the man represented a tradition that had been defeated, tortured, and abused by those who spoke of Jesus as their savior.

Melissa didn't know what to say, but then, to her relief, she saw Justin standing off to one side. He shook Enrique's hand, then nodded to Melissa, indicating that he was ready. Keep it simple, she thought. No need for a lengthy introduction. "Now, I want to introduce you to Justin Logos."

"Here he comes, Doc," Calloway called out from the family room of Doc's home in the tiny Colorado town of Ouray.

"I'll be right there," she called out from the kitchen, where she was making popcorn.

They'd just arrived an hour ago after spending most of the day traveling from Washington. They'd flown into Denver, where they'd waited two hours before catching their commuter flight to Durango. Then they'd driven an hour to get here. Calloway had spent his last night in the capital with Camila helping her recover from her unexpected encounter with Steve Ritter. She was confused and upset because she had no recollection of driving to the institution, but by evening she was recovering. As Doc put it, the committee now fully understood the potential dangers of remote viewing when carried to an extreme. But Calloway figured nothing had changed. The generals and spooks simply knew they had a bigger and better weapon on their hands than they'd realized.

Now he focused on the television as Doc came into the room and set a bowl of buttered popcorn on the table in front of the couch. Even though the CNN special was also on, Doc had insisted they watch this one, because it was live, and videotape the other. Justin, wearing his white smock, walked past the podium and over to a chair several feet away. A cheer rose from the crowd at the sight of him. But Justin didn't raise his arms, didn't wave or do anything to indicate that he was someone special, someone revered by his followers. He looked like a lab technician on his way to work.

"I guess we'll begin right away," Melissa Dahl said from the podium. "We'll start with the patients selected by the television stations."

A nurse, carrying a file folder, escorted a teenage boy named Duncan, who was missing his right arm below the elbow. Calloway doubted that Justin would be able to help him. As far as

Calloway knew, growing back missing limbs was clearly beyond Justin's capabilities. The camera moved in for a close-up of him. Justin didn't bother looking at the file. "Duncan, God didn't intend everyone to be healed. Sometimes we are faced with challenges that will allow us the opportunity to rise spiritually much faster than other people."

The kid looked disappointed, but nodded, resigned to his physical condition. "Poor guy," Calloway said. "He probably thought that Justin was going to grow back his arm."

Justin looked over the kid. "There is something else, though. What's wrong with your knee?"

Calloway hadn't noticed anything unusual in the way the boy had walked.

"The doctor said I may need surgery," Duncan said. "I have a torn ligament. I did it playing basketball."

Justin crouched and held his right hand a few inches from the knee. Justin didn't use ritual or high drama. He didn't call on spirits and didn't go into a trance. Instead, he proclaimed in interviews that he worked with energies and the patient's soul as he performed astral surgery.

"I bet you're a good basketball player, Duncan. You've got the right name for it. Dunk 'em."

The boy laughed. Justin stood up. "Have your doctor take another look at the knee. I think he might change his mind now about that surgery."

Duncan moved the knee from side to side and winced. "It still hurts."

"Hey, give it a chance. Healing takes time. At least a few minutes." Justin laughed and patted the boy on the back as he left.

Not an impressive start, Calloway thought as Justin moved on to the next patient, a woman in her fifties who had arrived in a wheelchair. She suffered from femoral arthritis in her lower back and couldn't get out of her wheelchair by herself. Two of Justin's assistants helped her to her feet as Justin moved behind her. "Are you okay?"

"As long as they don't let me fall."

Justin held his hands a couple of inches from her spine. He didn't move for nearly a minute. Then he told the nurses to lower her into the wheelchair. "You're going to start feeling better very soon. You're not going to need that wheelchair much longer."

She nodded. "I can feel warmth in my back. I think something is happening already."

After attending a couple more patients, Justin walked to the rear of the stage where more patients lay on beds. Within the next few minutes, he performed etheric surgery on a man with three malignant and inoperable tumors in his brain. Then Justin worked on another man with a clogged coronary artery, and again healing was promised to occur over time.

Calloway was starting to get bored when Justin approached a woman with a tumor growing on her lower intestines. He held his hand above the woman's belly, and within seconds the tumor started to rise through the skin.

"Look at that?" Doc said. "Do you see it?"

Calloway leaned closer to the screen as Justin touched the spot where a lump had formed. Suddenly, the skin ruptured. Carefully, he lifted out a bloody black mass about the size of a tennis ball. The woman appeared to feel no pain during the one-minute operation. "If possible, I would like you to come back next week with X rays and medical reports," Justin told the woman.

"That's pretty damned impressive," Calloway said.

"Now what's this?" Doc said as the broadcast was interrupted by a news update.

Dan Rather appeared on the screen, a somber look on his face. "The Centers for Disease Control is reporting a sudden and dramatic outbreak of a deadly virus in the nation's capital. Within the last few hours, emergency rooms in Washington have been overwhelmed, and three deaths have been reported. Stay tuned as we update this story throughout the evening and examine all of its implications, including the possibility, and I emphasize *possibility,* that the outbreak is related to a biological attack."

"Shit," Calloway said. "I better call Camila."

"Oh, Trent. I've got a bad feeling about this," Doc said, and stared at Justin Logos as he reappeared on the screen.

As Justin moved forward again, followed by the cameras, Betsy Lambert awaited her turn in the chair. Melissa moved closer to see what he would do. Justin came up behind Betsy. Again, he didn't look at the file the nurse held out to him. He didn't raise his hands, either.

"It's you," he said in a low voice. "I thought you would be back. I'm sorry, but I can do nothing for you. Your condition is terminal. You'll see to that yourself."

Melissa had never heard Justin say anything of the sort to a patient. Betsy didn't respond; Justin didn't move.

"Okay, that's all," Melissa said. "He's done with you."

Suddenly, Betsy stood up and spun around, knocking over the chair. She looked at Melissa, then to Justin. "Well, I'm not done with him," Betsy shouted. "You are a mistake, an evil mistake! You are lying. Your life is a lie, a total lie. Your father was a murderer and rapist. You are the devil's work."

"Betsy! That's enough!" Melissa reached for Betsy's shoulder, but she wrenched out of reach.

Melissa looked around desperately for Kirby. Where the hell was he? "J.D.! Help me get her out of here."

In that moment, when she'd taken her attention off the woman, Betsy pulled a gun from her purse. She aimed at Justin, fired. Once, then again, just as Melissa lunged toward her. Too late. Melissa wrestled for the gun. Out of the corner of her eye she saw Justin stumble, fall. Betsy pulled the gun away from Melissa and aimed it at her. Melissa flinched, expecting a bullet to pierce her forehead at any moment. Then, suddenly, Betsy turned the weapon around, stuck it in her mouth, and fired.

Melissa, gasping for breath, crawled over to Justin, who lay very still. A blotch of blood spread across his chest, and she knew it was too late, that Justin's worst prediction had come true, and she screamed, a long, mournful wail.

PART TWO

INTO THE PAST

Sixteen

Looking down Main Street with its two-story, red-brick buildings and the dramatic backdrop of a snow-crested mountain peak, Trent Calloway felt as if he were living inside a postcard. Pristine wood-framed houses with neat, fenced-in yards formed tight-knit neighborhoods on the sloping landscape. The town of Ouray, Colorado, possessed a sense of spirit. *Pleasant, refreshing, relaxing:* all those adjectives came to mind.

In spite of it all, Calloway figured the place would drive him nuts within a couple of weeks. It all seemed a little too quaint, too picturesque, and everything was up or down a slope. After the openness of the desert, the town felt cramped to him, and he especially didn't like there being only one road out of town. Every winter, residents here were snowed in, literally trapped for days and sometimes weeks after winter snowstorms.

He climbed into his Jeep and set the bag of groceries on the passenger seat. He felt a vague thickness in his chest and thought he needed a nap. He'd gotten up three or four times last night, and the interrupted sleep had left him feeling lethargic. As he headed down Main Street, he promised himself for a second time that he would leave Ouray this evening and drive down the Rockies to the Four Corners, to the desert and the open countryside he preferred. In spite of his plans, he felt anxious to get away. It was almost as if he suspected that if he didn't leave soon, he might never escape the town.

He passed Doc's bookstore, which closed for two weeks when Marla, her niece and co-owner, had left town on vacation. He turned up the winding road at the end of town, then onto Doc's street. He parked in front of her house. He'd told Doc he would spend Easter with her, then leave this evening. But now with the events in Washington consuming her interest, he thought he might be able to slip away after lunch, unless she insisted that he stay for the turkey dinner she'd planned. He would see if she minded.

As he started to get out of the Jeep, an image of Camila appeared in his mind. He dropped back into his seat, shut his eyes, focused. She stood at a podium and seemed to waver back and forth. Then she toppled over, collapsing to the floor. The image disintegrated like a mirror shattering and crumbling. He didn't know what it meant, but it probably reflected his concern for her, and there was plenty of reason for that.

He scooped up the groceries that he'd bought from a gas station convenience store, the only place open in town on Easter, and carried them inside. He suddenly felt woozy as he set the groceries down on the kitchen counter. Just tired, he told himself. He could hear the drone of the television in the living room and figured that Doc hadn't moved since he left.

"Anything new?" he called out.

"Yeah, and it's all bad," she responded. "Sixteen hundred and twenty-two confirmed deaths now. Almost all of them were people who worked in the heart of Washington. There's a full update coming in a minute."

Since hearing about the outbreak during the Justin Logos special, they'd followed the news closely. With each passing hour, the word from the capital had gotten worse. Both the president and the vice president had contracted the flu. Then yesterday afternoon, the nation was shocked by the sudden death of President David Dustin and the worsening condition of his vice president.

Calloway moved closer to the television as the familiar face of Ray Allard, a CNN anchor, appeared on the screen. All the networks and cable news stations had stopped their regular broadcasting to provide continuous coverage of the unfolding tragedy in Washington. Besides the frequent updates, experts were conjecturing on the source of the virus, and bioterrorism, although unconfirmed, was receiving the most attention.

"With our continual focus on the death yesterday of President David Dustin and earlier today of Vice President Rollie Mitchell, we've barely touched on the many other prominent people who have died from this still mysterious and deadly flu virus," Allard said. "At this point, eighteen members of Congress are dead, and another twelve senators and thirty-two representatives have contracted the virus. Among those battling the virus are Speaker of the House William Riley, who until hours ago was expected to be sworn in as the new president. Let's go to Tera Peters, who is reporting from inside the quarantine zone at Good Samaritan Hospital, for the latest on Representative Riley."

"Ray, we've just learned that Speaker Riley will be sworn in as president via a video hookup in his hospital room. He will then immediately transfer the powers of the presidency, at least temporarily, to the secretary of state. As you know, this same process took place yesterday when Rollie Mitchell was sworn in to the presidency from his hospital bed. Never in history has the presidency of the United States been transferred twice during one term, much less twice in twenty-four hours."

"Tera, I have to interrupt here. In a few minutes, we will be going to Jerusalem where Secretary of State Charles Vincent is about to board Air Force One. He apparently will assume the duties of the presidency of the United States while in the air above the Mideast. But first we're going to get the latest from the Centers for Disease Control here in Atlanta where a press conference has just begun."

"I can't watch any more of this," Calloway said, turning away. "I just keep thinking of Camila."

"I feel numb," Doc said, turning off the television. "Just numb."

"I'm going to try calling her again. Then I'll make a couple of sandwiches. Is tuna salad okay?" Before Doc responded, Calloway stomped his foot in annoyance. "Damn it, Doc. Why the hell hasn't she called? I don't understand it."

"Trent, she might be in the hospital."

"She could still call, couldn't she?"

"Listen, while you were out, they reported twenty-nine cases of the flu among the White House staff."

"Okay, what are you telling me?"

"They said nine are dead, but they only gave a few names. Harvey Howell is one of them. He might've already been infected when we saw him."

Calloway wasn't thinking about Howell. "They didn't mention Camila, though. That's good. I'm not giving up on her. Maybe she left town. Didn't they say something about setting up a temporary White House in Philadelphia?"

"Now they've changed it to Minneapolis after they found three cases of the flu in Philly among a family that had visited Washington a week ago."

He unpacked the groceries and tore open the top of the bag of jelly beans that he'd bought. He scooped up a small handful and popped several into his mouth. Suddenly, the sweet taste turned sour in his mouth. He spat them out into the sink as his stomach rebelled. No more. Ever. He tossed the bag into the garbage.

He picked up the phone and quickly punched Camila's cell phone, then her home, then her office. He listened to the ringing and the recordings where he'd already left messages. He didn't want to accept the image of her collapsing behind a podium. He thought of Tera Peters in Washington. If anyone else knew about Camila, it would be Tera. But could he reach her? He picked up the phone again. He called the CNN office in Washington and left his name for Peters along with Doc's phone number and a three-word message: "How is Camila?"

It was a long shot. But Tera knew him from when he and Camila were married, and if she had recently talked with Camila, she might take a minute and call him. He busied himself making the sandwiches. His head felt as if it were stuffed with soggy cotton. He tried to convince himself it was nothing and that he just needed something to eat.

"Trent, can you come here?" Doc asked weakly.

For a moment, he wasn't sure that he'd really heard her. He found her lying on the couch. Beads of perspiration covered her brow. Her face looked flushed; her eyes were glazed. "Oh, shit. What's going on?"

"I've got it, Trent," she moaned. "Damn it. That bastard general sitting across from me coughed in my face."

"But you were fine a few minutes ago."

She shook her head. "I've been feeling weird all morning. I just didn't want to say anything. But then it came on fast. All of a sudden."

He felt a scratchiness in his own throat. "Can I get you anything? Aspirin, soup?"

She slowly shook her head. "I've already taken three aspirins. It hasn't helped. It's not going to help. Call my doctor, Scott Roland. His number's in the address book, by the phone in the kitchen. He'll know what to do."

Calloway walked back to the kitchen and paged through the address book. He found Roland's number, rang it up, and left a message. He looked at the bread on the counter, the can of tuna, the celery, and the mayonnaise. The idea of eating tuna suddenly made him feel sick to his stomach. Chicken soup. Even if Doc didn't want it, he'd make it for himself, if he could find any.

He scoured the pantry and settled on vegetable broth. As he heated it, the phone rang. He snapped it up, amazed that the doctor would respond so quickly on a holiday. "Boyle residence."

"Trent, is that you? It's Tera Peters."

"Tera, have you heard anything?"

"I did." She paused and he braced himself. "I'm sorry, Trent. She died earlier today. The flu took her in about twenty-four hours."

Calloway slammed his palm against the counter. "Damn, I didn't want to believe it. Are you sure?"

"Trent, it's tearing me apart, too. She was a great friend. I've never known anyone like her."

"I'm sorry," he said hoarsely. His throat closed up. Tears welled in his eyes. He couldn't think of anything else to say.

"I've lost so many friends and acquaintances just overnight. Then of course the president and vice president. I'm overwhelmed by it all. But none of them were as close to me as Camila. When this thing settles down, we've got to do something special in her honor."

"Just let me know. I'll do whatever you want." *If I'm still alive.* He pushed away the thought. "Christ, I guess it's pretty bad there."

"It's terrible, really terrible, and it's not over. I don't know what's going to happen."

"What about you? How are you avoiding it?"

"I was out of town until the day before yesterday. I guess I'm taking a chance, but no more than hundreds of thousands of others who might come into contact with a carrier. At least now they know what it is."

"They do?"

"Didn't you hear? The CDC announced about half an hour ago that they've isolated the viruses. There are three distinct deadly contagions—anthrax, tularemia, and brucellosis. It's almost certainly the work of a bioterrorist."

"I'm not surprised."

"Trent, you don't sound so good."

Calloway heard Doc calling to him. "Listen, I've got to go. Thanks for getting back to me. I really appreciate it. Take care of yourself."

He hung up and moved over to the couch. "Doc?"

He didn't look forward to telling her the bad news. She didn't move. He touched her shoulder. She groaned, raised a hand, then let it drop. He felt her head. "You're burning up."

"Was that the doctor?"

"No, it was Tera Peters."

"What did she say?" Doc's voice slurred.

"Camila's on the list."

Doc tried to sit up, but slumped back down. "I'm sorry. I'm really sorry, Trent."

"Yeah, it's hard to believe." He didn't know what else to say, so he explained what Peters had told him about the three viruses. "I think I've got all three," Doc muttered. "I've got to try to sleep now."

Calloway backed away. He smelled the broth and moved

back to the kitchen. He poured himself a bowl and sat down. He started to eat, but his hand kept shaking and most of the broth fell back into the bowl. He could feel the flu slowly consuming him, and he wondered when the doctor would call. He picked up the bowl, drank from it, then left some for Doc.

He checked on her, saw that she appeared to be asleep, then made his way to the guest bedroom. He lay down and tried to relax. His thoughts immediately turned to Camila. He felt a deep ache inside him. Even though they'd been apart for years and their lives were so different, he felt closer to her now than ever before. Less than a month after their reconciliation, his greatest fear had been realized. He'd lost her again, lost her for good.

He clenched his fists. His sense of loss shifted to anger. Then he took control and willed himself to relax. He focused on the image he'd seen of Camila collapsing. He didn't know whether it had happened that way, but it represented the disaster.

Who did it? Show me.

He sank into his zone, but the harder he looked for his target, the less he saw. Maybe he was too sick to get anything. If Doc were monitoring him, it would be different, he thought. He could never work well by himself. Then he glimpsed a vague image of a building. He reached over to the nightstand where he'd put a notebook and pen.

He started sketching, and the image came to him in more detail. When he finished the first building, he drew another and another, a complex of related structures surrounded by open land and mountains. Separate from the main buildings, he drew a circle. Within it he drew other structures, but there was something impermanent about them. Outside the circle were oblong objects . . . vehicles. Like a parking lot, but somehow different. People lived there. Then he realized they were camping. It was a campground, and instantly he recognized his target.

He blinked his eyes as he fell out of his zone. It was Melissa Dahl's ranch in the Sangre de Cristo Mountains where he and Doc had observed Justin Logos. But Logos was dead. Calloway and Doc and millions of others had witnessed the ugly incident as it unfolded on camera. Sensational as the murder was, the death of the president and the spread of the deadly virus had quickly overshadowed it.

But maybe it was just his imagination. He was getting sick, after all, and working alone. Then an image of Harvey Howell came to mind, and suddenly he knew without a doubt that Howell had been right and he and Doc had been wrong about Justin Logos. Howell suspected that Justin and Dahl had bio-weapons, that they might use them, but he didn't have enough evidence.

He and Camila had tried to get supporting evidence through remote viewing, but Calloway and Doc had failed them. They'd failed the country and the entire world. Their concerns about abusing the psychic tool had blinded them to the dark side of the Justin Logos phenomenon, and now it was too late. Too damned late.

Seventeen

Melissa blended into the crowd that filled the big tent in a spirit of celebration and anticipation. At the podium, Suzie Carlson, a robust blonde from Minnesota, spoke about the four years she had worked as a volunteer for Justin. Melissa noticed that the devoted apostle referred to Justin in the present tense, as if he were still alive. It was just what Melissa had asked her to do. Everyone had to be in tune with the big event. If they all believed strongly enough, she knew it would happen. With Justin's hard-core believers dominating the crowd, their chances were much greater than if the tent had been packed with doubters, cynics, and skeptics.

"And now I'm extremely excited to introduce you to someone very special, the woman who first recognized Justin Logos as the incredible advanced being that he *is,* and who has faithfully and astutely managed the expanding phenomenon that has grown around him during these past six years."

Melissa felt a surge of energy ripple through the crowd, and it gave her confidence and the power she needed at this crucial moment. The clapping turned into cheers as she headed to the podium, and suddenly everyone stood up. She had worried that his ardent followers would blame her for Justin's death and that would dash any hopes of creating a unified energy field that she felt was needed at this crucial time. But fortunately her fears were unfounded. All she felt was wave after wave of empathy and support. With a sense of gratitude and relief, she let the crowd carry on for nearly two minutes as she soaked it all in. Finally, she raised her hands. The clapping slowly subsided and everyone sat down.

She looked over the crowd. Every chair was taken and people lined the walls, standing two and three deep. It almost seemed that nothing had changed, that Justin was still conducting his daily healing sessions and weekly talks. That was exactly the feeling she wanted to create. At all costs, she needed to avoid any reference to the sorrow and loss she had felt in the aftermath of his death. If she hadn't latched onto Justin's recurrent theme in his last days that he would return, that he would survive, she wouldn't be able to push off the sense of tragedy and devastation that still hovered over her like an impending avalanche. She would certainly never have been able to stand here today.

"Happy Easter, everyone!" she called out.

The greeting set off another cheer. This time she turned her palms up, soaked in the energy, and encouraged them to continue. They responded with another standing ovation.

"We're on a mission here, folks," she shouted above the cheering. "Many of us have experienced or witnessed Justin's incredible healing power at work, and we've all heard the naysayers tell us that such things were impossible, that they defied the laws of nature. But Justin is attuned to a higher vibration. He understands the laws of nature much better than any scientist.

"Therefore, I am telling you that Justin is definitely capable of returning to us. His body will simply vanish from the morgue in Santa Fe, as if it were never there, and he will walk among us. He predicted his death and he also said that he would return! I believe him. I believe him wholeheartedly. Do you?"

A thousand shouts—*"Yes, yes, yes"*—over and over again, reverberated through the tent.

She paused to let the words sink in. She wanted everyone firmly united in the belief that Justin was about to return from the dead.

"Now the way Justin described what will happen is a little complicated. He said that he would actually erase the defining event. It will be as if he were never killed. Now I'll be the first to admit that I don't know how that works or how we're going to perceive it, but that's how he explained it to me."

"Hallelujah!" several people shouted, and others joined them.

"Praise the reborn Lord!" someone yelled from the back of the tent.

"Yeah, this is a revival, all right!" Melissa shouted. "A real revival! And a great day for a resurrection!"

Applause and shouting filled the tent again. When everyone settled down, she started speaking again in a calm, relaxed tone. "I want to tell you a story about Justin as we're all waiting for this event to unfold. This is a story that, as far as I know, has never been told. A few years ago, a prominent magician came to the ranch to watch Justin heal, and he brought a reporter with him. The magician is known as a skeptic of the paranormal and he was very interested in seeing Justin remove a tumor or anything else from a patient's body.

"Justin knew the magician wanted to expose him as a fraud and get credit for it. He could easily have thrown the man out, but instead he invited the magician and reporter to stay. After a couple hours of healing patients without performing any operations that were particularly sensational, Justin came to a patient with a tumor. He made a two-inch incision in the man's abdomen with a scalpel, reached inside the opening, and removed a growth the size of a baseball. The patient did not receive any anesthesia and felt no pain.

"The magician had watched it all in silence. But now he asked Justin if he would allow the reporter to have the tumor analyzed. Justin agreed, but he already knew what was going to happen. The magician would deftly switch the tumor for a chicken liver. So a week later, when the reporter called and told him the results, Justin responded that the reporter should take a look at the before and after X rays of the patient. They would show that the tumor had been removed. Justin added that the patient had given permission for the reporter to talk to his doctor. Justin went on to tell the man that he should go to the magician's house and he would find the real tumor in a glass jar on a shelf in the magician's bedroom closet.

Melissa smiled as she reached the punch line. "The magician, of course, was caught off guard. He refused to let the reporter look in his bedroom closet for the jar, and the reporter, who had been skeptical of Justin, wrote the story honestly. But none of you read the article, did you? The reason is that the newspaper's editor killed it. The magician had complained that the reporter was biased and susceptible to fraud. The reporter told me himself what happened."

The crowd reacted with groans. "As all of you well know, the press has not been kind to Justin. As for that magician, he recently said that Justin was a very clever magician. That I suspect was supposed to be a compliment."

The crowd booed, then they started chanting, "Justin, Justin, Justin . . ."

She scanned the crowd expecting at any moment to see him step out into view and join her at the podium. But would they really forget that he'd been killed? She actually found that part harder to believe than his resurrection from the dead. No, that was wrong thinking. He never died, she told herself. *He's alive. He never died.* She said it aloud into the microphone and repeated it over and over, and everyone joined her. "He's alive. He never died. He's alive."

Twilight, moonlight, hope to see a ghost tonight. Calloway came awake in a darkened room with the rhyme from a children's game in his mind. The words had echoed in his head over and over again. He pushed himself up on his forearms. His body was drenched in sweat, and for a moment he didn't know where he was. Then he remembered that he'd lain down in Doc's guest room. He squinted at the glowing dial of the clock and saw that three hours had passed.

He reached for a bedside lamp, but knocked it over. He stumbled out of bed, feeling dizzy, and pawed his way along the wall of the darkened room until he found a light switch. He leaned against the wall, steadying himself. He felt a thickness around him as if his body extended a foot or more outside its normal dimension. He made his way to the family room, moving slowly as his eyes adjusted to his murky surroundings. He dropped to one knee next to the couch.

"Doc, wake up."

She moaned, mumbled under her breath, and turned over. He gently shook her shoulder. "C'mon, wake up."

Her eyes, red and bleary, blinked open. "Let me sleep, Trent. I don't feel well."

Calloway peered at her, knowing that his own eyes probably looked the same. "We've both got it. We've got to get ourselves to the nearest hospital. I don't know what happened to your damned doctor. He must be out of town."

Doc sat up, cleared her throat. "No, we can't leave. I talked to Dr. Roland while you were sleeping. He wants us to stay right here and out of contact with anyone else. We're supposed to drink a lot of liquids, take aspirin, and use ice packs to help keep our fevers down. He's contacting the CDC to find out exactly how he should proceed."

"Great. He's more concerned about getting it himself than in treating us," Calloway complained.

"Don't be so callous, Trent. He's just being cautious. He'll do everything he can. I trust Dr. Roland."

Calloway slumped down on the couch. "Meanwhile, here we are, awaiting the end."

"The end of what? Hey, don't get morbid on me. We're not going to die. I'm not ready to go and I don't think you are, either."

He rubbed his eyes and frowned at her. Doc's hair was mussed, her face looked red and feverish, her eyes glazed and watery. "You look like shit, Doc."

She glowered at him. "So do you."

They both laughed weakly and coughed. He clasped his head with his hand. "It hurts to laugh. My head is pounding. Doc, what the hell are we going to do?"

"Let's imagine how things were before this happened, before we went to Washington," she suggested. "We were both feeling pretty good out at Justin's ranch. That was kind of fun in a weird way."

"Yeah, I guess it was. Camila was alive and I was full of hope." Then Calloway recalled the images that he had received when he'd targeted the perpetrators of the virus. "Doc, we really screwed up. I think they're behind it."

"Who? What?"

"Justin Logos and Melissa Dahl." He told her how he'd targeted the source of the flu and what he'd gotten. "Dahl has the background for it. She's a microbiologist. Maybe she stole the viruses from one of the labs she worked for."

"Trent, I can't imagine them flying to Washington and merrily spraying viruses around and then going back to their healing work. She certainly couldn't have done it after he died. People were already getting sick by then."

"She probably got someone else to spray the stuff. Some of Justin's followers would do anything for him. We saw that while we were there." He knew he sounded irritated, but he didn't care. "This wasn't some feverish vision, if that's what you're thinking. I wasn't hallucinating or even dreaming."

"Hey, I didn't say you were hallucinating," Doc replied defensively. "But what if you're right? What can we do? I don't even know who we could report it to at this point. My guess is that everyone in that meeting with us is either dead by now or very sick."

"That's no excuse. We've got to do something. After all, we're partially responsible."

"Like hell we are. I am not in any way responsible for this virus and neither are you. Besides, we've both got it. We can't do anything but try to get well."

"Stop avoiding the obvious, Doc. We should've targeted Justin or Dahl."

"Hindsight is wonderful. You know exactly why we didn't do it. But let's stick with the present. Tell you what, I'll call the FBI and tell them what you've got."

He didn't want to stick to the present. He hated the present. He'd lost Camila and still didn't want to accept it. There had to be something else they could do. Doc started to stand up, but Calloway stopped her.

"Wait a minute. I've got a better idea. It's a long shot, but it's worth a try."

She sat back down. "What?"

"Let's go back and stop Dahl."

"Trent, we're in no shape to drive anywhere. We'd probably pass out before we got out of Colorado. Besides, the damage is done."

He shook his head. "No, that's not what I mean. Remember what you said about imagining how things were when we were at the ranch?"

"Yeah, so?"

"You were on the right track. We've got to try to go back in time, target the past, and stop her."

Doc coughed hoarsely. "What are you talking about? We've never done anything even close to that. Besides, the past is over. What difference would it make?"

"Maybe it would make a big difference. We don't know until we've tried." Calloway knew that the attempt would push his skills to the extreme. He wasn't even sure that he was well enough to get into his zone again. But it was worth the effort.

Doc poured them glasses of water from a pitcher on the coffee table. She wiped her brow with a cloth. "You're sick, Trent. You're not thinking clearly."

"I know it sounds nuts, Doc. But why not try it? I think we should target Melissa Dahl at a point in the past where I can take some action to affect her decision making so she doesn't send her bio-weapons to Washington. That's all I can think of right now."

"Okay, let's say you're right about the link between Melissa and the viruses and you were able to stop her. What do you think that would mean? What would happen to us?"

Calloway took a swallow of the water. His tongue felt thick

and dry. "Theoretically, we'd shift to a new present, one where Washington was never subjected to a deadly virus."

"And where Camila is still alive," Doc added.

"That's right, Camila and David Dustin and Rollie Mitchell and everyone else who has been infected are never exposed to the viruses."

Doc smiled. "If it were only so easy, Trent. It's a fantasy. I'm sorry, but it won't work."

"Who says?" he responded defiantly.

"Don't you remember our training? You can remote view the past, but you can't change what has already happened. Period." She was citing the standard response from the military's guidebook on remote viewing.

"I never bought into that. Besides, how do you know that it has never been done before? Maybe we don't remember it because of the very fact that we succeeded."

She shook her head. "You lost me. What exactly are you saying?"

"I'm saying that maybe part of the military's remote-viewing program actually was involved in attempting to alter the past. Maybe by succeeding we created a new branch of reality in which the act in question never took place. So we don't know about it. At least, not in the branch of reality where we live."

Doc threw up her hands. "I suppose it's all theoretical until we try it and see what happens. But I don't hold much hope for succeeding. I'll tell you that now."

"You've got to set aside your reservations and believe that it can work."

Doc wiped her brow again and held an ice bag to her head. "I'll do the damned best I can to make it happen. Anything to get out of this situation."

"That's all I ask."

Eighteen

Dusk had fallen on Easter Sunday when Melissa Dahl leaned over and peered into the telescope. She adjusted the eyepiece and the formless blur came into sharp focus. The crowd was still there, still waiting for Justin's resurrection. But after a few moments, Melissa conceded that only a few small clusters of true believers remained. In the distance, a long line of cars pulled away from the campground as the sun buried itself below the horizon. By morning, she guessed, only a couple dozen diehards would remain behind, a fraction of the throng that had crowded into the big tent to await Justin's return.

She turned away from the window, and the weight of disappointment pressed down on her. She'd lost her last scrap of hope. "Easter is over. It was all a lie, and I was an idiot."

"Don't give up yet," Kirby responded weakly.

She shook her head, a glum expression on her face. "No, it's over, J.D. There's no hiding it any longer. I was desperate. I wanted to believe."

"What else could you believe? Justin predicted his own death. He'd healed thousands. He'd performed miracles. Why couldn't he rise from the dead? Hell, you had me going. I expected to see him walk up to the podium."

"But he didn't. That's the fact of the matter." Scorn laced her every word.

"I don't know, Melissa. Maybe we're not seeing something. It just seemed so perfect, so right. I mean, he died on Good Friday and it made sense that he would rise from the dead on Easter."

"Stop it! I don't want to hear it anymore."

"Wait a minute." Kirby suddenly sounded excited. "Didn't he say that he would rise from his ashes? Maybe his body has to be cremated first. That's tomorrow, right?"

"Oh, J.D., let's not delude ourselves." She crossed her arms defensively. "He may rise in spirit from his ashes, but he won't reappear as his old self any more than those people dying of flu in Washington will ever return to their families and friends."

Kirby looked away. "I wish I'd never listened to you. I thought you knew what you were doing."

Melissa laughed, a sharp, cruel cackle. "Look on the bright side. If the media wasn't so preoccupied with the disaster in Washington, they would be here in full force, all of them picking us apart smugly trying to prove that Justin was just another fallible human."

Kirby shifted his weight from one foot to the other. "I remember what you told me a couple of years ago on Easter Sunday."

She frowned. "Which was what?"

"About the resurrection. You said you thought it was a symbol of rebirth, not a real event in the physical world."

"I guess I was right. But that was before Justin had said he was going to die."

In the distance, a voice boomed from the public address system and the words seeped into Melissa's bedroom. "It's a perfect evening for a resurrection. I believe Justin has already arisen and will be making his way to the stage at any moment."

Melissa walked over to the window. "Who the hell is that playing preacher now?"

"A believer."

"An idiot."

She slammed the window shut and pulled the blinds. "Justin's body is on a slab in Santa Fe. He's been autopsied as required by the state after a criminal death. He won't be climbing onto the stage."

"You've really flip-flopped, Melissa." Kirby placed a hand on her arm. His eyes searched to meet hers. "You were so filled with hope this morning."

She shrugged him off. "I don't want to hear about it. Just look at that!" She pointed to the television, which was tuned to CNN but on mute. Silent news about an invisible, silent killer. Tera Peters filled the screen.

"She's mocking me. Standing right there in the midst of the disaster. She should be dead like the others."

"You should've sued the bitch and her cable network for libel. You could've stopped them from airing that program." Kirby sounded exasperated.

"J.D., you're strong and handsome, but you're ignorant. You can't sue for libel before they libel you. So don't go telling me what I should've done."

None of it mattered now. Her faith in Justin, in the rebirth of the master plan, the salvation of her future, the resurrection of the god-man, had gone unanswered. There was no future. No plan. No salvation.

He shrugged. "At least we've got each other."

"Just leave me alone. I need some time by myself."

"Melissa, I don't want you getting depressed about this thing. We can work it out. The two of us together are strong."

She looked away from him. "I said I want to be alone."

He looked at her a moment longer, then left the room.

She sat on the edge of the bed and stared intently at the floor. Everything was coming to an end. She reached into the drawer next to her bed and took out a vial containing a lethal dose of arsenic. It would be a quick death. Her body would be racked with pain, but only for a few seconds. There was something cleaner about a fatal dose than a bullet to the head. No blood. No mess. No violent act. She held the vial for a long time. She felt neither sad nor happy, neither relieved nor fearful. She felt nothing.

She stood up, dropped the vial into her handbag, and slipped it over her shoulder. She descended the stairs as if she were in a trance. But on the second-to-last step she tripped over Omar. She fell to her hands and knees just outside Kirby's room. The cat let out a screech and bolted away.

"Damn it, Omar!"

She looked up and saw Kirby sitting on a chair in his room, his back to her, headphones clamped to his ears. The music was so loud that she could faintly hear it and recognized a song from Santana's *Supernatural* CD. Something about putting your lights on, over and over.

For once, she was pleased that Kirby didn't hear her. She picked herself up, moved quickly past the doorway, and into the kitchen. She took a bottle of water from the refrigerator and stepped out the back door.

The dusk deepened into night. A silver sliver of the waning moon hung above the eastern horizon. The air had cooled and smelled fresh. She walked down to the campground for one final look. She moved around the large tent and looked out at the camping area. A handful of trailers and RVs remained along with a smattering of tents and piles of refuse. It looked as though a flood had swept through the campgrounds and claimed most of the residents.

"Justin, are you here?" she whispered. No, of course not. She turned and headed for the clinic. As she approached the building, she felt emptiness and quiet where energy, excitement, and confusion had reigned. She unlocked the door and walked down the central aisle. She lifted the yellow crime ribbon and ducked under it. She moved to the place where Justin had died and crouched down at the spot. A dark stain remained behind, all that was left of his physical presence here. She reached into her handbag and took out a letter that she had found yesterday morning in Justin's desk. She carefully unfolded it. She again read the note to herself.

Dear Melissa—When you read this, I will be gone. But don't grieve, I will be back. You did the right thing in sending the viruses to Washington, but I couldn't let you take the variola.

A pox on all those who would stop me.

Your lover/son,

Justin

She placed a hand on the stain as if the contact would somehow put her in closer touch with him. "I started shaking when I read it, Justin. You knew so much more than you let on. You knew about my lab and you knew I sent Kirby to Washington with the viruses, and you took the variola. After all these years, you still baffle me. I don't know you. I don't understand you. You frighten me, Justin. You really do. *Who* are you, anyhow?"

She lowered her voice as if she didn't want to be overheard. "But what did you do with the variola? It was so hard to get. It took nearly two years of planning and I had top laboratory clearance. For some reason, you didn't want me to spread smallpox, but the others were okay. I don't understand. Well, I guess it doesn't matter now. You didn't come back for me like you promised, and now I'm leaving. I'm not waiting around here a minute longer."

She pulled her hand away from the stain as if it had turned hot. She stood up, took out the vial, and tapped the tablets of arsenic into her palm. She held up her bottle of water. "Goodbye, Justin. Or maybe I should say hello. Yes, hello."

She opened the bottle and chased the arsenic with a swallow of water. So simple. So deadly.

She lay down on the stain and stared at the ceiling. Within seconds, everything turned white, then streaks of red lightning shot down to her stomach. She wretched and her entire body twisted and contorted in excruciating pain. It felt as if every cell in her body were exploding. Each second stretched into an hour of unbearable anguish.

Then, she escaped the pain and felt nothing. She saw her body below her. Then she heard her name being called. Justin walked up to her, but now they were in India years ago and Justin was asking questions about her work with viruses. Abruptly, the scene shifted and Justin was talking softly to her as she sat quietly with eyes closed. He told her that she would join a group that was stealing viruses from the laboratory outside of Phoenix where she worked. Instantly, understanding flooded her awareness. Melissa knew that Justin had manipulated her into stealing the viruses, that she had released the viruses in Washington at his subtle command. He was not the naïve wunderkind-healer she had imagined, and she was not the independent manipulator, but the manipulated. He had provided her with the motives to act against her own will.

She glimpsed her contorted body below her again. She no longer felt any sense of attachment to it, no sense of loss. Then it faded as a sheen of white light rippled around her and she departed.

Calloway took a cold shower and tried to wash the flu away. He put on fresh clothes and told himself over and over that he felt fine. Then he took a couple of aspirins. Hopefully, his efforts would delay the symptoms from getting any worse. His fever still remained just below one hundred degrees, but he knew it might get a lot worse later. When he returned to the family room, Doc had just gotten off the phone.

"That was Dr. Roland again. He says that a pharmacist is driving here from Durango with an experimental drug that they've started using with patients in the capital. There's no guarantee it'll work, but it's the best bet right now."

Calloway nodded. "The sooner the better."

"It'll be a couple of hours." Doc refilled their glasses of water. "Roland wanted to come here right away and examine us, but I put him off. I told him to wait until he gets the drug."

"Good. I think."

She peered intently at him. "Are you sure you're up to this?"

"Let's get on with it before I'm too sick to do anything."

Doc turned on a tape featuring Andean flute music. Calloway could never figure out if that style of music was cheerful or mournful, but it seemed to depend on his mood. "I guess the route to the past is going by way of the Inca Trail," he commented.

"You want me to change it?"

"No. Leave it. I like it."

After Doc settled down in her chair and handed him a note-pad, she said she would direct him to a point where Melissa

Dahl had taken some action related to the release of the viruses. "Good. Let's keep it vague and see what happens."

His slight fever left him in a state of mind that seemed to actually encourage a swift entry into his zone. His mind drifted as he followed his somewhat ragged breath. With an effort, he let go of his concerns about his health and his future. Nothing else mattered besides his relaxed state.

He slowed his thoughts, released them. Finally, he lifted a finger, indicating he was ready. He barely heard Doc's directions. In his mind, he saw a woman wearing a long sweatshirt. Her legs were bare. She stood inside a tight, stark room with a counter. She examined several small spray dispensers.

He sensed he'd found Melissa and that the dispensers were extremely important to her. He moved closer to her and tried to impose himself on her thoughts.

What are you doing, Melissa?

No reaction. If she heard him, she made no response.

Destroy them. Kill the viruses.

Again he realized that he had no impact on her. He moved closer to her, tried to meld with her mind. She kept thinking the same thing over and over. Something concerned her and picked away at her, something about the dispensers that she didn't like. She'd made a discovery and didn't know what to make of it.

"Trent, are you getting anything?" Doc's voice sounded miles away. "What's Melissa doing?"

"She's looking at a container of spray dispensers. The viruses are in them. They're small and disguised as some sort of common objects. I can't quite pick it up yet. She's very possessive about the viruses, almost as if they're her children. They represent power to her, and the more power she has, the happier she is."

He frowned, focused, and pushed closer to Melissa again.

"There's something wrong with one of the viruses. It's supposed to be there, but it's not."

Calloway was going to look deeper into the matter, but Doc switched the subject. "How does she feel about everything that's going on around her?"

"She's confused and upset. She thinks, on one hand, that it's all over and she just wants revenge. She's worried that the CNN program will destroy her and Justin. But she also feels she has a mission. Chaos. She has to create chaos, and that will open the way for Justin. In spite of everything, they can still follow their plan."

"What plan is that?"

"A plan for Justin to become a global player on the scale of a religious leader, but one who transcends religion and national boundaries."

"Make her change her mind about using the dispensers," Doc ordered.

He pushed on Melissa again, harder this time. He told her to destroy the viruses. *Do it now. You don't need them. Everything will work out.*

Nothing. He made no impression on her whatsoever. "She's not responding, Doc. She's not even aware of me as far as I can tell."

Doc didn't reply.

"Bring me back."

He slumped farther into the couch, melting into the upholstery as his awareness returned fully to the room. He reached for his glass of water. Doc took an ice pack and pressed it against his forehead.

"Thanks. I'm okay. But I'll take a couple more aspirins."

She opened the aspirin bottle. "It looks like you found her right at a key point."

He shrugged. "For whatever good it did. You were right. It won't work. We can look in on the past, but we can't do anything about it. The past is over."

"I could say I told you so, but I won't."

Calloway looked up, surprised. During the years they'd worked together on intelligence targets, Doc had usually been quick to assert herself whenever she was right about something. During those times, she appeared belligerent and obnoxious, a fat woman with an "in your face" attitude. But she also cared about people, often placing their needs before hers, and that part of her personality had shone through for Calloway.

"Why not?"

"Because I wish you were right, Trent. I really wish the past could be changed."

"So do I."

When Doc turned the television back on for the latest on the epidemic, Calloway got up. He was sweating now, his fever breaking from the aspirin. He wished it meant he was recovering, but he knew that once the aspirin wore off, the fever would return. "I'm going out on the back porch and get some fresh air. Call me when the doctor gets here."

"Trent, don't be depressed. We'll figure something out. Besides, we've got help on the way."

He nodded. "Yeah."

He moved to the rear of the house and sat down on a swinging bench. He peered into the darkness and could just barely make out the small trees and rocks and the path leading through Doc's Japanese garden. He tried to relax, but he felt agitated, angry with himself. He should've left Ouray when he had a chance. It might have made a difference.

When he'd worked for Eagle's Nest in Colorado Springs, he once targeted his own future and had inadvertently glimpsed his death. He saw himself dying of an illness in a place surrounded by high mountains, and he'd never forgotten the brief encounter with his mortality. So after he'd left the military and his remote-viewing career, he'd favored the desert. But here he was in the mountains with a deadly flu virus. It didn't bode well and it didn't seem there was much he could do about it. If he headed for home now, he would miss the drug, which seemed his best chance at survival.

After a few minutes, he had an urge to walk out into the garden. It was almost as if someone or something were calling to him. He ambled slowly out into the night with only the light of the crescent moon to guide his way. He followed the path past a small pool, rocks, and shrubbery. Fences and shrubbery encased the backyard, and Calloway felt as if he were at a Zen retreat. He started feeling dizzy after several steps and sank down on a wood bench.

He tried to center himself. The dizziness vanished. He thought about his attempt to change the past again and tried to come up with a new solution. Maybe there was something that he wasn't seeing. But nothing came to mind. The longer he sat out here, the more he felt the aura of the flu descending over him again like a wet wool blanket. He hoped the doctor would get here soon.

He stood up to return to the house. The garden spun around him. He tottered and nearly pitched forward to the ground. He steadied himself and took a deep breath of the cool night air. He turned and headed back along the path toward the house.

Starlight, moonlight, hope to see a ghost tonight.

A tickling sensation on the back of his neck distracted him. He stopped and slowly turned. At first, he didn't see anything different in the garden. A slight breeze rippled the silvery leaves of a nearby bush. Then Calloway noticed a man standing near the corner of the property. In spite of the darkness, he could see him clearly, except for the top half of his head, which remained encased in shadow. He stood so still that for a moment Calloway thought it was a statue. But then the man raised a hand as if in greeting.

Calloway moved a couple of steps closer. "Hello, over there. Can I help you?"

No answer. Calloway squinted at him, trying to separate his face from the shadows. The man slowly lowered his hand. The dizziness suddenly returned, and Calloway steadied himself again by grabbing the back of the bench where he'd been sitting. He looked up and squinted again toward the corner of the garden. He hoped the man was gone, vanished, as if he were never there. But now Calloway not only saw his face, he recognized him.

"Justin? Justin Logos? Is that you?"

No answer.

Calloway shivered. His heart pounded. Maybe it was a ghost or a hallucination, but the man looked real, as if he'd risen from the dead. Calloway started to drop to his knees. Then he caught himself.

"I've got a problem with you. If you're Jesus, why did you allow Melissa to spread viruses? She's killing people. Can't you stop it?"

Justin pointed at him and he felt a jolt of energy. *Find yourself, Calloway. Then find what you need.*

Nineteen

So we have a new president sworn in under catastrophic conditions. The military is on high alert and President Charles Vincent is in full control. Yet, in this unprecedented situation, the former secretary of state cannot enter the Oval Office or even go to Washington to assume his duties."

Calloway heard the familiar TV voice of Peter Jennings from across the room. He moved over to the couch where Doc lay, covered by a blanket.

"Doc, can you turn that off? Something really strange just happened. I saw Justin Logos in your garden."

She bolted upright, one hand on the ice pack plastered to her forehead. "What did you say?"

"I saw him standing in the far corner of the garden."

Doc aimed her clicker at the TV and zapped Jennings. "Don't go bananas on me, Trent. You know damn well Logos is dead."

Calloway related what had happened to him, describing Justin's appearance and the cryptic directive he'd delivered.

"Then what happened?"

"He disappeared. I looked down a moment, and when I looked up again, he was gone."

"You've got a fever. You were probably hallucinating."

"I knew you would say that. Whether it was real or not doesn't matter. What matters is what he told me."

She shrugged. "So what? He's always telling people to find themselves. That's one of his regular messages. If he were really here, why didn't he heal you? Tell me that."

"I don't know. The message is what's important. I didn't understand either at first. But apply that to what we were just doing. I think it means we had the wrong approach when I went back in time."

"So what's the right approach?"

"Finding myself, of course. I want to remote view *myself* in the past and see if I can implant an idea in my past self to stop Melissa."

Doc set the ice pack in a bowl on the coffee table. "That's an interesting interpretation."

"But you think I'm chasing fairies with a butterfly net, don't you?"

"I don't mean to sound negative again, but I don't know if that'll work, either. I mean, even if you could influence your own past, your past self wouldn't know about the virus. So it would be sort of hard to convince yourself to stop Melissa from doing something that you, or rather your past self, is unaware of."

"Why couldn't I just tell myself what's going on?"

"Of course you could do that," Doc said, measuring each word. "But the question is whether your past self would believe that little voice in his head. I don't know."

"I want to try anyhow."

She squinted through bleary eyes. "Are you sure that you're up to this, Trent?"

"It's now or maybe never, Doc. Let's do it before the doctor gets here. Send me back to myself at some point in time that relates to Melissa."

"Help me out. Give me something specific."

"How about when we both met her when we arrived at the ranch?"

"That's a possibility. But I'd prefer that I wasn't in the scene. It might be too confusing with me in both places."

"Maybe. Wait, I got it. Just before we both saw Justin speak, I talked with Melissa briefly as she was heading to the stage."

Doc frowned. "Then we're dealing with a crowd scene. It's too confusing."

Calloway shrugged. "Okay. Let's target me and Dahl and just see where I end up."

Several minutes later, Calloway raised a finger indicating that he was ready for Doc to direct him to his target. He sank deep into his chair and almost felt that he was a part of it. Again, the fever seemed to easily trigger an altered state of consciousness. He silenced his concerns that his illness might misdirect him or block him from reaching his goal. Then as Doc told him to move to a target related to himself and Melissa Dahl, he began to sense himself in new surroundings.

"I'm in the kitchen."

"Whose kitchen?" Doc's disembodied voice asked.

"Ed Miller's."

"Okay. Who's there?"

"I am. You are, too. Ed and Camila." After a few moments, he added, "Now Ed just left the room." Was this wishful thinking, a vivid memory, or was he really remote viewing? "Doc, I don't know if this is working. This doesn't relate to Dahl." He started to come out of his zone.

"No, wait. I think it does. Stay with it. I think I know why you went there. Just listen and watch for a while. Try to make yourself a part of that scene." After a few moments she added, "When you're ready, try to contact yourself. You want to tell Calloway that it's important to remote view Melissa Dahl no matter what you thought before."

Calloway followed Doc's lead. He sank deeper into his surroundings. Now he had to ferret out his own memories from what he was seeing. It felt odd watching himself talking with Doc and Camila. He pushed himself further, merging with his past self, a silent observer, undetected. Gradually, he became aware of himself in Miller's kitchen in Utah, rather than remote viewing a target from Colorado.

Camila glowered angrily at him. "I'm disappointed in both of you. I'm sorry to barge in like this, but we need to straighten this out right away."

Calloway didn't mind her barging in at all. In fact, he was pleased that she was here and hoped that she would stay awhile.

He realized he was reading his own thoughts, his thoughts from the past, but the past felt like now.

"I think you're wasting your time coming here, Camila," Doc blurted. "We've made up our minds."

"Camila, we just don't feel that Justin Logos is a viable target. Sure, he's weird. He claims he's the Son of God, he's attracting a lot of attention, and he's even made predictions of a disaster. But that doesn't mean we should invade his privacy."

Calloway heard himself talking and realized he had to act fast before it was too late.

Doc nodded. "That's right. We've got to draw the line somewhere, and I think this is a good starting point. I personally do not want to go into Third Eye with a precedent like that hanging over my head."

Camila flicked her hair off her shoulders. "I understand your concerns, Doc. But you don't have the full picture. There's more to this than you realize."

"If you know something we don't, then tell us," Calloway said. "Maybe we'll reconsider."

That's good. We've got to reconsider. You've got to remote view Melissa Dahl. It's important.

". . . privileged information. Besides, I'd like to see if you can verify it psychically."

Calloway recalled something that had occurred to him while he'd been listening to Justin yesterday afternoon. "I think I already know what you're getting at. Justin sees himself becoming some sort of world leader, very influential."

"Yes, but how does he expect to achieve that goal?" Camila asked.

He saw his opening and pushed an image of Camila standing at a podium into his past self's head. She seemed to weave back and forth and then she collapsed to the floor. The disturbing image vanished.

"I don't know. I don't think he does, either."

Camila didn't like the answer. "If you looked a little deeper, you might find out that's not the case."

He felt uneasy about the image of Camila that he'd just seen and wondered what it meant.

Do what she wants. Target Dahl.

"I suppose we could take a look. But I'd like to target his handler, Melissa Dahl, first, before we try Justin."

Doc slammed her fist against the table as if to get his attention. "Trent, what the hell are you saying? We are not targeting either one of them."

Stand up to her. There's good reason.

"Doc, let's not get totally inflexible here. Let's consider what Camila is saying."

Doc looked momentarily stunned. *"Why are you backsliding? I can't believe I'm hearing this from you. It's like we never talked this over. First of all, this is about Justin, not his manager. And so what if the guy wants power, so do a lot of people."*

Doc turned to Camila. *"Today, it's Justin Logos. Next week we'll be remote viewing presidential candidates who want to knock David Dustin out of office. I'm sorry. This is totally unacceptable."*

"On the other hand, remote viewing offers a noninvasive way to make certain that Justin and Melissa aren't planning any acts of violence," Calloway said.

Camila gave him an odd look. *"That's exactly what I was going to say."*

"Who says it's noninvasive?" Doc shot back. *"When you go into someone's mind, that's about as invasive as it gets."*

"But there's no physical confrontation involved," Camila said patiently. *"We don't want to spy on their private lives or go on a fishing expedition to get dirt on them. We just want to protect the nation, particularly the capital, which might be a target again."*

Stick up for Camila. She's right.

"Doc, I've got to go along with Camila on this one. I'm sorry, but it feels like the right thing to do. I'm getting the impression that Melissa Dahl is the one we've got to look at."

Doc abruptly stood up. *"Well, you two lovebirds can do it without me. I am not taking part in any remote viewing of Logos or Dahl just to satisfy the curiosity of a few government officials."*

"C'mon, Doc. Let's talk it over."

"No thanks. I've done plenty of talking already and it hasn't

*done a bit of good." Doc walked out of the kitchen, the porch
door slamming after her.*

"I'm sorry about that." Camila shrugged helplessly.

*Calloway heard the engine of Doc's Explorer rev up. He
suddenly felt confused by his own flip-flop. Maybe she was right.
Why had he suddenly shifted his position? He bent over and
rubbed his temples. It almost felt as if another remote viewer
had been pushing on him.*

"What's wrong?"

"I've got a headache. I need to lie down."

Calloway opened his eyes to see Doc still holding an ice pack
on her head and staring at him. She immediately noticed that
he'd come out of his zone. "What happened?"

Calloway felt the aura of flu settling around him again, en-
casing him, but it didn't dampen his excitement. "I got inside
and I actually changed my mind, I mean, my past self's mind.
He agreed with Camila to go ahead and remote view."

"Were you going to target Melissa?"

Calloway hesitated. "I don't know. We didn't get that far.
You got mad and left."

Doc started to say something, but was overcome by a fit of
coughing. "That figures. That's exactly what I would've done if
you had sided with her. Well, maybe you changed the past, but
we're still in the same boat here. Nothing has changed, not that
I can tell."

Her voice trailed off and Calloway could tell she was frightened. Considering their prospects, she had plenty of reason for
concern. Maybe it was ridiculous to think that he could have any
effect on the present by remote viewing the past. He knew that
he should lie down and rest and wait for the doctor.

"Try again," Doc said in a weak voice. "Maybe you just didn't go far enough."

He wiped his warm, damp brow. "One more time. I'll try to push the ol' Calloway into action."

With difficulty, Doc adjusted her position on the couch so that she could monitor him again. "When you're out there, do you still have the flu? Are you aware of it?"

"Yes and no. It's kind of hard to explain." Calloway searched for the right words. "I'm aware of my condition, but now that I think of it, I didn't feel feverish at all. But my past self did get a headache just like I've got now."

This time he had trouble getting into his zone. His mind wandered. He felt drowsy, his head pounded. He felt the perspiration beading on his forehead and the fever pressing down on him. He was ready to give up when he started to drift off to sleep.

Gradually, he became aware of a sensation of movement, and for a moment, he thought he was inside a speeding train. At first, he enjoyed the feeling, but then he was moving faster and faster. He imagined he was being pulled toward a giant magnet. At any moment he would smash into it. He tried to stop, but it didn't do any good. He'd lost control; he started to panic. *Wake up! Wake up!*

It didn't do any good. He felt as if he were awake inside a dream, a nightmare in which he was being sucked up through an endless straw by some enormous, invisible creature. Finally, the sense of movement vanished. He seemed to hover in nothingness. He couldn't move, couldn't see, couldn't hear.

Nothing physical here. He willed himself away, but he couldn't get to his target, nor could he return to where he'd started. He tried to call out to Doc, but he couldn't speak. He'd lost contact.

Then he realized something was watching him, something cold and dark, an ominous presence that moved closer and closer until it penetrated him with its awareness. He felt like a rodent caught in the claws of an enormous bird of prey—a vulture.

Twenty

*H*ey, boys, news bulletin from the great beyond. Are you listening? Or, as we used to say back in Durango, back when I haunted the Strater Hotel, back before the shit hit the fan: Listen up.

Yeah, listen up good now. Here's the scoop. There are powers in the universe beyond our comprehension—way beyond it. Even I am impressed. Our buddy Calloway has awakened something that scared the shit out of me. Fortunately, it focused on Calloway and left me alone. Tolerated me. But, oh, the power, the enormous power.

This creature has been around forever, and then some. The more I think about it, the more I want to know about it. I think it's feeding me bits of information, because it knows I can't handle it all at once.

You see, it runs the show. Earth is its domain. It lives off us. And we're all a bunch of dumbies—yeah, dummies—because we don't have a clue. We're all caught up in our own little programs about what's what in this world, and that's exactly what the creature likes to see. People bowing down to the great god Asshole and chanting his name—Aaassss hooole. And they become as their god—assholes. First, they become little assholes in the early stages of initiation, and then they become big ass-

holes. *The ultimate, of course, is becoming the biggest asshole ever created.*

One of the top contenders for that job, without a doubt, is our buddy Harvey Howell. I was actually hoping we could work with the guy. Wrong. His asshole got in the way from the get go. He is so goddamned constipated that he can't see past his asshole.

Ah, no wonder they keep me locked up. I'm too much of a smart-ass. But you know what I learned from that terrible creature? I'm not locked up at all. Everyone else is. No sense telling them, though. They won't believe it.

But back to this creature. I want to stay on its good side. If you saw it, you would, too. Now that I know that it exists, that it deals directly in our affairs, I want to study it and I want to see how far it will let me fly.

Hey, are you guys paying attention? I don't hear any response. But I know you're out there. And guess what? Our buddy Calloway can hear me, too. But poor Calloway, he can't do anything about it. He's trapped. The creature's got him good. Doc can hear me, too, but she's so sick that she thinks she's hallucinating the whole damned thing.

Oh, now you boys are getting excited. Johnstone, Johnstone, it doesn't matter if they know you're working with me. Believe me, Calloway is trapped and Doc is on her way out. But just in case, let's check on Dr. Roland. That's Doc's doc. He's been waiting for a new drug and it just arrived a few minutes ago.

What's that, Timmons? How do I know so much? Because I live to snoop. It's my life. I live to travel. But, of course, my body stays behind. All the guards here see is a whacko staring at the wall all day.

Okay, I'm focusing on the good doctor. We're right on top of things today. He's got the drug and he's on his way. You see, that's why I called you guys. I need a little help here. The doctor lives about half an hour outside of town. Lots of curving mountain roads. Like the one coming up now.

Focus, boys. Follow me. Let's give him a little push. He needs some help driving.

Watch that curve, Dr. Roland. It's a sharp one.

Oops, he turned the wheel the wrong way and over the side and down the slope he goes. Boy, they need a guardrail there. Guess Roland won't be delivering that drug to Doc and Calloway. Too bad. A moment of silence for the doctor.

Okay, now back to Calloway. I've been keeping an eye on him, and I think the guy was onto something before he butted heads with that bird. He traveled to his own past and rattled his cage. He actually got himself—his old self—to change his thinking on Logos.

I'm curious to see if anything comes of it. I want to see what the old Calloway from the past, or maybe I should say the younger Calloway, can do about changing the future. Maybe I'll step in there myself and help him out.

Yeah. Let's play with that Calloway.

Are you guys coming along? Oh, stop whining, Henderson. So what if I'm taking up your time. And Timmons wants to feed his horse. Fuck all of ya then. I'll do it myself.

Twenty-one

In the dream, Calloway saw himself trapped in a dark place that was no place at all. He felt lost and knew he was neither alive nor dead. He couldn't move, couldn't escape. He remembered that he had contracted the flu, that an epidemic raged in the center of power, throwing the nation and the world into chaos. Like thousands of others, he'd been caught in a bioterrorist attack. Now he was at Doc's place and hoping for a miracle, a new drug that would save him. But maybe it was already too late.

Forget the drug, Calloway. Dr. Roland had a bad accident on his way to Doc's place. He won't be any help. You're in a bad way, a very bad way.

For an instant he saw a car tumble violently down the side of a slope and burst into flames. Then, from far away, he heard Steve Ritter's annoying cackle. As it faded, an enormous black shadow with wings folded over his body. A dark, foreboding sensation encased him, and razor-sharp talons clutched at his heart. He tried to scream out, but he felt as if he were suffocating. He gasped for breath and struggled like a helpless mouse caught in the deadly grip of a winged predator.

"Trent? Wake up! Are you okay?"

Calloway blinked, opened his eyes, and looked around in

confusion. He sat up on the couch in Ed Miller's family room and rubbed his face. For a moment, he was confused by Camila's presence, then it all fell together. The argument with Doc, her abrupt departure, his headache. "Jeez, I'm sorry. I must've fallen asleep."

"You did. You were making some groaning sounds in your sleep and twitching. That's why I woke you up."

He frowned. "Yeah. I was having a nightmare. I was feverish and this big, ugly bird swept down and grabbed me. I had a horrible feeling of dread. I really thought it was actually happening and I couldn't do anything about it."

He shook his head. "I don't know where stuff like that comes from. Maybe it was that breakfast I had, tortillas, scrambled eggs, and lots of salsa."

Camila smiled. "That would give anybody nightmares."

"There was more to the dream, too. Something about an epidemic that hit Washington, D.C."

"Were you in Washington in the dream?"

"No, I was at Doc's." He shrugged. "You know how dreams are, logic goes out the window." He smiled, glad to be alone with her again. He'd been surprised by how much he had missed her after she'd returned to Washington last week. The reconciliation had inflamed his desire to spend more time with her, and he was thinking of ways that they could somehow live together. "So what have you been doing?"

"I got a call from Tera Peters, then I talked to Ed for a while."

"I see Tera on the tube every so often." He had an urge to take Camila's hand and pull her down on the couch with him. "I hope Ed didn't carry on too long about the world's problems. He can get pretty long-winded."

"No, not at all. In fact, most of the time we were talking

about you. He really likes you, but he's concerned about you. He's worried that the remote viewing could destroy your mind."

Calloway laughed. "Maybe it already has."

She shook her head. "I don't think so. You've got a very good mind and you're surprisingly well grounded, especially considering what you've been through." She sat down on the couch just as he'd hoped. "I had a dream about you the other night. We were living together and things were good. Real good."

"I like that dream," he said, sliding his hand along the back of the couch.

Her fingers lightly touched his thigh and he instantly began feeling aroused. "So did I. But I don't see how that's going to happen anytime soon. Not unless you want to live in Washington."

He made a face. "I can always hope that Dustin doesn't get reelected."

She clasped her hands around his throat and playfully throttled him. "Don't you dare wish for that."

He reached for her arm, pulled her close. She pecked at his lips, drew her head back, and watched him. "Not so fast, fellow."

"Why not?"

She touched his lips with a finger. "Because I want to tell you about my dream. You see, we were having a picnic, just the two of us, by a lake. We had the place to ourselves and we got sort of carried away out there in nature and all."

Calloway nodded. "Ah, I think I remember a picnic or two like that one."

"You always liked to see if we could get away with something in the great outdoors."

"Outdoors . . . indoors."

She leaned over, kissing him with an urgency now. She slid

her hand around his back and pulled him closer. Suddenly they were grappling on the couch like a couple of teenagers. His hand slid under her T-shirt and he cupped her breast. Her nipple stiffened through her bra and he felt the years of separation melt away. He kept expecting Miller to walk in at any moment and destroy it all. He wished they could somehow transport themselves to his RV without missing a beat.

"Don't worry about Ed," Camila whispered in his ear as if reading his thoughts. "He said he and Guy were going to Blanding for supplies. He'll be gone at least two hours."

"That's good. That's very good."

Their clothes fell away, and like a blind man he read her body with his fingertips, recalling the past, renewing everything that had been good, and forgetting all that had gone wrong. His hands sculpted her soft curves, exploring and settling between her thighs. Then she rolled him onto his back and her tongue moved down over his chest, his belly, and she took him in her mouth.

He dropped his head back and felt the tingling sensations ripple through his body. Then she mounted him and they moved slowly, gently, both of them lost in the intoxicating sensations. He wished it would never end, that they could go on and on. But Camila's passion drew him deeper and deeper as she rocked forward and back. She urged him on, writhing wildly, and then they rolled off the couch and onto the thick carpeting.

Just as he reached completion, her legs scissoring him, Calloway felt another presence, as if someone lay next to him feeling what he was feeling. He felt invaded, assaulted, and he distinctly heard a cackle in his head, an all too familiar sound of the pesky Steve Ritter. His body tensed as a flood of anger doused his ecstasy. He would kill that bastard yet. He rolled away from Camila. He imagined himself pressing his thumbs deep into Ritter's throat and throttling him.

"Trent? Are you okay?"

He felt Camila's hand on his shoulder and turned to her. Her chest rose and fell, her body flushed with excitement. With an effort, he pushed away his thoughts of Ritter and forced himself to smile.

"I'm okay. How about you?"

She gave him a dreamy look. "Okay is not quite strong enough. I'm floating."

"How's that headache now?" Camila asked after they'd showered and dressed. They stood in the upstairs hallway outside of Miller's study.

"What headache?" *Ask me about Ritter.* The sense of his presence still lingered in his mind. He tried to tell himself that he'd just imagined the incident, but it didn't do any good. He knew Ritter had peaked into a private moment in his life.

She smiled. "Good. Then we can get to work."

"Now?" Calloway frowned. "Why don't we wait until after dinner at my place by the river."

She shook her head. "I'm sorry, Trent. I don't have the time. I've got a plane to catch tonight in Albuquerque. But I do want to see what you can get about Justin. Can we do it here before Ed gets back?"

"I suppose."

She looked into Ed's study, a large room with a desk and a computer and lots of file cabinets and bookshelves. "Do you think he'd mind if we used his office?"

"I don't think so."

"Good. Why don't you get yourself ready and relax while I go downstairs and leave Ed a message. That way he won't walk in on us."

He couldn't help but notice her change in perspective. Camila now acted as if she were talking to one of her staff members while getting ready for a meeting with the president. He didn't like being rushed into remote viewing, and he didn't like the idea that Camila might be disappointed if he didn't come up with something that confirmed her opinions.

It definitely wasn't the best circumstances for remote viewing. First, he knew who his target would be. He also knew that without a neutral monitor, the images his mind saw might conform to what Camila wanted him to see. It was the sort of remote-viewing challenge that had led psychics astray over and over again during the old Project Eagle's Nest. But then again, he knew his skills had advanced considerably since those early years. Besides, he'd already made the commitment. There was nothing else to do but proceed.

She started down the hall toward the stairs, but stopped. "Trent, I just want to say that I appreciate that you're taking the time to do this for me. I think Doc will appreciate it, too, once she realizes that turning down a request at this point would seriously endanger the funding of her program."

"Yeah. One thing, though. I'd like you to be very open-ended on the target."

She frowned. "What do you mean?"

"Don't tell me what you want to find. Just direct me to the ranch. Ask me what I see. Don't lead me."

"But I'm looking for specifics. I'm concerned about how Logos might be endangering national security."

He held up his hands. "I know. So once you've sent me there, just give me a key word or phrase."

"How about *national security?*"

"Fine."

She scowled. "That's all you need?"

"The less the better. Stay neutral. Think of Justin as if he were on trial—innocent until proven guilty."

"Gotcha."

When she returned several minutes later, he had already gone into his zone. An open notebook with a pen clipped to it rested on his lap. He stayed focused on his breathing, and as he waited to begin, he gave himself the suggestion that his vision would not be clouded by any of Camila's expectations.

She eased down into a folding chair he'd set up across from him. "Go ahead. Direct me to the target," he told her when she didn't say anything for a minute or two.

His first impressions came to him quickly. He picked up the pen and drew a rectangular-shaped object with something circular attached to either end. One circle was small, the other large. On the lower side of the object, three angled lines grew out of it. Below the drawing, he wrote: *for seeing and listening.* After a few more moments, he recognized the object as a video camera with a tripod. The rectangle was the body of the camera and the circular attachments were the lens and the eyepiece. The vision took on dimension. The camera faced two empty chairs. Several people waited in the room for the two who would sit in the chairs.

"Okay, I'm getting a television studio, but that's not quite right. It's a room that usually isn't a studio. I think it's at the ranch. I think Justin Logos and Melissa Dahl are about to be interviewed."

"That's good. What can you tell me about the person who will interview them?"

"A woman. She's trying to control her excitement. She knows something and she's planning some sort of surprise. She's going to put one or both of them on the spot. It's not really her style, but she feels it's very important that this information becomes known."

"Where are Justin and Melissa now?"

"Somewhere in the house. Not ready yet."

"Okay, see if you can find them."

After a pause he spoke up as another image appeared to him. "Justin is lying down. Melissa is sitting, waiting. I think she's anxious about this interview."

"What about Justin?"

Calloway shook his head. "It's almost like he's in a deep coma. He's revitalizing himself, regaining energy. He has some way of doing it in a very short time."

"National security."

She spoke softly but firmly, and he recognized the trigger phrase. At first, he couldn't get anything from Justin. He just couldn't read him. He moved closer. Immediately, he sensed an unusually strong energy field around the healer. It felt like a jolt of electricity; he pulled back. After a moment, he drifted closer again, adjusting to the energy. He reached into Justin's awareness.

This time the intensity of the energy multiplied. He tried to detach himself, to break contact, but he found himself in the grip of the energy field. He felt himself soaring as if he were riding a roller coaster through inner space. A swift blur of movement, waves of energy, and dazzling colors washed past him. Abruptly, the motion stopped. He found himself standing in a cool, soothing environment surrounded by a thick fog that made it impossible to see the ground or even his legs. He had no idea where he was and what had happened to him. He remembered that he'd been remote viewing from Ed Miller's house, that Justin Logos had been his target. He grasped on to the information as if it were a fragile vase. He feared that if he lost hold of it, he would never get back to where he'd started.

Now he noticed that the fog had dissipated. Astonished, he found himself perched on a mountaintop with a sweeping 360-degree view of blue sky, distant forests, and lakes. He heard a sound of footsteps and turned to see Justin Logos moving toward him, wisps of fog swirling around his feet.

Justin smiled and greeted Calloway warmly, like an old friend. He appeared vibrant, glowing with life. "There is nothing to fear, nothing at all. I've returned to earth to heal, not to cause pain." His lips didn't move, but Calloway heard his voice clearly.

In spite of the warmth Justin projected, Calloway felt uneasy, as if Justin were hiding something.

A frown creased Justin's brow. "I'm concerned about you, Trent. The Vulture hunts you. A part of you has already been captured in its giant claws. Unless you act quickly, you will soon merge with that part of yourself. You will cease to exist for all those who have known you on the earth plane. You will be trapped for an eternity."

A flash of panic seared through Calloway. "But what can I do?"

"To escape the Vulture's claw requires dedication and intense concentration. But more than that, you must kill your ego. Only then will you see the true path to freedom."

The mountain vanished and Calloway found himself back with Justin and Melissa in the bedroom where Justin was just waking up. At the same time, he was aware of himself with Camila in Miller's study. He felt as if he were viewing a split-screen television, except he was part of each of the scenes.

"Are you okay, Trent?" Camila asked.

"Something just happened. I was on a mountain with Justin. I'm losing the details now. It was like a dream, but it was much more real. Justin seemed friendly, even concerned about me."

"Do you want to end this now?"

He shook his head. Even though he was aware of sitting with Camila in Miller's study, a nonphysical part of him remained with Justin and Melissa. He felt drawn toward Dahl. "No, I want to know more about Melissa. There's something there. She's concerned that the interview won't go well, and she's right. Something is going to be revealed that she won't like at all."

He shifted his awareness to the tall, dark-haired woman. He moved closer to her. "Melissa knows that the interview is important, that it will be a turning point, but she doesn't want to go through with it. She knows it could backfire."

"National security," Camila said.

"Something secret, something hidden. She's been holding on to it. She's not really sure what she wants to do with it."

"What kind of secret?"

"An invisible weapon. I don't know what that means. Something very deadly, but it doesn't destroy buildings. It just kills people. Nobody knows that it's there until it's too late."

"Can you be more specific?"

Calloway was quiet for a while. "A bug."

"What do you mean?"

"Like the flu, but deadly. Okay, it's a biological weapon."

"How are we going to stop her?" Camila asked in a soft voice, more to herself than to Calloway.

But Calloway immediately sensed the answer. *Cancel the interview.* It was as if someone stood behind him whispering in his ear. "I don't know why, but the reporter is key. If Melissa goes through with that interview, it means trouble. Big trouble. She's got to cancel. I want to push her. I want to keep her away from that reporter."

"Do whatever is necessary," Camila hissed.

Calloway moved closer into Melissa's awareness. Again, he felt her concern about the interview. She noticed Justin stirring on the bed. "Are you ready, my love?"

"If you are."

Calloway implanted a thought into Melissa's mind. *Don't do it. Cancel it. It's not necessary. She's coming after you. It's too dangerous.*

Justin sat up and smiled. He seemed relaxed and refreshed. "Let's go show Tera Peters what you and I are all about, a partnership made in heaven." He laughed.

"You know what? I'm really worried all of a sudden. I don't think we should do it. It's just a feeling I've got. Something's going to go wrong. I don't want to do it."

"Really? That's interesting." Justin seemed calm, at peace, unconcerned about her shift in perspective.

Don't want to see her. "In fact, I don't even want to see her. I feel like staying upstairs."

"Well, good for you. Let's not do it."

Calloway pulled back. His impression of the room, of Melissa and Justin, faded. He looked up at Camila and told her that Melissa had decided to cancel after he'd nudged her. "It didn't take much. But that's all I want to do. Anything more and she might get suspicious."

Camila looked as if she were ready to bolt out of her chair. "Trent, this is really fascinating."

He held up a hand. "Just give me a minute."

He mentally released his contact with Melissa and Justin and moved his awareness fully into the room. He nodded. "Okay. What were you saying?"

"That was Tera Peters's interview! I'm glad I didn't tell you about it. She told me what she had found out about Melissa and you were right. It *is* explosive. Now it'll be interesting to find out if the interview really got canceled."

Calloway thought a moment. "Tera dug up something from the past. That's my guess."

"You're right."

"But she doesn't know how dangerous Melissa Dahl is. This isn't over yet. She's still got the weapons."

"I know. I've been thinking about that." Camila paused, frowning. "Unfortunately, there's no judge in the world who would approve a search warrant based on evidence obtained by remote viewing."

"You better do something. That woman is on the edge. If that story, whatever it is, comes out, Melissa will blow like Ol' Faithful and it won't be pretty."

Camila reached for his hand. "Leave that to me, Trent."

At the moment their hands touched, Calloway again glimpsed Camila standing at a podium. She seemed to wobble back and forth. Then she collapsed to the floor, and the image disintegrated. It was the same thing he'd seen earlier, when Doc was still here. But now he knew what it meant. He'd just glimpsed Camila falling ill to the virus that would still make it to Washington. It meant that he hadn't done enough to stop Melissa.

"Trent, are you okay? You look as if you were going back out there again. What happened?"

If he told her, she might panic. They couldn't afford either one of them overreacting right now. "I need your help again. I want to go back one more time just to make sure that the interview doesn't take place. I've just got a weird feeling that things aren't working out quite like I thought."

Camila frowned. She reached for her purse and took out her cell phone. "Wait. Let me call Tera right now. We'll see what's going on."

She punched the number and listened. After a few seconds, she lowered the phone, shook her head. "I guess she didn't want to be interrupted during the interview."

"Then I'll try again. But I want you to promise me that you won't go back to Washington if that interview wasn't canceled."

"Oh, Trent, be reasonable. I've got obligations. I can't just disappear because of a threat. We get threats all the time at the White House."

He reached for her hand. "I'm sorry if you think I'm overreacting, but I just don't like the feeling I'm getting about Washington."

She nodded, an expression of concern on her face. "Let's see what you get."

Calloway took a deep breath, exhaled slowly, and melted back into the chair. He sank quickly into his zone. He'd already started to pick up an image of Melissa sitting at a desk involved in some paperwork.

"Okay," Camila said, "I'll help you. But I don't have much time." Rather than guiding him, her voice interfered with his connection to his target. Melissa was talking with someone on a telephone. Calloway refocused and immediately a name came to his mind.

"Betty or Betsy. Something about a woman named Betsy."

Calloway's eyes remained open, and he saw the stunned look on Camila's face. "What about Betsy? What do you know about her?" she asked.

He hesitated. "All I know is that she's got to be stopped. She's the one who triggers the release of the bio-weapon."

"Oh, that's wonderful. Tera brought her to the ranch. Betsy knows something about Melissa's past, something very ugly. But you said the interview was canceled."

"So I thought."

Twenty-two

She'd made up her mind and she was going to hold firm. No interview. So what if Tera Peters didn't like it. If CNN backed out of the special because of her refusal to talk, then she would turn to one of the networks. They were all waiting for an exclusive on Justin. One way or another Justin's star would rise to new heights, and of course, hers would ascend along with it.

"I really appreciate that you're willing to go along with me on this," Melissa said.

Justin stood up from the bed and stretched his arms overhead. He clasped his hands together and pointed his index fingers. He leaned to one side, then the other. "It's no problem. Like I said, if you don't feel it's right, let's cancel."

He lowered his arms. "I'll go down and talk to Tera. I'll tell her that we've decided to cancel."

"Justin, don't bother. I'll get J.D. to tell her."

He shook his head. "No, I'll handle it. I don't want to offend Tera, especially not at this point."

"Then maybe I should go myself. After all, I'm the one bowing out. It's my decision."

He touched her arm. "No, I'll just tell her you're not feeling well and you'd prefer not doing the interview. I'll answer any remaining questions she might want to ask me."

Melissa conceded he was right. If she went down there, Peters would probably get hostile and she would be ready to throttle the redhead. "Okay, but I hate to see you get drawn into another extended interview. You've already given a lot to her. There's no need for it."

"Don't worry about me. I'll insist on keeping it short."

In spite of her reticence, Melissa was curious about what Peters would ask her. "Tell Tera that if she has any off-camera questions she'd like to ask, she can call me."

Melissa walked over to her office and looked at her appointment book. She just wanted to take her mind off Peters and the scratched interview, so she buried herself in the sort of mundane duties that she'd come to abhor. But as long as Justin was healing between five hundred and eight hundred people a day, someone had to manage details, such as garbage pickup and Porta-John cleanup.

After five minutes, she turned away from her desk. She hated it, hated all of it. She just wanted out and the sooner the better. Justin had to make the leap that he'd been talking about. She still couldn't quite envision what it would be like, but he had said that everything would be run by a corporation with international sponsors. People with money would flock to him to invest in his enterprise, which was healing the earth. They would move around the world from country to country working with the leaders, all the people who had power to change the world. Justin would heal them of their fears and their distrust, and international relations would soon begin to take on a new perspective. There would no longer be any need for civil wars or border conflicts or battles between ethnic and religious groups.

The phone rang and she let the machine answer it. "Hello,

Melissa. This is your mother. Can you call me today? I want to know what's going on with that CNN program you told me about. I haven't heard anything and I want to make sure I don't miss it. Call me."

She snapped up the phone. "Hi, Mom. How are you?"

"I'm fine, but I'm worried about you. I'm seeing so many things in the paper about Justin these days and a lot of it's so negative. It scares me. Why are these people attacking him, anyhow?"

"It's an organized effort from people who feel threatened by Justin. Most of them are old-line fundamentalists who want the reborn Jesus to act as if he were living in biblical times. Don't worry about it, Mom. Justin doesn't let it bother him."

"Well, what about you?"

"I look at it this way. If everyone just ignored what's going on here, that would be bad. The fact that we're getting attacked shows that we're making an impact. That's what we need to do."

"But what kind of impact? He should never have started calling himself Jesus. That was such a mistake. Your Jewish father would roll over in his grave if he knew that you were . . . oh, never mind."

She imagined her seventy-seven-year-old mother sitting in her Albuquerque condo with the television on in the background, a cup of coffee nearby. After her father died, her mother had refused to live any longer at the ranch, and Melissa had taken it over.

"Mom, we've been through this over and over. Justin represents change. Big change, and people are always afraid of it."

"What was it that I read the other day? Something about a big bird. Yeah, it said a big bird controls the world and took it away from another bird, and one of the birds—I can't remember which one—is going to attack Washington, D.C. Where does he get his stuff from, Melissa? That's not in the Bible, the Old Testament or the New. He's not really saying that, is he?"

"I suppose you read that in the *Enquirer.*"

"I did pick it up at the grocery store."

"These reporters take things and twist them around, Mom. They try to simplify it so people understand, but they don't understand themselves. Just stop reading those papers."

"It's a shame. I wish I understood. Do you think the CNN special will help?"

The intercom on Melissa's desk buzzed. "I hope so. Mom, I've got someone looking for me. I'll give you a call tomorrow."

"Don't forget, and take care of yourself, dear."

Melissa hung up and pressed the intercom. "What is it?"

"There's an old friend of yours down here," J.D. Kirby said. "She works with Ms. Peters and she wants to say hello to you before she leaves."

"She works for Peters? What's her name?"

"Betsy Lambert. She said you were friends when you were young, back in Chicago."

The name was vaguely familiar from a shrouded part of her past before her parents had moved to the Southwest. She'd buried her early teen years, when she was fat, as a tragic mistake. She'd been assaulted and had suffered temporary amnesia, and after that she'd lived in a fog. She'd been unpopular in school and hadn't really found herself until she was a senior in high school in Albuquerque, when her interest in science started shining through.

Somewhere in that obscure past lay the memory of a girl named Betsy who had been a friend. But why should she dredge up the past? There was no point to it.

"I don't want to see anyone now."

"She says she has something important to tell you."

Now Melissa felt apprehensive and she wasn't sure why. "I don't care."

"Should I tell her that you're not feeling well?"

She thought a moment. Maybe she should find out what was so important. It was probably something about a mutual friend from the past whom she'd completely forgotten. "No. I'll be down in a few minutes."

Maybe it would do her good to talk to someone who remembered something from those lost years. She considered calling her mother back and seeing if she had any recollection of the name, but quickly decided against it. She didn't want to hear her mother reminiscing about how she had raised three kids, rarely getting any help from a husband who worked day and night at his manufacturing business while he saved to buy his dream ranch. Besides, chances were she wouldn't remember the name, anyhow.

When Melissa went downstairs, the CNN crew was packing their gear. She saw Justin talking with Peters, who looked surprisingly upbeat. She even waved to Melissa, who forced a smile. Melissa hesitated, looked around, and then saw Kirby standing with a woman across the room. As she walked over to her, Melissa decided the woman looked like a candidate for a makeover. Her blond hair was dry and straggly, her face worn like old leather. But her blue eyes reminded Melissa of someone from the forgotten past.

Melissa smiled and introduced herself. "How can I help you?"

The woman seemed surprised by Melissa's abruptness. "Well, you must know who I am. Don't you remember Betsy Lambert from Chicago?"

Melissa shook her head. "I'm sorry, Betsy. You'll have to refresh my memory. A lot has happened to me since those years."

"We don't know each other anymore. But we did. Back in the bad days."

With each word and every sentence that Betsy Lambert spoke, the memories seeped back. The sound of bowling balls rolling on wood lanes and smashing into the pins came to mind. Melissa had avoided bowling alleys her entire adult life, and just the thought of entering one made her shiver.

"You remember now, don't you? I was with you when it happened, Melissa. We were lucky to get away alive."

Melissa shook her head. "What are you talking about? I don't remember anything."

But as she spoke, Melissa gathered a vague memory of a man in his twenties, sexy, blond hair, blue eyes. She realized that Betsy was telling the same story about the man. "Don't you remember how he talked to us as if we were eighteen and experienced with men. He was coming on to us and we were frightened, but we were thrilled, too."

"Stop it!"

"Then he raped us," Betsy said sharply, moving a step closer to Melissa. "After that, he killed a bunch of innocent people until the cops shot him between the eyes. Just what he deserved. But you were the one who got pregnant. You hid that pregnancy from everyone, except me. Your parents didn't even know. You were chubby back then."

Melissa didn't want to hear it, but the memories were coming back as Betsy spoke. "You had the baby in a bathroom in a restaurant. I'd just gotten a job there. You put it in the Dumpster in the alley like it was a piece of trash. I saw you do it. Then you went home. But a busboy found the baby and called the police."

Melissa's eyes reddened with tears. She shook her head. "I don't know what you're talking about. I really don't."

"That baby lived. Now I wished it had died." Betsy's tone turned unexpectedly dark and her eyes narrowed. "My mother knew what happened and she kept track of your baby. She told me that a couple in St. Paul adopted him and that his name was Justin, and now you live in sin with him. That's him right over there. The son of that devil-murderer."

"You're crazy," Melissa stammered.

"No, that's who he is. All the dates and places fit. You don't fool me. Neither of you do. I figured it out and I went to the TV station where Ms. Peters works and she proved I was right. Now everyone's going to know all about it."

Melissa pushed the woman away from her, then spun around, her face flushed, her forehead damp. She spotted Justin and Peters moving toward her and bolted over to the reporter. "So this was a setup. That's why you were so damned interested in interviewing me."

"Is it true, Melissa? Did you know Justin was your son?" Tera asked.

"That's a lie. If you put that on the air, we'll sue you and CNN so fast you won't believe it. You'll be out on the street looking for a job. Now get out of here and take this creepy little nightmare with you."

Peters seemed unperturbed. "I have proof—DNA from you and Justin and Harold Spiner, the man who raped you. There's an extremely high likelihood that you are Justin's mother."

Melissa saw the cameraman aiming at her from across the room. She felt trapped, pinned to the wall, under inspection.

"Turn off that camera. Get out of here, all of you! You'll pay for this. You have no idea of what we can do."

Justin stepped up to Melissa and put his arm around her shoulder as if to protect her, but also to keep her from assaulting anyone. Then he turned to Betsy. "I forgive you for what you are about to do."

"About to do?" Melissa snapped. "What do you mean? She already did it."

Betsy stepped back. But she pointed a finger at Justin. "You are the devil's own! The devil mocks us by trying to make us believe he is the opposite of who he is. But I know better!"

Melissa felt like throttling Betsy, but Justin kept a firm grip on her shoulder. No, she wouldn't attack the woman and get caught on camera in the act. She didn't really care about Betsy, anyhow. Tera Peters was another matter. She'd brought Betsy here. It was her fault, and Melissa vowed to get back at her. She didn't know how she would do it, but she would find a way.

"I'm going upstairs," she said to Justin. "I don't need this." She brushed past Betsy, ignoring her. But Melissa stopped as she heard a voice clearly in her head.

Turn around! Watch out!

She spun on her heels. Peters, Justin, and the cameraman stood in stunned silence. Then she saw the gun in Betsy's fist just as she aimed it at Justin's heart. Melissa lunged and grabbed the woman's wrist. The weapon fired, exploding next to her ear, as they struggled for it. Peters darted forward, knocking Betsy's arm to one side. The gun fired again, and a fierce burning erupted in Melissa's chest. She fell back, a long fall that seemed to never end.

Then she felt Justin's arms close around her as he lowered her to the floor. Blood bloomed on the front of her white blouse.

Another shot was fired. Someone else fell; the gun clattered to the floor.

Justin placed his hands on either side of Melissa's head and stared into her eyes. Her body relaxed. She felt no pain, but she knew she was dying, that her body's systems were shutting down.

"Help me," she whispered. "Help me."

Around her people shouted, and someone shrieked, "Call 911."

She felt herself fading. She glimpsed Tcra Peters's distraught face hovering above her. Then Justin leaned closer and whispered in her ear, "You and your old friend Betsy are leaving together on a long journey. As it was meant to be."

Twenty-three

*T*here are certain advantages to living in isolation. For one thing, I can control the influences on my environment far more easily than you guys on the outside. I don't have television or radio or even gossip. I don't need any of that. I can find out everything I want through my inner antennae without any distractions from electronic technology, which has replaced our innate abilities and made us zombies. Of course, when I say us, I don't mean us. I mean everyone else.

I can just imagine the fuss that the media is making about this deadly flu, especially with the prez and the vice prez stone dead and half of Congress on the way out. Oh, the madness and chaos. All I know about the flu is what I've picked up from Calloway and Doc. Those two, of course, are very concerned about it, since they've got it. Or maybe I should say they were concerned. I'm not picking up anything from Calloway anymore, not after that big, ugly bird swallowed him like some little morsel, and Doc's signal is weak.

But the younger Calloway from the past is another story. Remember, I tried to get you guys to come along on that ride. Too bad you're all so damned preoccupied with your own petty shit. But you have to listen to me, that crazy voice in your head.

Timmons says he doesn't know about any flu epidemic and he saw the president on TV this morning. Now that's interesting. No epidemic. No dead president. You agree with that, Johnstone? You, too, Henderson? I like it. I've contacted the boys from the past.

Calloway's good. I've always said that. I hate the guy, of course. Despise the ground he walks on. But I respect his abilities. After all, he got his past self to change his mind and look in on the so-called Son of God, Justin Logos, and one thing led to another. But I'm good, too. Because I'm right here in the same time. Just in time.

So, this Calloway from the past, this has-been, pretty soon discovered that Justin's sweet mama, Melissa, was going to release her bio-weapons as an act of revenge. What's that? Okay, you guys know this stuff. Even if you didn't go with me, it still seeps into your minds whether you want it to or not. Aren't you the lucky ones.

But I don't think you know everything that I do. In fact, I know you don't. You see, there's something else going on that I haven't figured out just yet. Calloway, who was showing off for his Camila, stopped that interview between Melissa Dahl and Tera Peters. But then he went back again because he figured he hadn't done enough to stop Dahl.

So that's when I picked up that someone else was pushing on Calloway, trying to interfere. It's a team of them working together, sort of like us, if you guys would get your psychic asses in gear. They were trying to stop Calloway from interfering. Whoever they are, they wanted Justin Logos dead and they didn't want Calloway getting in the way.

But it didn't work. Calloway felt their nudge all right, but he thought it was me trying to mess him up. So he went right ahead and pushed on Dahl. He ended up getting her killed for

the effort and Logos now lives on—reborn, you could say. That
must've changed everything out there. No bio-weapon released.
So it seems that Calloway got what he wanted. But who are
these other guys and what do they want? I'm at a loss. But I'm
fascinated by all of this.

So here's our chance to work together. I want you guys to
watch my back. Let's find out who they are and give them some
trouble. Should be fun.

Let's focus now. Pick up the strand. We'll follow it. I'm
already moving closer to them. Getting warmer, warmer.

"Steve Ritter, man of the moment. Welcome."

"Who are you? Where are you?" Ritter suddenly felt nervous, as if he were being watched.

"Focus, Steve. That's what you told your buddies."

"How do you know about us?"

"You're famous, Steve. Notorious, actually. You're going to
serve a purpose that you never imagined."

"A purpose for who?" The scene started to clear. He could
see a group of people sitting around a room. They were working
together, working on him. He moved closer. To his surprise, he
saw Doc, then Calloway, then the others, none of whom he recognized.

"We wanted our friends to experience your energy," Calloway said. "We mean you no harm."

"You sonufabitch, Calloway. What's going on? There's
something different about you."

"I suppose so. We'll let you figure it out. But you're not
going to be allowed back here again. So don't even try to reach
us."

"I go where I want and I don't take orders from you, Calloway. I don't know where you're coming from, but the last time I saw you in my time, you looked pretty dead."

The scene faded and Ritter knew that he'd lost contact.

The bastards. Did you see that? Did you see who it was? I know, Johnstone, I told you they didn't know about us. I was wrong. But that was not the Calloway I remember.

What's that, Timmons? You think they were looking at us from another time. I think you're right. Calloway and Doc are playing with time. But why did they bother with us? No reason for it unless Calloway wants something.

Cooperation. Yes, Henderson, I think you're right. They want to make sure that we don't interfere in their plans. Well, I've got news for them. We were born to interfere. I have no use for Calloway, whether he's from the past, present, or future. Now I just want to poke around more and see what else is going on.

Yeah, good guess, Johnstone. I think it must have something to do with Justin Logos. We'll keep closer tabs on him.

Twenty-four

Camila lowered her cell phone from her ear and looked over at Calloway, who was still sitting in Ed's comfortable office chair.

"No luck?"

"It's busy. I'll try again in a few minutes."

She glanced at her watch, but she no longer felt concerned about making her flight back to Washington. She would drive to Albuquerque as soon as she knew Tera was okay. Then, in the morning, she would take a flight to Dulles. Meanwhile, she needed to unravel exactly what was going on at Melissa Dahl's ranch.

Calloway had said very little while he was focusing on his target. But she could tell by the few comments that he did make that something out of the ordinary was taking place. Then he'd shocked her with his description of the confrontation between Melissa and Betsy.

"You're worried about Tera, aren't you?"

Camila walked over to the window that looked out on Calloway's RV. "If there really was gunfire, I just hope Tera wasn't hit."

"Like I said, I saw Melissa go down and I'm pretty sure I saw Betsy lying on the floor."

Camila still found it hard to believe that he could come up with that sort of detail. No sense worrying about it, though, she thought. She'd find out soon enough. She sat down next to Calloway. She liked his company; it was easy to remember why she'd fallen in love with him, why she'd married him. It felt comfortable with him, but at the same time she wondered if she'd made a mistake by getting involved with him again. She'd rekindled her love for Trent, but she wasn't willing to give up her life in Washington, at least not while David Dustin was president and he still wanted her on his staff. He had another year and a half left in office, and he was gearing up for his reelection campaign.

"You know you're welcome to stay here tonight," Calloway said, breaking the silence. "I'd really like you to stay."

Camila gazed out the window again. "Trent, I've got to get back. Do you see what kind of relationship we're looking at? We may be lucky to see each other once a month for a couple of days, unless you're willing to spend time in Washington."

"I've been thinking about it. In September, when the season ends here, instead of driving off to Baja, I'd like to join you."

She hugged him. "That would be great."

"One thing, though. I don't want to be part of your Washington social scene. At least, not full-time. I mean, the idea of going to dinner parties at some senator's house doesn't thrill me."

She smiled. "That can be arranged."

"You've got to remember that I've been a loner for years now. It's only been these past few months that I've started to think I could have another relationship."

"You mean a lot to me, and I know what you've been through. Sometimes, I think about you out here on the river while I'm running the gauntlet between reporters and Dustin and his staff. I know it probably sounds silly to you, but I sort of glamorize your life. You know, close to nature, the river, surrounded by the Navajo reservation."

"Well, then maybe you should join me for a while. I'm sure Dustin can find a temporary replacement, and I suppose I could find room for you."

She laughed nervously. "I'd probably go nuts after a week. I'd feel directionless out here."

"You could go to the local Navajo chapter meeting and raise hell with the BIA."

"I'm Mexican-American, please, not Navajo."

He smiled. "You're close enough. Anyhow, if you get tired of it here, we could just drive away to somewhere else and still be home. That's the nice thing about living in the RV."

"Let's hold that off for the future."

Calloway frowned. "Camila, are you still afraid of what I might do to you if we're together all the time? Do you think I might turn on you, like I did before?"

She shook her head. "I don't think you would ever hurt me. But your talents are so unusual that it would take me a while to adjust to that part of you."

"Hey, that part is invisible unless I turn it on," he said, sounding a bit too defensive.

She put her arms around his broad shoulders, hugging him. "I'm sorry. I shouldn't have said that. It's just that I'm so baffled when it comes to this stuff. I think it would take an incredible amount of courage to live with your abilities."

Calloway laughed. "You've got that backwards. It would take a tremendous amount of courage to do what you do every day. I just don't know how you do it. But I admire you for it."

He touched her face with his fingertips and her expression softened. Her lips parted and he leaned toward her. Their lips brushed once, twice, then as they were about to merge into a deep, passionate kiss, Camila's cell phone rang.

She pulled back. "I better get that."

Calloway snatched the phone from the table and feinted throwing it out the window. Then, giving her a glum look, he handed it to her.

She let out a quick, nervous laugh, then answered the call. "Tera, I was hoping that was you. Are you all right?"

"Yes, I am. But barely. Do you remember what I told you earlier this afternoon, about who I was taking here?" Tera gulped for air, as if she'd just run a couple of miles.

"Of course I do."

"Well, you won't believe what just happened a few minutes ago here."

"I might. But go ahead."

She listened as Tera explained everything that had taken place at the ranch from the time she'd arrived with Betsy until the woman had pulled out the gun and started shooting.

Camila met Calloway's gaze and nodded. "That's horrible, Tera. Are the police there yet?"

"They're on the way. It takes a while to get here."

"Are you safe there?"

"Sure. No one is threatening me. Everyone here is in shock. This whole thing was so horrible. It was a mistake bringing Betsy here. I had no idea she was so unstable."

"What about Justin? How's he handling it?"

"Very calmly. He's surprisingly calm. Wait a minute. Okay, the police are just arriving. Camila, I've got to go. I'll call you later."

Camila rang off and relayed what she'd been told. "You amaze me, Trent. You actually saw it happening, and when you warned Melissa, you prevented Justin from getting killed."

"But I didn't prevent the shooting. I wanted to stop Betsy, but I couldn't get into her. Something there was blocking me. So I had to go to Melissa."

Camila dropped her phone into her purse. "You mean she was blocking you?"

"No, not Betsy. I think it was my old buddy Steve Ritter. He's at it again."

"Ritter? How could that be?"

Calloway shrugged. "He must've figured a way of getting around the shield. Unless it's been turned off."

"I'll check on it as soon as I can."

"I'm not even sure it was Ritter, though. He's got a very nasty edge to his abilities. He usually gives himself away by throwing in little zingers whenever he gets into my head. But this seemed different. Then again, I've definitely been feeling him around."

"So you think it's Ritter and also someone else?"

"It's confusing. I don't know."

"Do you think it could be Ritter's buddies, the ones we were never able to prosecute?"

"I don't think so. They don't seem to act on their own. In fact, they seem to have shut down their abilities almost completely. I think they're all terrified of ending up like Ritter."

Camila slung her purse over her shoulder. "I'll let you know what I find out about Ritter when you and Doc come out to Washington next week. That should go very well now. You've got a good story to tell them."

"Yeah," he said uneasily, following her to the door. "I have to talk to Doc about that. What about that bio-weapon? I don't think I was imagining that."

Camila nodded. "I think you're on the right track. I have to check with Harvey Howell. He knows a lot more than I do. If you're on the right track, which I think you are, we've got to get the FBI involved."

"They should look for her lab right in the house. Near her bedroom, I think, in a hidden room."

Camila smiled. "You've been right so far, Trent. I'll make the calls right away."

"But you can't stay?"

She stopped at the door. "I need to get to Albuquerque so I can catch an early plane."

Just then a black Explorer crunched over the gravel driveway. "Is that Doc?" Camila asked, looking out the window.

Calloway moved beside her. "I think so. I'll go down and see what she has to say."

"I'll be on the phone."

"Okay."

Camila couldn't help noticing that Calloway didn't sound enthused by Doc's unexpected return. He'd wanted Camila to stay another day, and now she felt tension between the relationship and her career. Not a good sign.

Doc clambered out of her Explorer and walked into the kitchen where Calloway was waiting for her. In a way, he was glad that she'd come back. Now they could straighten out everything before Camila left. On the other hand, her arrival felt like a bucket of cold water splashed in his face. It washed away any hope of another sexual interlude. But maybe Camila would change her mind and stay the night, he told himself.

Doc ran a hand through her short hair, then braced her wide hips. "I see that Camila is still here."

"Yeah. She's upstairs making some calls. "So what's up?"

"Sorry for running off like that, but you know how I feel."

"I sure do. But if you've reconsidered, you're too late. Wait until you hear what happened."

Doc held up her hands. "Don't say anything more. Let me tell you what happened to me."

Typical Doc, he thought. Her story first. "Be my guest."

"After I left, I drove over to Blanding and ate lunch. By the time I finished, I started feeling drowsy and knew I better not start the long drive home. So I just curled up in the back of the Explorer in the restaurant's parking lot. You know, with the tinted windows in the back, no one can see inside. I slept for nearly an hour, and when I woke up, I knew I had to get back here."

"Why?"

Doc smiled and leaned toward him. "Something has happened in the future that changes everything."

He frowned and leaned back away from Doc. "What do you mean by that?"

"I mean I was contacted by . . . by someone from the future. I don't know exactly when he is living. It came to me just as I was waking up, and it had a really urgent feel about it."

Calloway turned up his hands. "So what's the message?"

"The message is that you've got to target the future."

"Why?"

"It's like I said, something has changed."

"Oh, for chrissake, Doc, that's pretty damned general. The future is a big place. Of course things are going to change in the future. You're not making sense."

"Shut up and listen to me. You don't understand what I'm saying."

"Then tell me."

"No!"

"Why not?"

"Because I'm not about to front-load you. I want this clean."

Calloway drew back and frowned. "What? Forget it, Doc. I've got enough problems with the present. I don't need to muck around in the future. Besides, I'm tired. We had a long drive today, and on top of that, I've been working with Camila. And, by the way, it looks like she was right, at least about Melissa Dahl."

Before Doc could object, he spilled out the story, and once he started, she listened closely. She nodded when he finished. "So it was Melissa. I'm telling you, though, this all has something to do with the future, Trent. There's something you need to find out."

Calloway looked wearily at her. He knew Doc would continue badgering him, but then Camila stepped into the kitchen and saved him.

"Hello, Doc. Did Trent fill you in on the news?"

"He certainly did."

"I just talked to Harvey Howell, and he said that Melissa Dahl was suspected of stealing viruses years ago, but there was never enough evidence to pursue it. But now with her murder, the FBI has some leverage. They're going to search the house."

"Good," Calloway said.

"My guess is that Justin is so involved in his work that he never knew what she was up to." Doc sounded defensive.

"What about his heritage?" Camila asked. "You would think he would've known who Melissa was."

"That whole thing is very strange. But why would he know about it? Just because he's a fantastic healer doesn't mean he knows everything."

"You know, of course, that everything is going to come out now," Camila said. "It's going to damage his image, and if they find bio-weapons, he could face criminal charges."

"Oh, I'm sure he'll be crucified." Doc's tone had turned vitriolic.

As Doc and Camila bantered back and forth about Justin, Calloway realized that Doc was ardently defending the controversial healer. Maybe when Justin had healed her in the crowd that day, he had simultaneously implanted a suggestion. Maybe he did it regularly with his patients.

"Trent, hello, did you hear me?"

He looked up at Doc. "Sorry, what did you say?"

"I said there's one way to find out how all this comes out, and that's to remote view the future, like I suggested before."

"I'm not sure that would bring any guarantees. You know as well as I do that remote viewing the future just shows a probable path. Things could change."

Doc nodded. "Sure they could."

Camila took a step closer. "I think it's a great idea. I'd like to stay for it, but I've got to get going. I'll be interested in hearing the results, though."

Calloway figured as much. As soon as Doc had arrived, Camila had made up her mind to leave, and he couldn't blame her. She wasn't on the greatest terms with Doc at the moment, and she had other plans. He met her gaze and nodded, resigned to the fact that they were once again heading in different directions.

"Are you sure about that message you got?" Calloway asked as they stood in Miller's yard watching Camila's vehicle disappear down the narrow road.

"You're damned right I am, Calloway. This was no ordinary daydream. This felt different. Now, are you going to get to work or do I have to twist your arm behind your back?"

He figured he might as well do it and get it over with. Otherwise, Doc would just hang around and bother him until he gave in to her. "Okay, but tell me truthfully what you think this is about."

"Even if I had an inkling, I wouldn't tell you," she answered bluntly. "I don't want to lead you or mislead you."

Calloway shrugged. "Whatever. Let's go in the RV. That way Ed won't disturb us if he gets home."

They entered the vehicle and walked to the rear where Calloway propped several pillows against the headboard of his bed. He found a notebook and pen and lay back on the bed.

Doc sat next to the bed on an upright lawn chair. "I'll just sit here and watch you vanish into the future."

He laughed. "Right. I'll be back to tell you about the mistakes you're going to make."

"Speak for yourself."

Calloway frowned. "How's this going to work?"

"Let's play it by ear. I'll suggest that you go to an important point in the future where there is a desire to make contact."

"Sounds good."

Calloway inserted a CD that contained a forty-minute continual chant of om. As soon as he heard the ambient toning, he started to drift into his zone.

"Why are you playing that tape?" Doc asked. "You know what happened before."

"Take it easy, Doc. I can handle it. I just had the feeling that this particular target needed something a little extra."

"Okay, but I'm not going to let you go off into never-never land again. There's no target there. I'll pull you back."

He pushed Doc's words out of his mind and slipped down deeper. He liked to use this CD when he wanted to go quickly into his zone and penetrate his target. But he had to be careful not to let himself sink too deeply into an altered state. He knew that, if he did so, he would go right beyond the realm where remote viewing worked and slide into what he and other remote viewers called the void, a higher plane of such intense energy that it was difficult to maintain self-awareness. He had dropped into the void a couple of times when working in Project Eagle's Nest and had come back feeling greatly inspired. But, as Doc had noted, he hadn't found his target, and he hadn't even remembered seeing anything.

"Go to a special place somewhere in the future where you will contact someone living at that time. He'll be waiting for you and he'll have a message for you. Something important for you to bring back."

Doc's soft voice played at the back of his mind. As usual, her instructions were clear and understandable. Although she had said she didn't want to lead him, she had provided him with direction. Within a few minutes, he started to hear voices emerging from the drone of the om. At first, he thought he was imaging them, but soon they took on a clarity that was distinct from the chanting. Slowly, he became aware of being among a group of people. They were seated in a circle in a large room talking. Some sat on cushions on the floor; others sat on a long, L-shaped couch.

Everyone suddenly fell silent. He tried to get a clearer image, but he sensed the scene more than he actually saw it. The group of people didn't seem to be doing anything, just sitting quietly, as if they were waiting for something. At the same time, he could still hear the om clearly, which puzzled him. Doc usually turned the volume way down or completely off as soon as she was certain that he had entered his zone. But even when she forgot to do it, he'd found that the music faded from his awareness until he returned.

Then, to his surprise, he heard a voice from the group call out to him. *Hello, Trent. We've been waiting for you.*

Instantly, he jerked away, as if someone had snuck up behind him and yelled in his ear. He felt the bed beneath him. Doc was writing something in a notebook. She looked up at him. "You're back. What happened?"

He heard the sound of a warbler in the cottonwood tree in Miller's yard and realized that the chanting had stopped. "I'm not sure. Did you just turn the CD off?"

"No, I turned it off about fifteen minutes ago, as soon as I saw you were gone. Remember, I said I didn't want you drifting off beyond the target."

"But I heard the music. I heard it clearly while I was out there right up until I came back. I was in a room with about eight or nine people."

"Who were they? Did you get a look at them?"

Calloway frowned. "I wasn't that deep. I didn't get a clear picture."

"So why did you come back?"

"Someone called my name. It startled me."

"Why?"

"Why? Because I was caught off guard. It was as if this whole group of people were remote viewing me."

Doc shrugged. "Maybe they were. Do you want to go back and find out?"

"Not really. It was kind of unsettling."

Doc leaned forward and spoke in the same gentle voice she used for monitoring. "Calloway, get your ass back there. You've got work to do."

He laughed. "Well, shit, if you put it that way, okay. But this time let's not play the music. Just give me a minute, then direct me back."

He took several slow, deep breaths; he struggled to quiet his mind. Thoughts of Camila and their unexpected tryst kept intruding, but finally he resettled into the state of mind that felt like remote viewing. Doc sensed it immediately and directed him to his target. He found the group of people again, and this time he could see more clearly. But he realized that he was directly above them. He only saw the tops of their heads.

Then he realized he could hear the om again as if it were actually playing at the destination. It occurred to him that the group might be chanting. He drifted lower, but stopped as he sensed that the chant was coming from above him. He redirected his attention upward and was surprised to see that the room extended high above the floor, like a rectangular shaft, at least three stories. He felt confused, because the odd-shaped space felt somehow familiar. Then he noticed two sets of walkways with railings circling the open area. On the lower walkway, several speakers were fixed to the railing.

He found his pen clipped to the notebook that lay on his lap and started drawing. While he could see the pad on his lap as he drew, he remained aware of a part of himself that hovered in the open space above the people. He jotted a single word below his drawing, *atrium*.

Then he knew where he was. "Doc, you're not going to believe this. It's Perez's old place, the underground mansion. That's where these people are meeting."

"Okay, I understand. Who's there?"

"Let me take a closer look." He drifted down closer to the group. He could see faces, but he didn't recognize any of them. *He's aware of us. Stay with him. Calloway, do you hear me?*

He scanned the faces, looking for the one who had spoken. He spotted a familiar face. "Doc, you're here, sitting at the end of the couch."

"Who else?"

He couldn't take his eyes off Doc. To his amazement, she

looked as if she had lost thirty pounds. "You look pretty good, Doc."

He was about to mention her weight loss when he saw another familiar face, one that shocked him upon recognition. "Christ, it's me. I'm here."

"How do you look?" Doc asked.

"Not bad. Maybe a few years older, hopefully wiser."

Yeah, that's right. It's us. Five years in your future.

The voice seemed to whisper in his ear. Calloway started to withdraw again, but this time he adjusted himself. *So you're really me. It looks like I made it okay, at least another five years.*

To his surprise, his older self responded to his thoughts.

Don't count on it. I'm only one version of your future. There's no guarantee you're going to get here. Besides, if you knew what was going on here, you wouldn't want to be here. That's why I contacted you. We want to get out of here.

Now Calloway felt thoroughly confused. *I don't understand.*

Come closer. Move into me, into my mind. I know you can do it. Just like going inside any human target.

Calloway hesitated. Something about the idea of going into himself in the future frightened him. Maybe he would get stuck there and lose five years of his life. Besides that, he didn't like the ominous implications his older self had made about the future world. Then he felt himself being pulled inward, as if he were being swirled down an invisible drain, until he sank into a point within himself where he encountered his other self.

Now it seemed they shared the same body, two versions of one person inhabiting the same body five years in his future. He settled into his familiar frame and acquainted himself with his future self. At first, he couldn't tell the difference from his younger self. Then he felt a pain in his right shoulder and a stiffness in the right side of the neck.

*A little rafting accident on the San Juan. You can avoid it
by not trying to carry all the supplies at once. Take two trips
from the truck to the raft.*

Calloway settled deeper into his future self and looked
around at the others. He felt as if he were actually here in the
room rather than remote viewing the scene from his RV. Suddenly, he became concerned about his physical self. He no longer
felt in contact with the part of him that remained in the bed.

*It's okay. Don't worry. You're still there and you're fine. It
appears that you're sleeping. We're working on Doc to make
sure that she doesn't disturb you.*

For a moment, he wondered who his older self meant by
"we." But then he knew. They were all remote viewers, Doc's
remote viewers, Project Third Eye five years in the future, but
now it was called Scanport. With the information came the understanding that he had access to all his older self's memories
and knowledge.

So what changed?

A storm of data flooded his awareness. A series of dramatic
incidents revealed themselves one after another. The information
came to him like a combination of headlines, pictures, and news
summaries imprinted into his awareness. Governments disabled
by terrorist attacks. Rapid social decay. Cities abandoned. Com-
munications and transportation systems interrupted. Millions
dead.

No, it couldn't be. Impossible. Not in five years.

*Think again, young Calloway. Virtually everything that was
taken for granted no longer works. Stay tuned. You haven't
picked it all up yet. Guess who's taking advantage of the chaos?*

Again, the answer to the question appeared as a series of
images and packets of information. He saw Justin Logos flying
in a private jet, escorted by an entourage. Everywhere he landed,

huge crowds greeted him. Presidents and prime ministers praised him, called him the savior with superhuman abilities that linked him directly to God. His influence spanned national borders and he was seen as the one person who could lead the world out of chaos and into an age of peace and harmony. He was the perfect ruler at a time when democracy was increasingly equated with violence and instability.

It all happened and is happening. Justin is at the heart of it. The internal voice, his own future self, assured him that what he was seeing was not a fantasy. *Most people are captivated by him. But we are not. We call him Justin, son of the Vulture. We don't use the term Christ or Antichrist for him, but if we did, Justin would be the latter.*

During your time, he believes that he is in the hands of the Thunderbird, but he undergoes great internal conflict until he learns that he is at the focal point of a struggle between the Thunderbird and the Vulture. He is guided and influenced by both of them, but from our point of view, the dark side dominates and manipulates many who come into contact with him.

Now, understand this: a part of you/me died at his hands. You are heading toward that death now.

Calloway was baffled by virtually everything that he was seeing and hearing. How could he die if he was alive five years in the future?

You are still thinking in linear terms. We have many selves, all existing simultaneously. Remote viewing, especially in the last five years, has verified that over and over. In my world, I escaped Justin, at least temporarily. But he and his kind have literally destroyed civilization.

In two years from your time, eighty million will die from smallpox as the result of a bioterrorist attack. Justin is behind it. As a result of all the changes, the population of the planet by

2010 is expected to fall to less than half of what it was in 2000. Calloway thought back to the incident at the ranch in which Melissa and Betsy died. *I saved Justin's life. What a mistake.*

Exactly. We tried to stop you. You sensed us, but you didn't listen. Now you must go back and stop Justin before it's too late. Don't count on the FBI to stop him. You need to go there yourself. We will help you as much as we can. If you succeed, we're going to try to escape this world and merge with our selves in that new altered world, free of the Justin-Vulture.

How can I can stop him? He must be incredibly more powerful than I'd imagined.

That's true. In order to survive, you need to change something within yourself.

"*What is it?*"

"*You've got to figure it out. It's got to come from you, in your own time.*

Calloway looked around and found himself back in his RV resting in bed.

"Hey, sleepyhead. I see you're back. You fell asleep and I just didn't have the heart to wake you up."

He rubbed his face. The images from the future that had flooded his mind seemed blurry now, as if their clarity related to the time frame. For several confusing moments, past, present, and future jumbled together as if he were living inside a dream and wasn't certain what was real. But then he found his footing in the present, his present, and one thought stuck in his mind. He had stopped Justin's murder and that act would ultimately cost millions of lives.

"I wasn't sleeping, Doc."

PART THREE

Now

Twenty-five

Calloway turned on the ignition of the RV. "Let's get going. There's no time to waste."

"Wait a minute," Doc protested as she moved forward and dropped into the passenger seat. "You want to drive back there now? It's been a long day. We just left the ranch this morning."

"You don't have to remind me. It's going to be a lot longer day before it's over."

"Why don't you call Camila? She can alert the FBI about the smallpox virus. If it's there, they'll find it."

Calloway shifted the vehicle into gear and pulled away. "I am going to call her, but I got the distinct impression from our future selves that we can't just phone this one in and go to bed."

"I suppose I can sleep on the way," Doc said, amending her thoughts.

"Yeah, you sleep; I'll drive," he said as the small town quickly dropped away behind them.

Doc gave him a guilty look. "Well, one of us should get some rest, and you don't want me driving this thing."

He picked up his phone to call Camila, but then remembered his commitment to Miller. "Damn, I've got to call Ed and leave him a message. He's not going to like it, either."

"I got news for you. He's home. I saw him come back while you were touring the future."

Miller answered, as Doc had predicted, and Calloway told him his change in plans. "I'm sorry, Ed. It's an emergency. I can't avoid it. I'll be gone a couple of days. I'll explain when I get back, and I'll make it up to you, too."

"What the hell, Trent. For chrissake, you just got back and we've got two groups coming in tomorrow. I want you to lead the Scout trip. Can't you go to the ranch tomorrow after you're back? The schedule's wide-open after that."

"Listen, Ed. Believe me, when I say it's an emergency, I mean it. I can't wait a day."

"What am I going to do, Trent, tell them to wait until my wandering guide gets back?"

"Why don't you try Charlie? He can fill in for me."

"Charlie's drinking again. I can't trust him, and I don't know if I can trust you anymore, either."

"There's got to be somebody who can help out. I know, let Guy take out one of the groups."

"He's a kid, Trent."

"I've taken him on three or four trips now, and I let him take the helm for a while. I think he can do it."

"Like I said, he's a kid."

"He's seventeen. I trust him. He's going to be down there tomorrow morning. Keep the two groups together. Then you can keep an eye on him."

"All right. Hurry back, and I want to hear more about this emergency. Does this have something to do with that Jesus fellow again?"

"I can't talk about it right now. I've got to go. I'll tell you more later."

Calloway shook his head as he disconnected the call. "Damn, I almost had to forget about saving the world so I could go rafting to keep Ed happy."

"We all have our priorities."

They followed the winding road out of the river valley between jagged sandstone cliffs. "Right now my priority is to contact Camila. We're going to need her help."

He punched her number and she answered her cell phone on the second ring. "Camila, you've got to turn around and meet Doc and me at the ranch," he blurted.

"Calm down, Trent," she said after a pause. "What's going on? What are you talking about?"

He explained what his future self had told him about Justin and the state of the world five years from now. "That's interesting," she replied in an even tone. "If there is a smallpox virus on the ranch, the authorities will find it. They're on top of it, Trent. In fact, the FBI is on the scene right now and they've got a warrant to search the property for stolen viruses. Apparently, they had someone undercover on the ranch for several months. She worked her way into Justin's inner circle and got enough evidence to justify a search."

Calloway recalled what his future self had said. *Don't count on the FBI to stop him.* "I still think it's important for you to meet us there. I want to help out."

"Actually, there's really nothing you can do," Camila said. "It's under control."

"I'm still going."

"Why?"

"Camila, we're talking about stopping an epidemic. I can help them find the virus."

"But you don't need to be there."

"Yes, I do."

She didn't say anything for several seconds. "Is it the virus you want to go after, or is it Justin?"

"Maybe both."

"I'll call the FBI and tell them you're going to the ranch to volunteer your services. I'll explain what you do and how you do it. That's the best I can offer."

"All right. That's fine."

"What happened?" Doc asked after he hung up.

"She's going to call it in."

"Meaning what?"

"She'll give us a reference. The FBI is apparently already searching for viruses." Calloway stared pensively ahead. "I just hope that Camila isn't flying into a death trap. Justin could've already sent the viruses to the capital, for all we know."

"I'm just not sure about this yet," Doc caviled. "I'm sorry, but I still have a hard time believing that Justin is a terrible person. He probably doesn't know anything about the viruses. That was Melissa Dahl's scheme."

"Well, if our future selves are correct, he catches on real fast."

"I wonder," Doc said doubtfully.

"Look, you were the one who thought it was so urgent to peek into the future. But now that I've come back with bad news, you don't want to believe it."

"As I remember you saying, Mr. Calloway, that future is only one probability."

"That's exactly right, and it's not the future that I care to live in. So let's get our asses to that ranch and see if we can change it." He wondered again how Justin might have influenced Doc's thinking during the healing. If his future self was correct,

Justin was clearly capable of implanting such suggestions.

"So what are you planning to do, go there and shoot him?" Doc asked defensively. "If that's your plan, you can turn around and drop me off at Ed's place."

Calloway gazed upward, supplicating the sky. "Give me a break, Doc. I'm not going to kill anyone. Except maybe Steve Ritter, but that's another matter. I want to make sure that the authorities find that smallpox virus. That's all."

She considered what he'd said for several seconds. "I can go along with that as long as the authorities understand that we don't have any concrete evidence that Justin is hiding smallpox or any other viruses."

Calloway laughed.

"What's so funny?"

"Now you're sounding like the skeptics. *No concrete evidence.* That's what they always say about remote viewing."

"I know. But in this case, they would be right. It's not like remote viewing an object across the country that can be verified with a telephone call. We're dealing with the future, with something that hasn't happened yet."

"Agreed. So let's see that it doesn't happen."

"You're impossible sometimes, Calloway," she muttered. "I just want you to be very conscious of the fact that we're dealing with a man who has saved hundreds, maybe thousands, of lives and helped many thousands more."

"No problem as long as you recognize the possibility that he may have a dark side that's far worse than the best that we've seen from him."

Doc turned quiet, sullen.

"Do you think he might have affected your thinking when he healed you?" Calloway ventured.

"How so?"

"You know, he might've implanted a suggestion so that you only see his good side."

"That's ridiculous," she bristled. "I would've known it. Wouldn't I?"

"I don't know."

Tera's head throbbed with pain; she felt terrible. Nothing like this had ever happened to her before. Even though she had had no indication that Betsy might be violent, she still felt at fault for Melissa Dahl's death. She'd just been interviewed for an hour by sheriff's office investigators, then went over everything again with two FBI agents.

Now she headed from the big tent to the clinic where Justin had gone to meditate and escape all the chaos. She wanted to apologize to him and ask his forgiveness. If he turned her away, she would certainly understand. But she felt that she needed to make an effort to tell him how sorry she was for what had happened.

She'd already called her producer and had heard the anxiety in his voice after she'd explained the outcome of the interview. Hal Russell had been excited about the project. He'd worked hard editing more than fifteen hours of videotape that included her previous interviews, tape of Justin healing, follow-ups with patients, and some amateur videos of Justin working miracles. Russell had been excited about what she'd found out, and he thought the revelations would be one of the top stories of the year.

But when he'd heard what had happened, she could tell he saw it all falling apart and turning around on them. Their role in sneaking Betsy Lambert into the interview as a fake crew member and the resulting murder would complicate everything.

Tera could just imagine the new twist it might take. *Enterprising reporter's efforts to expose self-proclaimed new Messiah leads to on-camera murder.*

Wonderful.

There was a good chance the special would be canceled or downgraded. Certainly the impact would be substantially altered by Betsy's actions. Even if it was canceled, Tera's efforts would still be the subject of news stories and endless analysis of how far reporters should go to get their stories. Ultimately, she might be forced to resign, even though she'd gotten Russell's approval to sneak Lambert into the interview.

She pushed away her concerns as she reached the clinic. She found the front door locked, so she moved along the side of the building until she came to another door near the rear of the building. She knocked. No one answered, so she tried the door and found it open. She stuck her head into the gloomy interior.

"Hello!" she called out. "Anyone here?"

No answer.

She stepped inside. Several lights burned along the walls, but the interior of the building remained gloomy. She moved farther inside and saw that she was near the first of several examining tables with screens that blocked the view from the waiting area. On a previous trip here, she had spent two days watching Justin work.

She called out again, feeling as if she were intruding, even though no one seemed to be around. Maybe Justin had gone for a walk to get away. Then she heard a door close from somewhere at the rear of the building. She moved around the examining area and looked behind a partition and saw Justin Logos walking her way.

"I'm sorry to intrude like this, Justin. I certainly didn't mean to interrupt you."

"Hello, Tera. I'm glad you came looking for me. I want to talk to you."

Her heart pounded. Her throat felt dry. "Oh, you do? I wasn't sure that you would."

She felt nervous now in his presence, even though she'd been relaxed during the interviews, at least until the one today. Her recurring headache was back and it pounded against her temples. When he didn't say anything, she continued, "I was hoping that you'd be willing to let me apologize. You don't know how terribly sorry I am for what happened. I feel at fault."

Justin touched her arm. "You were doing your job. I'm sure you didn't know the woman's intentions or you never would've allowed her to come with you."

Tera's shoulders slumped. "You don't know how relieved I am to know that you feel that way. It really helps."

Justin stared deeply into her eyes. After a few moments, she blinked and looked away. She felt as if he were looking inside her, examining her life. "Tera, would you mind sitting down in a chair over here?"

She followed him over to the examining area. "I guess so. But why?"

"I'd like to work on you for a moment. You've been having headaches, haven't you?"

Even though she had witnessed Justin's uncanny ability to diagnose illness on several occasions, she was still caught by surprise. "Is it that obvious? I've been getting them off and on for about six weeks. I've gone to a doctor, but I didn't get much help."

"Don't worry. I'll take care of it. You'll feel much better very soon, and it won't come back."

·   ·   ·

*Look at this, boys. Here we go. Watch how the God-son operates.
He's so smooth. She doesn't have a clue.*

*Johnstone. Glad to see that you're with us now. I know you
were trying to block me out while you fixed yourself something
to eat. We all have our special interests, don't we, Henderson?
Meow, meow. But you almost missed Justin. Watch him now.*

*Yes, Timmons, he is healing her. But there's a lot more going
on. I swear Justin is not the same person we met last time. He's
changing like a big ugly moth emerging from a cocoon. It's
happening right before our eyes. Let's move in closer and get
inside for a peek and see what this is all about.*

This was going to be easy, Justin told himself as he held his
hands above Melissa's head. She had come to him asking for
forgiveness, just as he had expected. It had taken longer than
he'd thought, but he was patient. The medication was wearing
off now and he knew he was coming into his own. He was
already feeling stronger and capable of doing things that he
would never do when the lithium controlled his life.

Now he was here for Tera, and, yes, he would get rid of her
headaches. No problem there. But he would go much further. He
would put her to his own use. Why not? She had used deception
and had intended to destroy him. But her ace in the hole, Betsy
Lambert, had decided to take matters into her own hands. If
Melissa hadn't stepped in the way, Betsy would've killed him.
Besides, he needed Tera now that Melissa was gone.

He made sure her eyes were closed. He spoke softly to her,
relaxing her deeply. Carefully, he reached into his pocket and
pulled out a small package wrapped in plain paper. He dropped
it into Tera's handbag, which she'd set next to the chair. He
continued talking until he was certain that she'd slipped into a

highly receptive state of mind. He told her that she would not consciously remember him telling her anything. But when she came fully awake, she would be open to his suggestions and willingly go along with them.

He told her that she would resign her job and join him to work as his chief administrator in charge of operations. She would replace Melissa. He also told her about the package that he'd given her and what she was to do with it. Gradually, he brought her fully awake.

"Now, how's the headache?" he asked, smiling.

She touched her temples, then looked around, puzzled. "It's gone. But what happened? Did I fall asleep?"

"No, you weren't sleeping. You just got very relaxed as I gave you a hypnotic suggestion that will allow you to work without concern about headaches. I could've cured the headache quickly, but instead I chose to get to the root of the problem so you could be done with the headaches for good."

"I think it worked."

He smiled. "Good. I knew it would. Before you leave, Tera, there are some things I would like to talk to you about."

He is so smooth. I'm guessing she'll be working for him within a week, if not sooner. She's totally programmed. But first she has a job to do. Did we all see how he slipped Tera a very special present? Now she's ready to take it to Washington to spray the town, and spray it good.

Twenty-six

Dusk encased the landscape as Calloway and Doc turned onto the dirt road that led the final ten miles to the ranch. Several cars moved in the opposite direction, apparently leaving the ranch.

They passed a few more vehicles. Then, a mile before the entrance to the ranch, Doc pointed to her right. Calloway slowed and in the fading light saw a battalion of National Guard troops and vehicles parked in an open area off the road. "I wonder what they're planning."

"It must have something to do with the viruses. That's my guess," Doc answered.

Calloway touched the brake as a roadblock appeared. Two vehicles were stopped in front of them. State troopers talked to each of the drivers, and after a short discussion, each vehicle made a U-turn and headed back. Calloway pulled ahead and a state trooper approached the RV.

"You need to turn around, sir. The ranch is temporarily closed. It's a crime investigation scene."

Calloway told him his name. "We're here to talk with an investigator. I've got some information that will be useful. The FBI should be expecting my colleague and me."

The trooper told him to wait, then moved off and spoke with

another uniform, who walked over to the RV. "Can I see some ID from both of you?"

Calloway passed their driver's licenses to the trooper, who examined them closely, then handed them back to him. He moved away several yards and made a phone call. After a long wait, the trooper exchanged a few words with someone, then hung up. He ordered two troopers to move aside the roadblock, then walked back to Calloway and Doc.

"Drive directly to the campground, then report to the large tent. Agent Thompson will meet you there. Stay away from the house."

They drove along the dirt road leading to the campground. Halfway there, Calloway slowed and pointed toward the ranch house. "I wonder what that is?"

A huge bubble-shaped, white enclosure, illuminated from the inside, had been erected next to the house.

"I think we'll find out soon enough," Doc said.

To Calloway's surprise, the campground remained full. Now he realized that the vehicles they'd passed were probably all people who had been turned away. In spite of the problems here, no one was leaving. He drove back and forth along the rows of campers, RVs, and tents and finally found a spot near the end of one row.

As soon as they parked, a crowd of people gathered outside the RV. When they stepped outside, everyone watched them closely, as if there were something unusual about them. Then he realized what it was. They were arriving at a time when no one was being allowed into the camp.

"Hey, I recognize you," said a young woman in an ankle-length, green dress, whose hair looked as if it had been brushed with an electric sander. "You were here yesterday. How did you get back in?"

"Lucky, I guess," Calloway responded.

"Are you a reporter? I heard that's all they were letting in now."

Calloway shook his head.

Now a tall, angular man in baggy jeans and suspenders spoke up. "I bet I know what it is. When they found out you were just here, they wanted you back with the rest of us."

"Why?" Doc asked.

"That's what we're all trying to find out," the man said. "They won't let anyone leave. They're saying this place is under temporary quarantine, because of a virus."

"But that's a lie," Green Dress said. "We can't find anyone who's sick with a virus here."

"And if they were, Justin could heal them," Tall Guy said.

Now Calloway was getting a better idea of what was going on. But he was curious about how much else they knew. "So is that why all the cops are here?"

A man with a trim white beard and half-frame glasses hanging on a chain around his neck stepped forward. "They say that Melissa Dahl is dead, but we want proof. We want to see Justin."

"That's right," Green Dress concurred. "Two hours ago, they promised us that Justin would come out and explain everything. We're still waiting and now we're getting suspicious."

She deferred to White Beard, who continued, "We think the government might be trying to stop Justin from healing. As he gets more and more well known, he's getting more powerful. They're afraid of him. They don't know how to deal with this sort of person."

"They want him to disappear," Tall Guy said. "They want everyone to just forget that he ever existed. But we're not going to let that happen."

"We heard that the FBI had an undercover agent here working as a volunteer," Green Dress said. "But Justin figured it out, and when Melissa confronted her, she left real fast. Now they say Melissa is dead."

Doc took Trent by the arm. "We're going to look around now and see what else we can find out."

They headed toward the big tent. "I thought you were in a hurry to talk to the FBI," Doc said.

"I am. I just wanted to find out what they know. I should've figured they'd think there was a government conspiracy behind it all."

"Maybe they're right."

Calloway patted his pockets looking for his jelly beans. But he'd forgotten them in the RV. Just as well, he thought. The sugar would make him sleepy and he was tired already.

The stage came into view and a couple of thousand people were gathered in front of it, waiting for Justin. Doc paused a moment on a knoll, taking in the sight below. "If I didn't believe in your talents at remote viewing, I'd probably be right down there with them talking up the conspiracy theory."

They continued on, moving along the outskirts of the crowd and over to the circus tent. About a dozen reporters, including at least three television crews, were stationed outside the tent waiting for something to happen.

Calloway approached a state trooper. "We're here to see Agent Thompson."

As soon as they told him their names, the trooper nodded and motioned for them to follow him. They stepped into the tent and were surprised by the changes that had occurred since their recent visit. No longer a meeting place, community kitchen, and information center, the interior of the tent now looked liked the staging ground for a small war. They were led toward a gray-haired man in a coat and tie who was talking to a slender, blond woman in her thirties whom Calloway recognized as one of Justin's apostles.

"I've got Trent Calloway and Miriam Boyle here to see you," the trooper said.

The man in the suit finished what he was saying to the woman, nodded to Trent and Doc, then walked away. "Hi, I'm Agent Jean Marie Thompson," the woman said, turning to them and extending a hand.

Calloway recognized the woman as he shook her hand. "I thought your name was Claire something."

"It was until yesterday. I was undercover."

"Now what are you?"

"I'm in charge of the investigation here. Not the murder, but the theft of viruses from government labs."

She sized him up a moment with a practiced eye. "Camila Hidalgo told me a little about you, Mr. Calloway. She said you're good. I'm glad that you're both here to offer your services, but at this point we've got everything under control."

"Did you find the smallpox virus?" Calloway asked.

"Smallpox, anthrax, tularemia, and brucellosis. We found Dahl's secret lab and we found the viruses hidden in her security chief's dresser. They were kept in mist dispensers that looked exactly like plastic cigarette lighters and fountain pens."

"How do you know that's what's in the dispensers?" Doc asked.

"We don't know for sure," Thompson admitted. "That's what the labels say. But we're working at it. We've got a portable airtight lab in place outside the house. The analysis is going on as we talk."

"Why did she steal viruses?" Doc asked.

"She was among a group of researchers who believed that eliminating viruses, like smallpox, was a mistake, that it upset a delicate balance in nature," Thompson explained. "But later, it became a power struggle when a couple of the researchers saw the viruses as weapons that could be sold to the highest bidder."

Calloway was more concerned about the immediate problem. "How do you know that you found all of the viruses?"

"If there's more, we'll find it," Thompson said brusquely. "We're continuing the search. We're also keeping everyone in the campground here for at least twenty-four hours. We want to see if anyone comes down with a viral infection."

"But what if Justin already sent some of the smallpox virus to Washington?" Calloway persisted.

"First of all, we have no evidence that Justin knew anything about the viruses. Dahl was extremely secretive. She kept things from Justin, like her relationship with the security chief."

"Do you think the security chief was involved?" Doc asked.

"Kirby's under arrest. We have information that Dahl confided in him."

"Maybe she told Justin about it, too," Calloway suggested. "After all, he predicted some kind of disaster in Washington. Maybe it was their plan."

Thompson looked off to her right toward a red-haired woman who was waiting to talk to her. The woman looked vaguely familiar, but Calloway couldn't place her. "I spent months undercover here. I got to know the lay of the land. Justin was preoccupied with his work. Dahl was the schemer. Now, if you'll excuse me, there's someone waiting to talk to me."

Thompson walked over to the woman and Calloway leaned toward Doc. "So what do you think?"

She shrugged. "Like the lady said, they've got everything under control."

Calloway peered at the redhead and realized it was Tera

Peters. He rubbed the back of his neck. "Funny, but I don't think they've got this thing under control at all."

Something new and unexpected zipped through Tera Peters as she entered the tent and looked for Thompson. She thought of it as a feeling of hope and deliverance, a sense of mission, something that had always been lacking in her life. She had just spent two hours alone with Justin in his clinic, and he had not only healed her, but had infused energy into her that had transformed her life. She had learned more about him in those two hours than she had in all of her interviews with him. But she'd also learned something about herself. She realized now that she longed to set off on a quest, on a new path.

She spotted Agent Thompson talking to a black man and a pudgy woman in the part of the tent that used to be the information center. She stopped short and stared at the FBI agent until she caught her eye. While she waited for Thompson, her thoughts drifted back to Justin. On one hand, he seemed so human, so vulnerable. Yet, there was something about him, something she couldn't quite grasp, that intrigued her. She knew, without a doubt, that she had fallen under his spell.

She saw everything differently now. Never had she felt so strongly about anything in her life as she now felt about her future alongside Justin Logos. She knew it sounded crazy, but she was committed to him. Melissa Dahl had been dead only a few hours, but everything was speeding up. She would step smoothly into Melissa's place, but first she needed to help Justin through this transition.

"Tera, can I help you?"

She smiled at Thompson. "I talked to Justin. He wants to address the crowd now. He's ready."

Thompson glanced at her watch. "He still wants to go out there? It's getting a little late."

"Not for his people. They'll listen to him at three in the morning, if that's when he's speaking."

"How well I know. Did he give you any hints about what he was going to say?"

"He said he'll explain the situation so everyone understands why they are being required to stay here."

Thompson frowned. "You spent quite a bit of time with him. How does he seem to you?"

"He's amazing. I've never met anyone like him."

The agent considered what Tera said. "You know, when I was undercover here, I found that I was becoming more and more attracted to him the longer I stayed. He's a very charismatic character, yet you wouldn't know it by watching him. He seems so normal, so approachable."

"I know exactly what you mean. After every interview with him, I felt like I was on a high for a day or two. It was incredible, and I just wanted more. Maybe I was a little jealous of Melissa, but when I found out about her past, I couldn't overlook it."

She noticed the agent's brow furrowing. Stop babbling, Tera told herself. She looked over at the man Thompson had been talking to. "By any chance, is that Trent Calloway?"

"Yeah. Do you know him?"

"I met him once a long time ago, but his ex-wife, Camila Hidalgo, is my best friend."

"Hidalgo? That's interesting. She called me and told me that Trent was coming. If it wasn't for her, he wouldn't have gotten past the gate."

"Is he going to remote view for you?"

"Are you asking me as a reporter now?"

Tera didn't think she'd be doing any more reporting on this story. In fact, she might very well be finished with her career as a journalist. She smiled. "Off the record."

Thompson nodded. "He made the offer, but I don't feel it's necessary. We've found what we were looking for."

"Good. I think it was Melissa, all the way. I had a feeling that there was something very odd about her. Of course, then I found out just how odd she was."

"Do you think she knew he was her son?"

"She denied that she knew it, but it seems pretty far-fetched that she would just happen to meet him in India."

Thompson shrugged. "Then again, when it comes to Justin Logos, a lot of things that sound far-fetched are happening all the time. I can attest to that myself. Are you going to get all that stuff into your program on Justin now that Melissa's dead?"

Tera had told the authorities what she knew about Melissa's past because it related directly to why Betsy had shot her. "I haven't really had a chance to think about it. The whole thing is up in the air now with these new developments. I'm not sure what's going to happen."

Tera felt like telling Thompson that she didn't care any longer, either, that she was going to work for Justin and help him through this difficult time. But she thought it best to keep that to herself for now.

"Do you think I'll be able to leave in the morning? I really need to get back to Washington. Everything has gotten complicated."

Thompson considered the request. "I don't know. It depends. We'll see what the situation is in the morning."

The agent's cell phone rang. She answered and listened a few moments. "Okay, I'm on my way."

Thompson snapped the phone closed. "Don't count on leaving just yet." With that, she headed toward the doorway of the tent.

Calloway looked up to see the woman with the auburn hair walking toward him. She extended a hand, introducing herself.

"I knew that you looked familiar," he said, smiling. "It's been a long time."

Doc extended a hand and introduced herself. They exchanged a couple of comments, then Tera turned to Calloway. "Trent, I think your work is fascinating. But do you think you can be any help here for the FBI?"

"Not according to Agent Thompson, but we'll see."

Calloway suddenly had a bizarre urge to grab Tera's handbag and turn it over to Thompson. The handbag dangled in front of him, held by just two of her fingers. He started to reach for it, then his rational mind took over, and he asked himself what he was doing. He realized that the impulse came from outside him. He tensed, thinking that Ritter must be at it again. No doubt his idea of a joke.

"Grab it!" Doc said.

He looked sharply at Doc, startled by her words.

At that moment, a voice boomed through the loudspeaker system. "Folks, we haven't been waiting in vain. The man is here. The moment is here. Let's welcome Justin Logos."

Cheers reverberated from the stage and suddenly everyone in the tent stopped what they were doing and listened. Tera slung the bag over her shoulder. "I have to go. Nice to see you both." She hurried toward the entrance.

Calloway turned to Doc. "What did you say?"

Doc shook her head, a puzzled expression on her face. "For

some reason, I thought you should grab her purse. Can you believe that?"

"Yes, I can. I had the same idea in mind. That proves it, Ritter and the gang are active and messing with us."

"Do you think?" Doc asked as they joined the flow of bodies moving toward the door.

"That bastard is dead meat," Calloway muttered half to himself. One way or another, he was going to stop Ritter from invading his brain.

The crowd had doubled in size by the time they stepped out of the tent. Calloway followed Doc, who plowed ahead toward the stage. The applause and the cheering continued even though Justin still hadn't appeared. Then shouts rang out as he walked to the microphone. A surge of energy rippled through the crowd; the cheering intensified.

They stopped a hundred feet from the stage when Doc couldn't get any closer. Calloway spotted Tera just as she crossed through the line of security guards. "I guess Tera has a backstage pass," he shouted in Doc's ear. Doc nodded, but continued to stare at Justin. If the crowd bothered her, she didn't show any sign of apprehension. That, more than anything else, proved to Calloway that Justin's power to heal was astonishing.

After nearly a minute, Justin motioned with his hands and leaned toward the mike. "This is not exactly a time for cheering."

The applause instantly faded and everyone seemed to lean forward to see and hear him. He wore jeans and a sweatshirt and a cap that seemed to be pulled so far forward so that it was difficult to see his eyes.

"I said there would be changes, that there would be turmoil. You are all experiencing it. We have sheriff's deputies, state troopers, and the FBI operating out of our tent. I understand that several hundred National Guard troops have been mobilized and are just outside the ranch waiting for orders.

"Melissa Dahl, my longtime associate and the owner of this ranch, is dead. We have heard that the authorities have found dangerous viruses on the ranch. These are not good things. We are in the time of chaos. But are we in a time of danger?"

He paused and raised his head, and his blue eyes glistened in the bright stage light. "There is no danger, unless you believe there is danger. If we give in to fear, the Vulture moves in and eats us alive. But make no mistake, the Vulture is real and its unwitting emissaries are among us. They are bringing on the chaos, and the high drama, which will raise everyone's emotions. It will be a great feast for the Vulture and it will help keep them all in his control. Don't give in to it. You can stand above it."

Calloway swore that Justin was staring at him, as if he were talking directly to him. But he guessed that most of the audience felt the same way.

"They say that everyone must stay at least another day because of the quarantine. I suppose that's not so bad. We can do that, can't we?"

Cheers and thunderous applause greeted the comment. The same voice, but a different message. Friendly, outgoing, nonconfrontational. Yet, Calloway sensed something different about Justin, a sharper edge, an underlying energy that hadn't been present during the other talks he'd witnessed. It almost seemed that he was a different person inside the same body.

Then he heard a voice in his head, Justin's voice. *The closer you come to me, the quicker you die.*

Twenty-seven

With Justin's approval, cots had been set up in the circus tent for reporters, while the investigators who wanted to sleep were assigned to the cottages. Tera felt restless, and after everything that had happened to her, sleep was the farthest thing from her mind. She had a strong urge to get out of here and head back to Washington tonight, but she didn't know how she was going to do it. Not with the damned quarantine in force.

She noticed several reporters and camera crew members, including Louie, her cameraman, huddled together near the information area where the last press briefing of the day had been held shortly after Justin's talk. Even though she didn't think she would continue working as a reporter for CNN or anyone else, she still gravitated toward the other reporters. She quickly sensed that something was going on and asked if they were still under quarantine.

"Yes and no," said one of the reporters, a blond-haired young man with a perfect television face—believable and sincere.

"What's that mean?"

"Hi, Tera. Art Drysdale from KRML-TV, Albuquerque. It means we can leave, but we can't go far. I was just telling everyone that we've just gotten approval to go see what the National

Guard troops are doing down the road. Would you like to come along? I've got a Suburban with plenty of room."

"That's a good idea. But if you don't mind, Art, I'd like to follow you with my cameraman."

"No problem. I'll let them know at the gate."

It was just the break she needed. She would get out of here ahead of time without Thompson's seal of approval. She thought she should say something to Justin, but realized that would attract too much attention. She would contact him after she got to Washington. Besides, by then she would know if she was really committed to making the leap.

Synchronicity, boys. We're back in business, back to destroying the capital. It must mean we're in the groove, attracting the experiences to us that we want to see happen. When you think of it, an epidemic is much cleaner and more effective than a bomb. We won't destroy buildings; we'll just kill people, and the epidemic will spread and spread and spread.

Timmons, you don't think there's anything clean about a virus? Don't worry. You won't be anywhere near the capital.

But Tera will need our help. We're like guardian angels, you see. Tera is on her own, and as far as I can tell, she doesn't even know what she's doing. Justin programmed her to carry out his mission, but she won't take any evasive actions to avoid getting caught.

That's where we come in. We'll guide her through any rough points. Yes, Johnstone, we are working for Justin, but not officially. I'm not sure he's even aware of us, although it seems that this new and improved Justin may know more than he's letting on. We'll see.

Meanwhile, let's pick up the action. Tera is heading to the

Albuquerque airport. She made a clean break. But we'll make sure that no one stops her in case Thompson puts out an APB. I don't think that's going to happen, though. There's so much confusion back at the ranch that they probably won't know Tera's gone until morning.

No, Johnstone, we're not going to kill any cops. If she gets stopped, they will simply realize they made a mistake. We alter their perception. It'll only take a few secs. We've done it before. Meanwhile, we've got to make one other little nudge. We want to convince Tera that she should get a room at the airport in Washington instead of going home. Her apartment will be too hot by morning.

Ah, Timmons thinks that's a good idea. Of course it is. I thought of it. With any luck, our lady will be spraying the town before the noon hour tomorrow.

And so the chaos begins.

Calloway bolted upright and nearly hit his head on a cupboard door. Morning light crept through the windows. He felt the narrow fold-down cot beneath him and remembered it was Doc's turn to sleep in the recreation vehicle's queen-size bed. He heard pounding and realized someone was at the door, that the knocking had awakened him. He stumbled to the front of the RV and opened the door.

"Calloway, I decided I need your help."

He stared at the blond FBI agent, who looked as if she'd been up awhile. He tried to focus on what she'd said. "What time is it?"

"Quarter to eight."

"Why do you need my help?"

"The test results are back. The containers labeled variola

were empty. We're missing the smallpox virus, if there ever was any."

"I'm sure she had it."

"Then help me find it. I'd like to see what you can come up with."

Calloway rubbed his face, then looked at Doc, who had joined them. "Let me get a cup of coffee. We can do it right here."

Fifteen minutes later, he sat back against the headboard of the bed with two pillows behind him. When he turned on the om tape, Doc frowned. "Don't worry," he told her. "It'll speed things up."

Calloway drifted into his zone. He could tell right away that he was going deep this time. Maybe too deep. He heard himself saying something about Tera's handbag. But he kept going, deeper, deeper. He found himself in the underground mansion and realized he had merged with his future self.

Calloway paced about the large central room of the under-ground mansion. He gazed up the atrium toward the skylight three stories overhead. Even though the place was roomy, he was getting cabin fever, living here with seven others. Except for two tense days in St. Paul where he was interviewed by a commission investigating the epidemic, he had remained on the isolated Colorado property for the past eighteen months. None of them even dared to go to town. Smallpox was so widespread and virulent that there was no guarantee that the vaccine worked. Certainly, the old smallpox vaccinations that had been given to schoolchildren up to the early 1960s were useless. The soaring death toll of baby boomers attested to that.

But smallpox was only one of the problems they faced. It was just a matter of time before Justin Logos's World Militia forces, which operated as an international private army with close ties to the U.S. military, came after them. They needed to make their escape soon, an escape like no other that he had ever imagined.

"It didn't work. You didn't do it," Doc groaned. "All you had to do was grab the bag and you would've had the virus."

Calloway shrugged. "Same as last time. I didn't do it then, either."

"No, it wasn't the same! This time I told you to take the bag. I listened. I heard, but you ignored me."

"Sorry." It felt odd apologizing for his inability to change his past actions.

"Now what are we going to do?" she asked. "Our best shot is to get them—our past selves—to stop Peters before she leaves the ranch. But I don't see that happening now. The problem is that you're so damned mad at Ritter at that point that you can't see straight. You think that any outside nudges are from him, so you just ignore them."

"I had good reason," Calloway said defensively. "Besides, that's not the only reason. Don't you remember how tired we were? We listened to Justin and went right back to the RV and fell asleep."

"I remember. By the next day, when we figured out what was going on, it was too late. Maybe we should try again and go back to that same point in time in the tent."

Calloway shook his head. "No, it's not going to work. It's like you said, I'm convinced it's Ritter telling me to grab the purse."

Doc turned up her hands in frustration. "So we can't do anything. Is that what you're saying?"

"Maybe we're looking at the wrong target."

"What do you mean?"

Calloway looked up as he heard the elevator. He touched a button on the remote control for the security system, and a screen on the wall lit up showing Joyce Evans and Rick Ferraro, two members of the remote-viewing team who stuck close together. Joyce, a twenty-five-year-old black woman looked up at the camera in the elevator and waggled her fingers. Ferraro, standing behind her, wearing his ever-present black beret, a goatee, and an earring, raised his middle finger and smiled.

"Do you get the feeling that Rick doesn't like us spying on him and Joyce?"

Doc laughed. *"That's a good guess."*

The elevator door hissed open after descending three stories, and a few seconds later the pair moved into the central room. *"Why do you always turn that camera on, Trent? Who else would be coming in?"*

"I don't know. That's why I look, Rick. I don't want to be surprised."

"Everything's fine out there," Joyce said. *"We checked the entire perimeter."*

"Even though we could do it electronically at any time," Ferraro added sarcastically.

"It's important to do a visual inspection," Calloway said patiently. *"There's always a chance that the equipment is misreading the data."*

Originally installed by Eduardo Perez, the somewhat paranoid builder of the underground fortress, the system had been turned off and in disrepair during Project Scanport's first years. Calloway had taken it upon himself not only to repair the system, but to learn all the details of its operation. As a result, he was

*protective of the system and didn't like anyone making light of
the need for it.*

Ferraro shrugged. "Yeah, I suppose."

*Kevin Gurney, a slight man with round glasses, walked into
the room with a sheet of paper. "We've got E-mail from Washington. Take a look at this."*

*Doc took the page and Calloway glanced over her shoulder.
"What is it?"*

"Uh-oh. The shit has hit the fan, folks."

"Should we duck or run?" Ferraro asked.

*"The Office of National Security has advised us that we have
forty-eight hours to vacate these premises. We've been evicted."*

*Calloway's shoulders slumped. "I wonder what provoked
them to act now."*

"It's surprising we lasted so long," Doc said.

*In spite of the chaos that had resulted from the smallpox
epidemic, Project Scanport had been funded by the Charles Vincent administration. Vincent, the former secretary of state who
had succeeded David Dustin, was a strong supporter of remote
viewing. Concerned about renewed terrorist attacks, Vincent had
gotten the project moving, and within six months the old Perez
mansion had been renovated. But with the election of Bobby
Royalton a year later, coupled with the rise of Justin Logos, the
assignments had dwindled and there had been none for the past
year. Meanwhile, the distant outpost had virtually been forgotten
and the remote viewers ignored.*

"So what are we going to do?" Joyce asked.

"At least we got a warning," Ferraro said.

*"Let's not respond to it," Calloway said. "We've got to de-
lay them as long as we can. We're not ready to make our move
yet."*

"I agree with you there," Doc said. "Trent, just before you heard the elevator, you started to say something about the target, that maybe we were going after the wrong one. What did you mean?"

"I was saying that maybe we've been pushing the wrong buttons. We should be going after Thompson. She's the one who can stop Tera."

Calloway blinked his eyes and looked up from his bed in the back of the RV. Doc sat next to him, and he heard Thompson's voice at the other end of the RV.

"Doc, you're not going to believe where I went."

"Way beyond your target. I know that much. But at least you caught something on the way out."

"I did? What?"

"You said the variola is in Tera Peters's handbag, the same one you wanted to grab."

He frowned. "I did? I don't remember saying that. But I believe it."

Doc nodded toward the front of the RV. "We're looking into it right now. Jean Marie is getting Tera's bag confiscated. So, where did you go?"

Oddly, Calloway couldn't recall anything about targeting the smallpox virus. "I went ahead five years again."

"Back to the future!" Doc turned up her hands. "Why not? So what happened, anything interesting?"

"We were just getting evicted from Perez's place."

Just then Thompson moved to the rear of the RV. "Well, our suspect has left the ranch. She slipped out last night with some reporters who were going to report on the National Guard activity, but Tera and her cameraman just kept going. We're going to her apartment right now. We'll catch up to her."

A few minutes after Thompson left, Calloway sipped his second cup of coffee and puzzled over the meaning of his inadvertent trip to the future.

"It actually seemed like I was there. I can still feel what it was like being me in his time. I don't think he was aware of me at all."

"So what did you learn?" Doc asked from the gas stove where she scrambled eggs.

"That we should've grabbed Tera's handbag. They were the ones who were pushing us to take it."

"Who do you mean by 'they'?"

"You and me, our future selves. It wasn't Ritter at all."

"Interesting. It fits."

He thought about how it felt to be himself in that future world. Camila was dead and his future self silently mourned her loss. Camila and tens of millions of others had died. He shook his head. "I'm glad I got back."

"That future is not going to happen," Doc said firmly. "As soon as they find Tera and collect the virus from her, we shouldn't have to worry about any of that stuff coming to pass."

"Somehow, I've got the feeling that it's not going to work out that smoothly. And what if someone here comes down with the virus?"

Doc scooped the scrambled eggs from the pan onto a couple of plates. "Trent, don't even think about that."

Before he could respond, he heard a knock at the door. "I hope that's Thompson with some good news."

He opened the door and was greeted by a cheery, round-faced blond, an Amazon who stood an inch or two above his six-foot frame.

"Mr. Calloway?"

"Yeah."

"Good morning. My name is Suzie Carlson. I don't want to intrude, but I have a message for you from Mr. Logos."

"Really? What is it?"

She hesitated and tried to look past Calloway as if she were concerned that Doc was listening. He stepped out of the RV and closed the door.

"Thank you. Mr. Logos enjoys meeting certain people who are known to have special abilities or talents. He would like to see you at your earliest convenience."

Calloway frowned. "How does he know who I am?"

"I believe that Tera Peters, the CNN reporter, told him about you. He'll be at the clinic waiting."

"I'm about to eat breakfast."

"Then after breakfast."

Calloway hesitated. "I'll be there in half an hour."

She nodded toward the RV. "Fine. And please, come alone."

Twenty-eight

*C*onfession time. I know that I'm the best remote viewer alive, that this life in prison has improved my skills. The truth, though, is that I have a hard time focusing on my life in the future. Of course, I want to find out if I will get out of here, and I keep thinking that by helping Justin Logos, I will be writing my ticket out the door.

But then, when I look ahead, I get mixed results. I've focused on five years in the future, because that is the time the other group is working from. In case you've forgotten, we encountered another set of remote viewers who were messing with Calloway. I pushed toward them to see what I would find on my own. I thought I could sneak a peek at them by myself. But they blocked me just like I'm now blocking Calloway and Doc.

So I just focused on myself in that time frame. I picked up two conflicting pictures, one in which I was alive, but still incarcerated and the shields were up—the EMF had been turned back on. In the other one, I wasn't in prison any longer, but I wasn't here at all. I hate to sound morbid, guys, but if those are my choices, I might just prefer moving on right out of this world, instead of spending boring, endless years here without even the option to escape through my mind.

Now I hear Johnstone, a small voice in the dark. *What about us?* he asks. *What happens to us?* I can't answer that, but I've *got the feeling your fates are linked to mine. With either choice, you guys lose. Without me, you're left to wander in a psychic minefield. Sooner or later, you'll take the wrong step.*

Then it occurred to me that we don't have to settle for those two options. Why can't we create some other, better choice? After all, Calloway escaped his own death and went back in time. Yes, I know, you guys don't remember that. But I do. I followed him back.

So, what can we do? How can we improve our options? Any ideas? Johnstone thinks we should just lie low so no one comes after us. Sorry, that's not an option. If we are passive, then we don't have any control. We leave our future up to others, and I'm not about to do that.

Here's what I think. We go right to the top. We go to Justin Logos and plead our case. Let's get it out in the open. We'll work for him. Stop shaking, Timmons. He's not going to infect you with any germs. But go ahead and wash your hands if it makes you feel better. Sometimes I think I'm running a nursery. Believe me, if you guys weren't so good, I would be spending my days figuring out how to destroy this psychic network.

Okay. Let's focus now. We're going to visit Justin Logos, wherever he may be at this moment.

Whenever he was working, Ritter sat on a stool that was bolted to the floor of his cell and faced the back wall. Now, just as he was moving toward his target, he heard a noise behind him. It sounded like ice cubes jangling against a glass. What the hell was it now? The damned guard had to be at the door trying to get his attention.

Reluctantly, he turned his stool around. To his surprise, someone stood inside the room, a man dressed in white who reminded him of an orderly in a mental hospital. But Ritter hadn't heard the door open or close.

"What do you want?"

"Don't you know who I am?"

Ritter was about to say that he didn't know and didn't want to know, either. But then he realized he was staring at Justin Logos. "I don't get out much, but I recognize you. How did you get in here?"

Justin ignored the question. "I think you get out a lot."

Ritter stood up and hobbled over to him. He reached out and touched his arm. "I feel like the guy who stuck his finger in Christ's wound to see if it was real. You are actually here, but that's impossible. They would never have let you in my cell."

Justin leered at him. He looked dangerous, on edge, Ritter decided, nothing like the kindly, godly healer he was supposed to be. "I heard that you could appear in two places at once, but I didn't believe it. I didn't think that could be done."

Justin laughed. "Steve Ritter, you think if you can't do it, it's not possible. You can travel far with your mind, but there are many things you can't do."

Ritter nodded, dumbfounded. "What can we do for you? We want to help your cause."

"Then you can force Calloway to kill you."

Ritter laughed nervously. "Yeah, that's good. I like that. He can try, but he's the one who will die. Not me."

Justin patted him on the shoulder. "You can do it. For me. For the future."

Do what? Die or kill him? He didn't ask, because he didn't want to hear the answer. He was not going to let Calloway kill him.

"Any more questions?" Justin asked.

"Yeah, I've got one. If you're in two places at once, what else are you doing right now?"

Logos stared at him with such intensity that Ritter looked away. "I guess it's none of my business," he said uneasily.

When he looked back, Justin was gone. But the answer to his question rang inside his head. *What else am I doing? I'm talking to Calloway.*

Twenty-nine

As he walked along a well-trod path among a grove of oaks to the clinic, Calloway tried to figure out what he would say to Justin. He didn't know whether he should confront him about his suspicions regarding the missing virus or wait to see if Justin brought it up.

The path curved and he looked up, expecting to see the clinic. He suddenly felt dizzy and everything seemed to waver around him. He blinked trying to get his bearings. He sucked in his breath. He was no longer on the trail, or at the ranch, or even in the same time frame. Without warning, he found himself in the underground mansion.

Calloway touched the remote and the big screen on the wall of the central room lit up. The screen was divided into six different news broadcasts: three U.S. networks, one cable, and two foreign stations. He looked at the images and clicked on one of the networks. The image grew larger, the others shrank to half their former size, and the sound for the selected station came on.

Even though they were isolated in the underground mansion and never saw a newspaper, they followed world events on television and the Internet. But they had to be careful using the latter. They could no longer communicate with others of like mind. E-mail was easily invaded, on-line privacy a thing of the past.

The broadcast began with a breathtaking report on a medical-genetic breakthrough, a story on the first human to "re-grow" a limb. A forty-two-year-old man, whose lower right leg had been amputated sixteen years earlier, had a new leg and could walk normally. The medical advance was said to be five to ten years ahead of previous expectations in genetic engineering.

It was the type of story that usually led the news these days, anything to avoid gloomy reports on smallpox. Clearly, the smallpox epidemic was the biggest story of the new millennium, but according to polls, most people were weary of hearing about it and felt bombarded by the constant reminders in the media.

In spite of those sentiments, the next story dealt with the presidential task force that was directed to reopen the investigation into the source of the epidemic. Kira St. Clair, the young anchor of CBS News, said that the task force was close to announcing that they had found the perpetrators. St. Clair hinted that she would provide inside information when they returned from a commercial break.

Calloway called out to the others. Doc, who had been in the kitchen, came out with Kevin Gurney.

"What's going on?" Doc asked.

Calloway pointed to the television. "It's coming out on the investigation. Let's see if they listened to us."

Over the years, the story behind how the epidemic had started had become more and more blurred. It was still considered a terrorist act, but no terrorist or group had ever been identified as the source. But in recent months, there had been growing demands among politicians for a solution. Doc and Cal-

loway had been among those subpoenaed to appear before the task force. They were each interviewed for two hours, then returned a second day for follow-up interviews.

"I don't have much hope for that," Doc said. "They were so negative about everything we said. Half the time they didn't even seem to be listening."

"Here it is," Gurney said as St. Clair appeared on the screen again.

"Although the findings won't be officially released until the middle of next week, a source close to the investigation of the smallpox epidemic says that investigators have pinpointed a domestic plot that involved three government employees, including an FBI agent and two members of a secret intelligence project."

"Holy shit!" Calloway leaped up. "They're sticking it on us."

"And Agent Thompson," Doc said. "I can't believe it. What the hell would be our motive?"

"Listen!" Gurney shouted, pointing at the television.

"The source said that the three conspirators, who have not been arrested, and I quote, 'intended to link the viruses with Justin Logos as a means of destroying the illustrious healer and statesman's reputation.' More on that story as it develops."

Rick Ferraro walked into the room at the tail end of the report. "Well, I guess we know now why we're being evicted."

"That's the least of our worries," Calloway said.

"Let's not panic," Doc said, patting the air with her hands. "It's a trial balloon. That's all it is. That's what they do in cases like this that are so political."

Calloway stared at the smiling, cherubic face of Bobby Royalton, the thirty-seven-year-old president of the United States. He hit the mute button on the remote, but couldn't take his eyes off Royalton. The youngest candidate ever elected to the highest office, Royalton was also the first president elected from the three-year-old Unity Party, which was closely associated with Justin Logos and his followers.

"Now we're really up shit's creek," Ferraro said. "They'll probably nail the rest of us as coconspirators."

"We've still got time," Doc said. "We can make our break. We've got to calm down and focus."

"That's right," Calloway said. "Forget about dinner for now. Rick, get Joyce and the others in here. We've got work to do."

"Do you really think we can actually move ourselves to the past?" Ferraro asked. "I still find this whole idea hard to believe."

"Well, believe it, Rick. I've told you the story. It's not only possible, but I did it. I moved back several weeks and integrated with my past self. I escaped another version of the epidemic that was about to kill me and Doc."

"How do you know that other life is not just a dream? There's no proof that other reality happened. You're the only one who remembers it. Besides, tell me this, what happened to the other you, the one you left behind?"

Calloway glimpsed the image of himself trapped in a non-place under the control of the most formidable bird that he had ever seen. He didn't know whether the image was symbolic or real. It had taken him a long time to sort things out and recall the events leading to his escape. But he was sure it had happened. "But I think both Doc and I died of the flu. But it's not important, because I'm here."

Ferraro turned to Doc. "You don't remember any of that, do you?"

"No, I don't, because I didn't go back in time, but Trent did."

Gurney took Ferraro by the arm and led him away. "Let's do what Trent says, unless you've got a better idea."

Calloway looked over at Doc. "Let's hope they stop Tera. Otherwise, there's no point in making the effort. Even if we succeed, we'll be right back in the worst of it."

"Let's see if we can help them this time," she said.

Unexpectedly, Calloway found himself standing outside the clinic. It took several moments for him to get his bearings. The entire experience that had just unfolded seemed like a daydream now. Yet, while it lasted, he'd not only witnessed the future, but he'd actually experienced his future self's life.

Now he remembered that he was about to visit Justin. He felt like going back to the RV and telling Doc what had happened, but the door suddenly opened. Suzie Carlson smiled and motioned him to come into the clinic. "I thought I heard something out here. There's no reason to be afraid of meeting Justin. He's really just like a regular person most of the time."

They walked past the desk near the front of the empty clinic and between rows of chairs, past the examination area, and over to a closed door. She tapped on it, opened it a few inches, then called Justin's name. Calloway heard a murmured reply. Carlson stepped aside and told him to enter.

As soon as the door closed behind him, a feeling of dread descended over him and he knew he'd made a mistake coming here. The air felt cold and clammy, dimly lit and hazy. A couple of dozen candles burned on the floor, and it took a moment for him to see clearly. He couldn't believe what he saw. It not only defied logic, but it sent a shudder of terror through him. He wanted to turn and run, but he couldn't move.

Justin Logos sat in a lotus position in the center of the room, his eyeballs rolled up into his head. He was naked and blood dripped from his palms and side. But even more startling, he hovered two feet above the floor. Calloway backed toward the door, reached for the doorknob. He cried out as he touched it. The knob was so cold that it burned his hand.

"You've just arrived. Don't leave yet."

Justin's voice boomed inside Calloway's head as if he wore headphones with the volume set high. But Calloway didn't see Justin's lips move. "Partake in the spectacle. You are so privileged to be here."

"What do you want of me?" Calloway managed to say. His body trembled from the cold that permeated the room.

"What do you want of me?" Justin mimicked him, but his mouth remained sealed.

"Who are you? What are you?"

"I am everything that has been said about me—goodness and hope, a vehicle to everlasting life—the Almighty Thunderbird. But also the Great Keeper of Darkness—the ruthless Vulture."

"How can you be both?"

"Ah, you think they nullify each other. But, no, they complement. They are the essence of what we are. Goodness depends on evil; evil on goodness. Where would one be without the other?"

"You've misled and misguided everyone. You're not what you appear. You talk against the Vulture, but now you say you are one and the same."

The room seemed to grow even colder. "The truth is that I am neither the Savior nor Satan, the Christ nor the Antichrist, the Thunderbird nor the Vulture. I am a projection in flesh of the great cosmic battle that wages beyond time and space. Life on earth, as always, is a reflection of that conflict."

That might be, Calloway thought. But at the moment, it clearly seemed as if the dark side prevailed. He felt helpless, trapped. Alone. *Why me? Why am I here?*

Justin responded as if Calloway had spoken aloud. "You are here because you have broken free of your pen. You are honored by the Thunderbird for seeing that there is much more beyond the borders of your pen, but you are a threat to the Vulture, who must reinforce the strength of the boundaries that hold you captive."

Justin raised a bloody hand. "See for yourself!"

Instantly, Calloway was no longer in the room, but in a place that was no place. He saw himself dangling from a hook that pierced the skin and muscle at the back of his neck. Then he realized it wasn't a hook at all, but the claw of an enormous bird.

"Do you remember what happened, Trent? You were infected by a virus and dying. You await a doctor who will never arrive. You live many versions of your life simultaneously. That life is every bit as real as the one you are living now. I show it to you because it relates most directly to this life.

"Now you will see another version of yourself, one who is aware and very interested in you. Look!"

Calloway rested in a comfortable chair in a room on the second level of the underground mansion. Soft music played and Doc sat in another chair a few feet away. He was trying to reach out to his earlier self, the one that was on the same path as his current life. He knew that Calloway must change something to alter the course of events. Although it seemed obvious that the answer lay in stopping the smallpox virus from being released, he sensed that for that to happen something else had to be changed. He'd faced this same dilemma himself five years ago and had failed. Ironically, he still didn't know what was missing. But if he failed this time, he would die.

"What are you seeing?" Doc asked.

He shook his head. "I'm having trouble focusing. I've been sensing him as if he's been around here with me. But I can't seem to get back to him."

"Concentrate."

He sensed static around him. He tried to push through it. Now he sensed he was being observed. "I think he's right here with us again. It's like he's me now, but I want to become him. Oh, shit!"

"What is it?"

"There's someone else here, too. I can't see him, either. But he's here watching."

"Who is it?"

"Justin Logos."

He heard a disturbance somewhere nearby. A knock, Doc's voice talking to someone. Everything went fuzzy around him. He couldn't sense Logos, but he remained out somewhere in a sub-space realm that lacked clarity.

"Okay, Trent. I'm bringing you back now," Doc said. "Focus on my voice. Stay with me."

He felt a hand on his knee. He sensed others nearby, just outside the room. "Are you okay, Trent?" He heard a frantic undertone to Doc's voice.

"I'm okay. What's going on?"

As she spoke, a piercing blast ripped through the structure as the alarm sounded, and he knew the answer to his question.

"They're here," Doc sputtered. "Three black helicopters have landed. They're coming to get us."

Calloway found himself back in the room with Justin Logos amid the flickering candlelight. The chill had left the room and Justin was no longer hovering above the floor. No blood dripped from his hands or sides, and he was garbed in a white tunic as if he were about to be cast for a role in a Roman drama.

"So, you see how it is, Trent. Things are not so good in your future. Now you face the challenge of learning from what you have seen. You have a chance to change what is becoming into what could be. But how will you do it?"

Thirty

When she woke up in a room in the Howard Johnson's the next morning, Tera wondered why she hadn't just taken a taxi home from the airport. She'd been tired, but she'd taken many trips and come home exhausted without staying at the airport. At least she didn't have to deal with all the telephone calls that would be coming in.

She climbed out of bed, ran a hand through her thick auburn hair. She could imagine the messages on her machine. Her producer, Hal Russell, would be sounding desperate. He would probably imply that their story and their jobs were in jeopardy. There would probably be a call about an important meeting, and if she couldn't get to the office, she needed to get on a conference call. On second thought, she'd made the right decision staying here.

The entire Justin Logos affair was a big mess, but she felt surprisingly at peace. As far as she was concerned, the story was dead. She didn't want to pursue it. She just wanted to quit her job, clear up her life here, and return to Justin as soon as possible.

Her sentiments left her with an incredible sense of relief. She'd worried that she would wake up this morning and find herself back in the old mold, ready to fight for the story and her job. But she could only think about Justin and joining him to begin a new life. That was all that mattered.

Just the thought of the healer sparked something inside her, a sense of excitement, of adventure.

Her phone rang and she jumped at the sound. Who knew that she was here? She hadn't told anyone that she was staying at the airport. She picked up the receiver and realized it was a wake-up call. But before the operator hung up, she was reminded to pick up a package that she'd left at the front desk.

What package? She couldn't recall checking a package any more than she remembered making a decision to check into the motel. She called the front desk and identified herself. "I checked a package last night. Could someone send it up to me?"

She slipped on a robe and retrieved the package when she heard a tap at her door. She recognized her own handwriting on a large envelope and remembered leaving it at the front desk as a security precaution. Although she couldn't exactly recall how she'd gotten it, she knew it was something from Justin. She opened it and a hand-sized package wrapped in plain paper slid into her hand. She examined it a moment, then tore off the paper wrapper. Inside were a half dozen expensive fountain pens, the kind found in specialty shops. Each one was labeled: *White House, Justice, Congress, FBI, Pentagon.*

Now she remembered that Justin had asked her to carry out an important mission for him. It was as if he had planted a packet of information inside her and now that she held the fountain pens in her hand, it was all available to her. The fountain pens were actually mist dispensers that contained liquid incense. Justin had blessed the incense, and when it was sprayed, it would open minds. A few days ago, the idea would've sounded preposterous to her, but in the aftermath of her solo encounter with Justin, it made sense.

She had to take the pens to the appointed places and release their contents. Everything would be okay. It was for the better. People would finally understand that Justin was here to heal the world, but first a major shake-up would occur. She would play a key role in saving the planet and bringing about a new world order with Justin Logos at the forefront.

She ran her fingers over the pens and picked up the one labeled *White House*. She felt a sense of urgency to move ahead in her mission. She touched a hand to her forehead. So much had happened in the last day; her thoughts and memories ran together. But the one thing that prevailed was her sense of commitment to Justin Logos.

She punched Camila Hidalgo's number and left a message with her assistant. She showered and was dressing when Hidalgo returned her call.

"Camila, thanks for getting back to me. I need to see you about something important related to Justin Logos. Any chance I can get in this morning?"

"Let me look at my schedule. It's crazy this week. How are you doing? You must be under a lot of pressure."

"I'm dealing with it."

"Let's see. I can squeeze you in for fifteen minutes at ten-thirty. That's about the best I can do."

"I'll be there."

"Are you sure you're all right? You sound different."

Tera laughed. "I feel different, too. I'll tell you about it when I get there."

•　•　•

Calloway nearly bumped into Doc as he left the clinic. She gasped for breath and placed a hand on his shoulder. "I'm glad I found you. You've got to call Camila right away." She handed him her cell phone.

"Why?"

"She called for an update and when I told her about Tera . . ."

"What did she say?" Calloway asked impatiently as Doc tried to catch her breath.

"She said Tera Peters had an appointment with her in a few minutes."

Calloway's brow furrowed. "I hope you told her to cancel it."

"Tera was already in her waiting room. She said she would take care of it. But I don't like the sound of it."

"Neither do I."

He quickly punched the White House main number. He had Camila's cell phone number in the RV, but he didn't want to wait that long. He was put on hold.

They walked away from the clinic toward the campground, the phone clamped to his ear. After about a minute, the line went dead. "You did tell her that Tera might have the dispensers, didn't you?"

"Of course I did. We weren't talking about the weather. So what happened with Justin?"

"Doc, I can't even begin to describe what happened."

"Give me a hint?"

"I'm not sure you're going to understand, because I'm not sure I understand."

"Try me."

"The gist of it is Justin is not who people think he is."

Doc frowned. "Which people are you talking about, the ones who think he's the Son of God or those who want him to be the Antichrist?"

Calloway gave her wry smile. "Both."

"You're right. I don't understand."

"Think of it this way. Imagine the returned Savior was manic-depressive. Jekyll and Hyde. The Christ and Antichrist all rolled into one."

"Now that is *scary.*"

He told her, as best he could, what had happened during his encounter. Doc listened closely. "That doesn't sound like the same Justin Logos we've been seeing."

"I know."

When they reached the RV, Calloway found Camila's number and called her. This time he got her recording. "Camila, it's Trent. I need to talk to you immediately. This is an emergency. Please pick up."

He waited, then left his number and repeated the urgency of the matter. He shook his head as he hung up. "She's not taking calls or she's not by her cell phone."

"I think we need to go to work right away and track Tera," Doc said. "If we can't get through using technology, we'll connect through the ethers."

"Right. But let's focus on Camila. She may need some extra help."

Moving right along. There she goes.

You see, it only took a little nudge on the guard. There was really no need for concern. After all, Tera has credentials. She's in the White House all the time. The guard searched her, even examined her fountain pen and saw it for just that, a fancy pen.

Now it's just a matter of time. But let's not take any chances. We need to stay close to Tera, real close, and make sure she shows Camila how the fountain pen works.

"I'm really glad you could see me on such short notice," Tera said as she walked into Camila's office.

Camila moved around her desk and gave Tera a quick hug and motioned for her to sit down. Camila leaned back against her desk. Tera seemed remarkably relaxed for someone who had witnessed a murder-suicide during the most important interview of her career. "So, after everything that happened at the ranch, I'm really surprised that you would find time to see me today. What's so important?"

"I want to tell you my plans. Things have changed for me. You're going to be surprised when I tell you."

Camila nodded, encouraged her friend to continue. Just moments ago, Doc had told her that Tera might possess dispensers containing smallpox virus, but Camila doubted it. She knew Tera well enough to know that she was hardly a terrorist. "How so?"

"I turned in my resignation just before I came here."

"What? You quit?"

Tera beamed. "Yes."

"What about your story?"

"It's dead as far as I'm concerned."

Camila needed to ask her about the dispensers, but she wanted to wait until the right moment. "Tera, you were so excited about it. You said it was your biggest and most important story ever. You certainly couldn't help what happened. It wasn't your fault. Did they pressure you into resigning?"

"No, not at all. Well, I never even gave them a chance to pressure me."

Camila shook her head. "I don't understand."

"I went through a very transforming experience yesterday, first seeing two women die right in front of me, then having a long talk with Justin. I'm going to work for him."

A warning alarm sounded in Camila's head. If what Tera said was true, then anything was possible. She might even have the virus. "Whoa. Tera, have you thought this through?"

"Of course I have. I hope we can stay friends, too. I know that Justin would like to be on good terms with the president and get beyond the threatening rhetoric that's been flying around."

Camila was baffled by the turn of events. "I hope we stay friends, too. But the only threatening rhetoric I've heard has been coming from Logos."

"Maybe so. On the other hand, an FBI agent was sent undercover to the ranch and spent months there."

"And for good reason. They found a lab with deadly viruses right in that ranch."

At that moment, an impression of Calloway flashed before Camila's mind's eye. Another warning. Something was seriously wrong here. She needed to call security.

Calloway moved in close to Camila and tried to impress his awareness on her. *Stay calm, Camila. Keep Tera occupied.* He could tell that Camila sensed him, but she seemed to interpret the thoughts he was trying to impress upon her as a warning to get away.

"Tera, I've got another meeting. You'll have to excuse me. We'll have to talk later."

"Okay. But I want to show you something that Justin gave me."

Take it away from her.

"I'm sorry, but I really don't have time right now."

Calloway realized it was useless. Camila wasn't going to stop Tera no matter how much he prodded her. She wasn't listening to him. She was going to call the Secret Service, but by then it would be too late.

"Let me just show it to you real quick," Tera insisted as she opened her purse.

Now he knew he had to stop Tera. He shifted his focus to her. Over and over, he pushed the image of Camila dying and Tera spraying a mist in the White House. But no matter how hard he focused on her, Calloway couldn't stay with her, and the image he projected seemed to wash away like steam evaporating from a bathroom mirror. Then he realized that he was being pushed away by a force outside of Tera.

Sorry, Calloway. We beat you to it. You're not getting near Justin's new lady. She brings deliverance unto those who need it most.

He felt a surge of anger rise when he recognized Ritter's foul presence. He heard him cackling, enjoying his ability to interfere. Calloway had to work around him. He imagined himself leaping over Ritter and settling right into Tera's mind. But when he made the move, he just kept going as if he were soaring away. Then his connection with Ritter vanished, and to his surprise, he found himself snuggled inside his future self again.

It sounded as if a half dozen fire-rescue vehicles, sirens blaring, were racing through the underground mansion as Calloway quickly led the others into the walk-in closet at the back of the room where he'd been remote viewing. But the repetitious din of the alarm didn't prevent him from feeling a sudden concussive jolt as the invaders set off another explosive somewhere on the surface.

He worked the combination on the steel door at the back of the closet, pulled it open, and moved into a tunnel. Joyce Evans, the last to enter, slammed the door shut. "They're not here to help us move out. They've got orders to terminate all of us."

Calloway knew Joyce as a natural psychic, someone born with the talent, but it didn't take psychic ability to figure out they were in trouble. He couldn't help thinking of the irony of the situation. Six years earlier, he and Doc, along with Eduardo Perez and Camila, had fled down this tunnel after an attack by a white supremacist militia. Now it was happening again, but this time the attackers were probably Justin Logos's paramilitary troops. Perez had built this fortress to escape conflict and disasters, and yet he had died in the first attack. Now, Calloway heard pounding coming from the far end of the tunnel, and he knew they all might follow Perez in death.

"They've got us trapped," Doc said, aiming her flashlight down the dusty tunnel. "They're way ahead of us."

Calloway nodded. "I guess Perez's tunnel is no longer a secret."

"What are we going to do?" Kevin Gurney asked.

"Make our escape, as planned," Calloway said.

"Isn't there any other way?" Rick Ferraro asked. "I'm still wary about that route."

"None that I know of." Calloway stopped about midway through the tunnel. "I say we take our chances. We do it now, or not at all. We've got a few minutes to get into our zones."

"Everyone sit down and focus," Doc said. "Let go of any

fears. Breathe deeply. We're using powerful group energy. When you're ready, find yourself five years in the past at a meaningful and appropriate time and place. When you hear them coming for us, you will release and fully integrate into your past self. You will be that person. This future will be like a dream."

"Does that mean I have to repeat all the same shit I went through?" Ferraro complained as he slid down the wall.

"Not at all," Doc said. "Maybe this time you can get it right."

"Once you change something, other things change," Calloway said as he relaxed himself. "It all compounds and pretty soon you're not living your old life at all."

At that moment, Calloway lost contact with his future self. Instantly, he felt Ritter's caustic presence swelling around him. He tried to push him away, but he felt the others closing around him. He pushed at them, but they just pushed back harder.

No, Trent. No, no. You're not getting away from me so easily. Me and the boys have been savoring this moment. Now we've gotcha. Gotcha good.

Thirty-one

*O*kay, here we go. Head-to-head with Trent-O. We stop him cold. Stop him dead. I'm tired of dealing with him. We're wasting too much time and effort blocking him. Eliminating him is much better.

Yeah, guys. He can hear me. So can Doc. So what? Our little psychic network, the psi/net as our ol' boss Gordy Maxwell used to call it, is finished. Over. Kaput. Just like Max. Dead.

Come get me, Calloway. I'm waiting. Can't wait to tangle with you again. First, I'll tangle, then I'll strangle. But where should we go for our showdown? How about the moon? We could throw moon rocks at each other.

No, I can see that wouldn't work. I'd get to the moon and you'd be back dealing with Tera. Just leave her alone, pal. Let her squirt that pen around the White House. That's why she's there.

Calloway was fed up with Ritter's chatter and his heckling. He couldn't get the bastard out of his head, and now the guy was picking a fight. Frustrated that he couldn't help Camila and aware of the devastation that would result from the release of the smallpox virus, he felt his rage surge. He lunged his awareness toward Ritter, but at that moment, the scene shifted.

He stood in Camila's office just a few feet from Tera, who held up the fountain pen. Calloway realized he was actually in the room with her. Baffled, he lurched toward Tera and grabbed her arm. To his surprise, she fought back with surprising strength. He struggled with her, and the tip of the pen turned directly at his right eye, and for a moment, she seemed about to plunge it into his pupil.

He heard a cackle and realized that he was fighting Ritter, not Tera. Camila's office vanished, replaced by a dirt ring surrounded by a shouting crowd. The entire scenario was a psychic manifestation.

It's a cockfight, Calloway. Let's see which one of us is the biggest, meanest cock.

Ritter leered at him and pushed the fountain pen another inch closer to Calloway's eye. "Yes, I do think the pen is mightier than the sword, especially when it's filled with a deadly virus. Don't you agree, Trent?"

Calloway took advantage of Ritter's babbling. He slammed a leg against the back of Ritter's calves. His knees buckled and they both tumbled down. Ritter managed to roll on top of him, and now the pen transformed into a vicious-looking blade the length of Ritter's arm.

"On the other hand, there's nothing quite like a sharp, deadly sword, either," Ritter said through gritted teeth.

He pulled his arm from Calloway's grip, raised the weapon, and slashed down at Calloway's head as if he were about to cut a cabbage in half. Calloway jerked away at the last moment. He wasn't sure what the results of such a strike would be. Even though he knew that he was actually remote viewing from his RV and that Doc was seated nearby, an aura of tangible reality filled this odd realm.

Calloway struggled to get away, but he felt Ritter's strength multiplying and knew that the others in the psychic web were applying pressure. Then, he realized that all the faces in the crowd around the ring were the same, images of his old remote-viewing associates—Johnstone, Timmons, and Henderson—over and over again.

Ritter slipped the blade beneath Calloway's jaw and pressed it against his throat. "If I chopped off your head, you might die of a heart attack back at the ranch," Ritter said, answering Calloway's unspoken question. "Anything goes here, and you are going next."

Calloway felt the blade pressing harder against his throat, cutting off his breath. From a distant place, he heard Doc calling to him. But he couldn't escape from Ritter's hold.

"You changed the past, Calloway. Now I'm going to change the future. I saw you alive in five years, and I wasn't around. You killed me right here. But now it's my turn. In the new world, the boys and I will work out of Perez's old place, but we'll work for Justin. Yeah, a brand-new world, and you're not in it."

A surge of energy ripped through Calloway. He twisted around and pushed Ritter off him. He grabbed Ritter's arm and twisted it until he dropped his weapon. Calloway scooped it up and it changed into a leaded nightstick. He seemed to possess extraordinary power. Around him the crowd shrank back as if they suddenly feared him. He pressed the nightstick into Ritter's windpipe.

"Now you pay, Ritter," he seethed.

Calloway's fingers squeezed over the weapon, a psychic project of his hate and anger toward his former associate. At that moment, he knew that he could kill Ritter, that he had the power to do it and finally rid himself of the madman. He pushed harder; Ritter gagged, his eyes widening.

It all seemed too easy, as if he was getting outside help. An image of Justin, wild-eyed and manic, came to mind, and he felt another surge of strength. Justin Logos wanted him to kill Ritter. But why? Then he remembered his encounter with his own future and the warning he'd received. To survive, he must change something within himself. Now he knew what it was.

He needed to release his hate, specifically his hate for Ritter. He struggled with himself. Ritter deserved to die. But healing comes through forgiveness. *Forgive us our trespasses as we forgive those who trespass against us.* With an effort, with a will he never knew he had, he let go of his anger, his loathing. In spite of everything that Ritter had done to him, he absolved him.

"Steve, it's all over. I'm not going to kill you. I forgive you, man. It's not easy. But I forgive you."

Calloway held up the nightstick and it changed into a knife with a jagged blade. Then he turned it on himself. He plunged it into his heart. Shocked by his act, he stumbled back as blood ran over his chest. How could he have done it? Then he realized that the act had been symbolic, that he hadn't killed himself. He'd killed his ego.

An explosion rocked the tunnel. Calloway heard it and he knew that he and his associates were about to die. He let go and the scene vanished. He knew he would never go back, that he was fully connected with his younger self, who had just forgiven Ritter.

Camila shrank back, confused, frightened. "Tera, don't, please don't."

Tera looked at the fountain pen that she held in her hand

above her head like a weapon. Then she peered at Camila and a feeling of surprise and confusion spread through her. "My God, what am I doing? Do you know what this is?"

Camila gasped for breath, but tried to calm herself. "It's not a pen, is it?"

Tera shook her head. "I had the idea that it was some sort of blessed incense, a liquid incense that would help heal the world. But it's not. It's a virus. He tricked me. He's trying to get me to infect the capital with smallpox."

Camila took a cautious step forward. "Tera, who are you talking about?"

Tera looked up and met Camila's gaze. "Justin, of course. He programmed me."

"Would you put it down on the desk?"

Tera hesitated as if she wasn't certain what she should do. "I feel like I've just woken up. I was supposed to spray it in here and all over the capital. We would've both died."

"How did you figure it out?"

"It's the strangest thing. As I held up the pen, I had a strong impression of Trent Calloway telling me to stop. I tried to push away the image, but then I had a clear vision of myself spraying something from the pen, and then immediately I saw you falling down next to a podium, and I knew that I'd killed you."

Tera moved forward and dropped the pen on the desk. "It's not going to happen."

"Trent, are you okay?"

He opened his eyes and found himself inside his RV. Confused, he looked around. "Where are we?"

"At the ranch." Doc looked worried. "What happened? Are you all right?"

He smiled. "I'm fine. I made it back."

He blinked and everything started to fade. He felt unhitched in time, and he knew that it wasn't over yet.

In the dream, Calloway dangled in darkness in the grasp of the Vulture. But now the creature's feathers rustled as if it were distracted by something. Its enormous wings created a tsunami of energy. It let out an eerie cry that swirled around in a vortex of sound. Then the claw that held Calloway lost its grip.

For a moment, Calloway felt himself soaring. Then he plummeted, wingless and helpless, toward earth. An instant before impact, he opened his eyes.

He looked around the sterile room, confused. "Doc?"

"Trent, you're awake! How do you feel?"

"I'm not sure yet. Where am I?"

The chair scraped against the floor as she stood up. "Just what it looks like. You're in a hospital in Durango. I better get a nurse."

He held up a hand. "No, wait. Why am I here? I don't remember coming here."

"Take it easy. There's a good reason you don't remember." Doc sat back down. "You went into a coma and nearly died after an allergic reaction to penicillin. You never told me you were allergic to it."

He frowned, trying to remember what had happened. "Why was I given penicillin?"

"For the flu, of course. We both picked up a case while we were in Washington."

He closed his eyes. "Now it's coming back. The epidemic. How many are dead now?"

"There's no epidemic. It's just a minor flu outbreak, and as far as I know, no one has died of it."

"So David Dustin is still president and Camila is okay?"

Doc frowned. "As far as I know, they're both just fine. Why do you ask?"

"I'm trying to work things out. I remember being trapped by a big ugly bird, the Vulture. But while I was trapped, I was aware of different time frames. We were trying to go back and stop the flu before it started."

"You were hallucinating."

"So you don't remember any of that? I can see you don't. What about Justin Logos?"

"Who?"

Calloway raised up on his forearms. "Wait a minute. You do remember going to the ranch, don't you?"

"What ranch?"

"Doc, Justin Logos, Melissa Dahl, the viruses. Don't tell me it was all a dream. I don't accept that."

Doc shrugged. "I can't say that the names ring a bell."

Calloway dropped back onto his pillow. "I see there's been some new wrinkles."

"What do you mean?"

"Wait a minute. Why were we in Washington?"

"To get the project started."

"But you don't remember Harvey Howell asking us to remote view a prominent healer?"

"Trent, I think you need to rest."

"The problem with my memory, Doc, is that I'm remembering too damned much." He didn't think he was allergic to penicillin, and why would they get penicillin for a virus? "I'm sorry, but this just doesn't make any sense. It doesn't feel right. What about Ritter?"

"What about him? He's in prison."

"You don't remember anything else about him?"

She smiled, an oddly aggressive smile. "Just that he's the damned best remote viewer ever encountered."

Calloway looked sharply at Doc. "What did you say?"

She gritted her teeth, leering at him. Her features wavered and then Ritter sat next to the bed grinning like a madman. "You didn't think you'd get away from me that easy, did you, Trent-O? Just because you forgave me out of the goodness of your silly heart doesn't mean that I was going to disappear."

Calloway realized that the hospital room was just another psychic projection, a construct of Ritter's. He'd cleverly disguised himself as Doc, as he'd done with Tera. Nothing here was real, Calloway told himself. He struggled with the thought that he might not find his way back, that he would be pursued by Ritter until the maniac finally finished him off.

"So you don't want to kill me. That's good of you, because I'm going to hold you to that, Calloway. Yes, I am."

Just as Calloway started to get out of bed, Ritter lunged for him and clamped his hands around his throat. "Take your medicine, Calloway. Now you die for your sins."

Calloway knocked Ritter's arms away with a surprising burst of strength. Ritter stumbled back and reconsidered his approach. "That won't do, Trent. You're acting far too aggressive for a forgiving sort of guy."

Don't listen to him. He's weaker than he thinks. His sidekicks have abandoned him.

Calloway didn't know where the thought had come from. He knew it could be another trick.

It's me, Trent. Calloway from five years ahead. I'm with you and I'm staying with you. I'm becoming you. Let's take away his power to manipulate the setting. Let's put him back where he belongs.

Suddenly, they were inside Ritter's prison cell. Ritter looked puzzled, then surprised when he looked at Calloway, then at a second Calloway standing a few feet away. "We're here from your past and your future. We're shutting you down," both versions said simultaneously.

"You can't trick me," Ritter shouted, and charged into one of the Calloways. Instantly, the image vanished and Ritter tumbled to the floor of the cell.

Calloway felt the other part of himself merging with him, two versions of the same soul blurring, melding. "The electromagnetic field is back on, Ritter. You can't get out."

Focus on Doc. This time the thought felt more like his own. He pictured Doc sitting next to the bed in the RV. *Moving back . . . moving back.* He heard a distinct pop and he disengaged from the mind grip that Ritter had held over him. He breathed deeply and felt the bed beneath him. He opened his eyes and turned his head to see Doc leaning toward him.

"Jeez, Trent. I thought I'd lost you. You just passed out. I couldn't wake you up."

"I know. I had some trouble with Ritter."

Suddenly, someone shouted outside the RV. More shouts followed. Several people ran by. Doc pushed aside the curtain and looked outside. "There's something going on. I'll take a look."

Just as she left, Calloway's cell phone rang. He reached over and answered it.

"Camila, what's going on?"

She sounded breathless as she told him what had happened in her office. "I'm glad they found the virus," Calloway replied, "but it wasn't Tera's fault. You've got to understand that Justin has extraordinary abilities."

"I think you do, too, Trent. Tera said an image of you came to mind at about the time she snapped out of her strange infatuation with Justin."

"That's interesting, because I didn't think I was getting through."

Just then the door burst open and Calloway looked up expecting to see Doc. Instead, Justin Logos, wearing a purple robe, charged toward him.

"What the hell!" Calloway managed to sputter. Justin knocked the phone from his hand, wrapped his arms around him, and drove him onto the bed.

Instantly, Calloway felt a jolt of energy. Light flickered around him, then darkness prevailed. He lost track of where he was and what was going on. Nothing seemed to matter. He heard a noise, then felt himself plunging downward. He sucked in a deep breath and opened his eyes. He was lying on the bed, but now he was alone. He noticed the phone on the bedside table even though he was sure it had fallen on the floor. He picked it up. The call had been disconnected.

He had no idea what had just happened to him. But he was sure that Justin had attacked him. The door of the RV opened and Doc walked calmly toward him. "Trent, you're awake."

"I wasn't sleeping. What happened to Justin?"

"What do you mean?"

He told her how Justin had rushed in just after she'd gone out to see about a disturbance outside.

"That's a strange dream."

"I wasn't dreaming." He looked around. Something seemed different now, but he wasn't sure what it was.

Doc laughed. "Trent, you were sleeping. You were tired from the drive and wanted to take a nap before you looked around."

"Wait a minute. What are you talking about? What drive? When did we get here?"

She gave him an odd look, then glanced at her watch. "About half an hour ago. There are a lot of people here. I don't know if I'm going to be straying too far from the RV."

Calloway frowned. "Crowds bother you now?"

"Of course they do. Are you all right, Trent?"

"Are you saying that we just got here for the first time?"

"Boy, you have been dreaming."

He sat down heavily on the bed. "I don't accept that."

"You are acting very strange."

He tried to calm himself. "Let's start from the beginning. Why did we come here?"

She frowned. "We came here at the request of Camila and Harvey Howell."

"That's what I was afraid of. I've done this before. This has already happened. I can't go through this again."

"Go through what? You're not making sense."

He was starting to lose track of everything that had happened. "Don't trust Justin Logos. Can you remember that?"

"Trent, let's give him a chance. Remember, we said that we weren't going to react to Harvey Howell's fears. We're going to go one step at a time and see for ourselves."

"Howell knows something and so do I."

"What's that?"

He looked down at the floor and shook his head. "I can't remember now."

Go outside.

He shook his head. "I'm going to take a walk."

She nodded and gave him a worried look. "Don't get lost."

He stepped out of the RV and saw that a crowd had gathered near the stage. A voice announced that Justin would be speaking in fifteen minutes. He realized that Doc was right. They had just arrived. What had he been thinking?

No. Don't fall for that.

Where had that thought come from?

You're getting trapped. There's a way out. Find your way.

He had no idea what that meant. But he still had a strong sense of déjà vu. Then an idea came to mind and he knew what he had to do.

He walked back to the RV and found Doc making lunch. "I want to go for a target."

"I thought we said we weren't going to target Justin until we made sure that there's a reason for it."

"I don't want to target him. I want you to direct me to myself at a future time."

She frowned. "Are you serious?"

"Very much so." He moved to the rear of the RV. The sooner the better.

"It's an interesting idea, but what's the point?"

"The point is that I've got to move ahead."

"What's the specific target?"

"I'm not sure. Just send me to a critical moment in the future that relates to what's going on right now."

"That's obscure, but direct, I guess. Okay, relax. I guess we'll eat lunch afterwards," she said with a sigh.

He drifted down in his zone. He heard Doc's voice saying something about the future. He drifted deeper. Then he was soaring through inner space as images unfolded in his mind's eye. All around him the darkness was receding as a cosmic specter unveiled itself. The Vulture shrank away and retreated. The Thunderbird, replacing it, spread its wings, its warmth and light, over the planet.

He wanted to stay right here, in the light, in the warmth. He felt exalted, ecstatic, fulfilled. But it all faded, and when it was gone, Justin Logos stood at the center of a revolving gyroscope. His arms were held straight out to the sides forming a cross, and he was garbed in a luminous robe. The gyroscope spun faster and faster and then Justin vanished. But his voice resonated inside Calloway's head.

Am I a demon or a god? Whichever you answer, you are right and you are wrong. The light and the dark are all part of the same thing. I am all things to all people. I bring you awareness.

You showed compassion, love, and forgiveness when it seemed that you should kill. In doing so, you freed the Thunderbird within you and scorned the Vulture. You are free.

Calloway opened his eyes. He was still resting against a pile of pillows stacked in front of the headboard. He was alone.

"Doc? Where are you?"

She didn't answer.

Then he saw Justin lying on the floor of the RV, his body shrouded in a purple robe. Suddenly, the door swung open and Doc clambered inside, out of breath. "Justin? Trent?"

Her gaze settled on the body. "Oh, no. What happened?"

He realized that he was back to the present, a term that was starting to become exceedingly obscure to him. "I don't know."

Agent Thompson followed Doc into the RV. She pulled out a two-way radio and called for a medic. She knelt over the body and felt for a pulse.

"We heard shouting outside," Doc said. "I went out to see what was going on, and I saw him running around shouting and babbling, totally flipped out. He almost knocked me over. Then he ran right in here."

Thompson looked up to Calloway. "Did he say anything?"

Calloway hesitated. He was about to say that Justin hadn't said a word. Then he changed his mind. "He told me everything I needed to know, then he left."

Thompson stood up. "He's gone, and I don't think he's coming back."

Epilogue

Seated in the back of his RV, Calloway stared at the monitor of his computer as he read over his notes. Two weeks had passed since he'd returned to Bluff, and now he was back into his routine of leading raft trips and helping out Ed Miller, who had forgiven him for leaving on such short notice. Last night, they'd watched the CNN special on Justin Logos and Melissa Dahl, and like millions of others, Miller had been astonished at what he'd seen. But no matter how hard he tried, Calloway could find no way of accurately explaining his role in the affair. There was just no way of casually saying that he had traveled in time and changed things.

The more he thought about it, the less sense it was making. The idea that he had literally created a new world sounded too outrageous to talk about. So, instead, he was writing about it. And why not? Other former government remote viewers had written books about their experiences. Why couldn't he do it, too?

The phone rang, interrupting his thoughts. He answered, and when he heard Doc's voice, he walked outside into the night. "So next week is the big meeting in Washington."

"That's right. Do you want to join me?"

Calloway grimaced. "Not unless you really think you'll need me."

Doc laughed. "I thought you'd feel that way. Hey, that's okay with me. Camila says everything is lined up. After what happened at the ranch and all the publicity, everyone is ready to get things rolling. I even think I can get money for repairing the Perez place. It'll be the headquarters in a year."

"That's great. But what exactly are you going to tell them about what we did?"

"Just what happened. We pinpointed the missing virus, and with Camila's help we stopped a smallpox outbreak that could've become a deadly epidemic."

He wandered toward the river. "I guess that sounds pretty impressive."

"You bet it does. By the way, the reason I called is that Camila said Ritter has officially been transferred to an undisclosed military base in the Southwest where an electromagnetic field surrounds him twenty-four hours a day."

"That should keep him out of our heads. By the way, how do you feel about telling the brass in Washington about time travel and the ability to change the past?"

A couple of beats passed. "I don't see any need for it. I know we talked about it and tried it, but that part is all sort of vague to me now. I think it's best that we don't raise any red flags. Don't you think?"

"Yeah, I guess."

He rang off and gazed out over the river as beams of moonlight reflected off the rushing waters. That was another reason for writing his book, he thought. If he didn't do it now, he might gradually forget all that had happened, like an astonishingly vivid dream that dissipates over breakfast. He would write it all truthfully, as he remembered it, and hope for the best. If it didn't get published, maybe he would change the names and circumstances and make it a novel. Then, instead of being called a liar by all the doubters, people might read it and think, "Hey, what if?"